THE FIXER UPPER

Echo Springs Book One

MAGGIE MAE GALLAGHER

Published by Blushing Books
An Imprint of
ABCD Graphics and Design, Inc.
A Virginia Corporation
977 Seminole Trail #233
Charlottesville, VA 22901

Maggie Mae Gallagher
The Fixer Upper

EBook ISBN: 978-1-947132-65-8
Print ISBN: 978-1-947132-66-5
v1

Cover Art by ABCD Graphics & Design

This one's for my mom.

Chapter One

From Old Man Turner's Journal:
In life, as in love, expect the unexpected.

Oh, brother!

The house her dearly departed Great-Aunt Evie had left her in her last will and testament reminded Abby of a Victorian horror film, complete with a set of ugly as sin gargoyles guarding the front porch entrance. Gingerly, Abby opened the front door, the hinges creaking as she pushed, with the set of keys that her aunt's attorney, Clark Biddle the Third, had mailed her. Clark Biddle was a crusty codger who had been in business since the invention of the American legal system, and her aunt's attorney for over forty years. Aunt Evie had never married and, in a way, must have felt a bit of a kinship with Abby, since she was the only one in her family line who was unwed and didn't have a passel of kids running helter-skelter on her sanity. While Abby remembered visiting here as a child, she had been five, shy, and really had not looked at anyone above their knees.

Unsure of what she might find, she had brought all the essentials with her: wine, chocolate, toilet paper and bug spray, the important things—at least while she figured out what to do with all her aunt's possessions and, in the meantime, finished her dissertation without her family constantly butting in and hovering with their judgmental, albeit well-meaning, interference.

As luck would have it, she'd been able to finagle an adjunct faculty position at the start of the fall semester at the local Echo Springs Community College, where she'd instruct bored freshmen in basic college composition classes with an American Literature Lecture series tossed in just to keep it from getting too snooze-worthy on her end. The previous professor, David Northrup, had eloped with one of his students at the end of last term. With the school being a small-town community college two hours from the nearest metropolitan area, they had been desperate to fill the spot on short notice.

Abby spent the next hour carting in her belongings from her well-used Land Rover. This baby had seen her through undergrad and then graduate school. It was a high school graduation present from her parents, two esteemed professors working in physics and engineering, as an attempt to bribe her into following in their rather forbidding academic footsteps.

And for a full year she'd let them guide her, until her sophomore year and what her parents had termed the unfortunate mistake. After that, Abby had switched majors and colleges, then entered a field that caused her parents to view her like one of their science projects instead of as their daughter.

Abby admitted that their dissatisfaction had created a distance between them. It wasn't that she didn't love them, she did, but she'd decided to live on her terms, which seemed to confound them on a daily basis. Now that she had been living the way she wanted, following her own star, she could never return to the listless, staid course her life had been on to please her family, not at the cost of her soul.

The inside of Great-Aunt Evie's home was a cross between 1950s Cold War décor and Barnum and Bailey's, with Victorian architecture that had been spliced with *Little Shop of Horrors*. Abby imagined Dracula would feel at home and comfortable here. She knew her aunt had been rather eccentric, which was her parents' nice way of saying her dad's aunt had been bat-shit crazy.

Once she'd hefted the final box inside, Abby decided her best bet would be a quick tour of the place she'd be calling home for the next few months. Then she could break out the cleaning supplies, starting with whatever room she'd use as her bedroom.

The main floor had a living room parlor, complete with inlaid ebony wood shelves and an ivory marble fireplace in the front. In the rear of the house were the kitchen, dining room, and laundry room, which all had a nice filmy layer of dust coating every surface. She prayed dust was her only houseguest, and that it didn't extend to mice, cockroaches, or spiders.

Her aunt's home was located in the tiny mountain town of Echo Springs, Colorado. It was one of the many stops along the interstate leading to ski resorts, a strip of parceled land with the majority of its residents living in homes surrounding the two-mile stretch of Main Street. The bulk of the town was situated along the northern edge of the interstate, with the mountains beyond forming a natural crescent shape.

Her aunt's house was in one of the residential areas set farther inland and away from the civilization of the tiny strip. Her street boasted all of five homes on acre lots. The house backed up to one of the foothills, still large by her estimates, but a baby mountain among the fourteen-footers nearby.

There was a bit of contention with her parents over the fact that Evie had willed her estate to Abby and not her father, Phillip, as would have been the proper thing to do. Her parents objected to anything that was outside of normal, acceptable behavior.

She guessed that was why Aunt Evie had left the home to her. She'd always enjoyed coloring outside the lines, preferred it over her parents' compartmentalized and sterile existence, and had corresponded with her aunt almost weekly. Their unlikely friendship had come about through an assignment in fourth grade where she'd had to select a pen-pal. Instead of picking a perfectly acceptable grade-schooler her age, she had chosen her great-aunt. In recent years, their communications had declined some, but Abby had still found the time to write her aunt in the old-fashioned, letter-writing, non-computerized way. It had been Evie who had championed her desire to change majors, encouraging her to strike out and follow her own path in life.

Abby climbed the wooden stairs in the center of the house, wooden floorboards creaking under her weight as she ascended, the scrolled ebony wooden railing smooth from a lifetime of hands trailing over its surface.

The house boasted four bedrooms at the top of the double L-shaped staircase, with the master bedroom, her aunt's, at the rear of the hallway. Abby chose the second-largest room, which had a window that overlooked the gardens, and in the distance, she could spy her neighbor's driveway and darkened house beyond. The room held an old four-poster number, a chest of drawers, and an antique writing desk. She could set up camp with her laptop and work on her dissertation in here if she wanted.

The room also held a portion of her aunt's prized doll collection. Not the modern, plastic ones, but the old porcelain dolls, with creepy as hell faces. The damn things gave her the willies and would be the first casualty in her decluttering of the house. After setting her meager belongings on the bed, Abby carted and removed all the dolls from her room. She'd never sleep with all those beady eyes staring at her. And the ones with clown faces, forget about it—those suckers, she might just have to torch.

Abby spent the next hour cleaning her new room as best she could for the night. She'd work on the full house and give it a proper cleaning come morning, but she'd spent the better part of the day in her Rover and could feel the onset of fatigue settling in her bones. There was a semi-modern bathroom across the hall, with one of those claw-foot tubs she'd take advantage of when she wasn't dragging her feet and ready to go horizontal for eight hours.

Settled in for the night, she made herself a small picnic of her wine and cheese offerings and added hitting up the local market for all the essentials to her to-do list for the morrow. Her parents would only shake their heads if they could see her in her thermal pajamas, drinking chardonnay directly from the bottle that hadn't even sported a cork, but a lid that twisted off.

She was toasting her own brilliance when she heard the creak of the front door opening. Grabbing her trusty nine iron, a little gizmo she'd inherited from an ex-boyfriend some years back, Abby cursed at her phone's low battery.

"Figures," she muttered under her breath.

She left her room, tiptoeing down the stairs, her movements muffled by her thick socks. She rounded the corner, and a beam of light blinded her.

"Gah!" Screaming, she swung the iron, ready to take on her intruder. All the self-defense classes her parents had scoffed at hadn't been for naught. Who knew that in a sleepy little mountain town, burglars and vagabonds were a problem? The golf club whizzed over the intruder's head.

"What the?" a deep baritone barked.

She swung again, determined to fend off whoever the hell thought he could invade her aunt's place with mischief on his mind. The shadowed outline of a large man loomed behind the beam of light. When he didn't back off, only kept advancing, her internal panic button hit overdrive. The nine-iron connected with flesh with a thudded whack.

"Ow, fuck, cut it—"

"Get out or I'll call the police!" she swore, her pulse hammering, her grip on the nine-iron so tight her hand was fusing into a claw formation. She reared back to strike again when his next words halted the forward progression of her swing.

"I am the police."

She blanched, almost dropping her weapon, but then thought

better of it. What if he'd lied to disarm her and then would attack?

Nice try, buddy. She wasn't falling for it.

"Prove it." She wasn't the atypical heroine who idiotically descended into the darkened basement, despite the light mysteriously not working, to investigate the strange noise. She'd studied horror films and knew she was not the dumb bimbo, but the smart woman who survived. His indicating that he was the police was a sub-plot straight out of a B horror film and was precisely the type of thing the killer would say.

She raised the nine-iron into a defensive position as the man moved to her right, flipping on the overhead light while pulling a shiny silver badge from his belt. He held it toward her so that light reflected off the silver star. Blinking as her eyes adjusted, Abby wondered if she was dreaming. Cornflower-blue eyes studied her, dressed in her flannel pink pajama bottoms, tank top, and fluffy purple robe. He was larger than the darkness had suggested, probably a good six-three, and lean. His dark midnight hair fell in curly waves to his jawline, which was covered in dusky stubble. There was a ruggedness to him, indicating that somewhere in his make-up he preferred life outdoors, and it showed. He reminded her of the men gracing the covers of the romance novels she'd hidden from her parents growing up, and still hid from her colleagues.

She'd always had a bit of a thing for men in uniform, but the only defining mark that even suggested he was an officer was his black jacket with an emblem embroidered into the right shoulder. Otherwise, he looked like a mountain man, in a button-up emerald flannel shirt and blue jeans that rode low over his muscular hips.

Then she focused on the badge. Oh, sweet heavens! The badge read: *Sheriff, City of Echo Springs.* Why did this have all the beginnings of a campy horror flick? Woman goes to the wilderness to find herself, makes acquaintance with the local law enforcement, and then the army of dolls stuffed inside the home come to life, possessed by a demon spawn from hell, to try to kill the heroine.

This was why Abby needed to get away from her daily life. When a person started comparing her life to horror movies, she was on a one-way train to Crazyville.

He gave her an identical head-to-toe assessment. Abby felt his gaze clear down to her center, then he finally responded to her dare. "I'm Nate Barnes, Sheriff of Echo Springs. Would you mind telling me who the hell you are and why you are trespassing in Evie Callier's home?"

She'd just assaulted the freaking sheriff! Great. Just perfect. Some of the wind deflated from her sails and her defensive stance slackened. She loosened her shoulders and grip a teensy bit. But she didn't lower her nine-iron, just in case. This was always the part where the psycho killer did an *I'm just kidding* and sprang in for the kill. "Abby Callier. Evie was my great-aunt, and I'm here to help settle her estate."

His stiff demeanor slackened somewhat. "I hate to ask this, especially at the risk of you beaning me with that thing again"— he nodded toward the iron she held—"but I need to see some identification to verify you are who you say you are. It's procedure and all. We've had a rash of break-ins here recently."

That tiny bit of news didn't settle her anxiety any. What had she been thinking when she'd made the decision to come live in Evie's place in the middle of nowhere Colorado? Granted, she could be in Denver inside of two hours, but still, she wasn't the reclusive type. Much.

"Let me get my wallet. Stay here, please." She gestured, holding her hand up while holding the nine-iron in her other hand like she'd stepped into the batter's box and was waiting for the pitch. Abby was already wired up. The last thing she needed was to have him follow her up to her room. Her grip on the iron tightened again. Sheriff Barnes nodded as he clipped his badge back on his belt. Abby backed up, retracing her steps to her room. She raced up the top half of the stairs, her heart thumping madly in her chest, like she'd just run sprints, from the adrenaline rush of the last few minutes. Her hands visibly shook as she dug in her purse and withdrew her license from her wallet.

Mentally, Abby added a new, heavier-duty deadbolt to her internal shopping list for the following day. With her New Jersey license gripped in one hand, holding on to the iron like it was a lifeline with the other, she left her room and headed back downstairs to Sheriff Barnes, who should be given an award for being one of the sexiest lawmen west of the Mississippi—so much so that in her mind, she had already dubbed him Sheriff Stud Muffin. That hunk of law and order was currently nosing through the living room, paying particular attention to the pile of dolls she'd deposited on the red velvet loveseat. The doll heap looked eerily reminiscent of a horror film, *Night of the Living Dolls*, or like sacrificial offerings to the Lord of Darkness, surrounded as they were by the dark burgundy red of the couch.

"I've got to ask. What's with the dolls?" Sheriff Barnes quirked a dark brow in her direction. The corners of his lips twitched as if he was trying not to laugh as she handed him her license while maintaining a reasonable distance between them. His long, piano-player fingers brushed against hers as he took the license to inspect it, and a zing whipped through her body.

Well, hello, libido, you do still exist. I was beginning to wonder about you. Although, hormones and horniness in general typically preclude the mass-murdering zombie apocalypse, so...

"Aunt Evie loved collecting those things, but I find them creepy as hell. There's no way I'd get any sleep tonight with those beady eyes watching me."

A hint of a grin shrouded his lips. "So, you're moving in?"

"More or less, for the time being. Until I decide whether I should keep or sell the house. If you think this pile of dolls is bad, you should see my aunt's room." She clamped her mouth shut on what had sounded like an invitation. She would not invite a strange man anywhere near her bedroom, or her aunt's. Even if Abby found Sheriff Stud Muffin incredibly attractive, she could virtually hear the opening strains of a horror flick should she do something like have a one-night stand—not that she would, although it would be nice to be rid of her sexual dry spell. But that would tank any possibilities she had for this place and making it permanent. Abby didn't want to head back east only to have her parents greet her with their holier-than-thou *I told you sos*.

"Well then, let me be the first to welcome you to the neighborhood," he murmured, handing her license back.

Abby accepted it from his outstretched hand. She avoided his touch this time, not wanting a repeat of the livewire current that had sliced through her system before. Wait, neighborhood? Between the wine and the eight hundred miles she'd driven today, her brain wasn't firing on all cylinders. "You live around here? And is this your normal MO? Sneak into a person's home and scare the crap out of them?"

"No, it's not typical, but I'm bound and sworn to investigate when I discover something out of place. I live next door to the left of you, noticed the light on in the room upstairs, and had not heard that any of Evie's relatives were moving in. Since no one came to the funeral, I just assumed."

"I was out of the country, in England, when she died. My parents didn't let me know about her passing until after the services had occurred. If I'd known, I would have made the trip," Abby explained, restraining her desire to fidget under his direct gaze. And if he was her neighbor on the left, that meant her bedroom window looked out directly over his home. She might have to rethink the location of her bedchamber.

Abby wasn't used to being observed so intensely, and his cornflower gaze roamed over her from head to foot. In fact, he did that to the entirety of the room as well. There was nothing that missed his stare, which she assumed was a good trait to have when you were the sheriff.

Normally, it wouldn't have offended her, but this made her feel like she was being dissected and judged, which got her back up. Part of why she was here was to escape from her parents' constant judgment and condemnation of her life choices. They were hers. She didn't want to be a carbon copy of the exalted Doctors Callier, or try to make herself fit into their academic niche, which was why she'd struck out on her own. Yet even now, on the eve of her completing her dissertation and being awarded her doctorate, her parents couldn't seem to keep themselves from passing judgment on her choice of subject matter. The exasperation in her mother's voice during their phone call that morning as she'd enquired when Abby was going to stop all this nonsense and join a *more promising academic field* still smarted. It was her mother's code for the sciences or mathematics—none of the subjects like literature or, heaven forbid, philosophy, were considered up to par.

"I see. I'm truly sorry for the intrusion," he said.

"That's okay. Nothing like a little excitement before bed to get the blood pumping."

The man laughed outright. Crinkles appeared at the corner of his eyes. She'd thought he was attractive before, but his smile transformed him from merely handsome into a gorgeous hunk of man meat that made her ovaries give him a standing ovation. This was why she rarely went out. She had constant foot-in-mouth syndrome, where her brain chose not to connect with her mouth.

"I mean, um…" Abby stuttered and felt heat flush her cheeks, wishing there was a hole that would open up so she could crawl into it and hide from the embarrassment.

"Don't worry about it, Abby. I will let you get back to your evening. If you need anything, I'm right next door," Sheriff Barnes murmured, heading toward the door. "Make sure you lock the door behind me. Like I said, there has been a rash of burglaries in the area."

"I will." She followed him to the front door, holding it open as he stepped outside.

"Good night, Abby." He gave her a small salute and sauntered off her porch. His police cruiser, an SUV, was parked next door in his driveway.

"Night, Sheriff," she responded as she shut the door and flicked the lock. She tested it before she marched to the back door and made sure it was firmly locked as well.

Then, just to be on the safe side, since she knew it would be a while before she succumbed to the oblivion of sleep after the night's festivities, Abby decided to check all the windows in the house and ensure those were locked up tight as well.

The last thing she wanted was to end up splashed across the local newspaper as a cautionary tale. Although, it would make her parents blow a gasket, which would be pretty satisfying. She could see the headline now:

Evie Callier's great-niece found slain! Local police suspect it was the army of undead dolls...

NATE'S long legs ate up the distance between Miss Evie's home and his. A sliver of moon shone down, casting the yard between their houses in a murky darkness. The nightly weather had begun to dip into colder temperatures even though it was only mid-August.

So, that was Abby. She wasn't conventionally beautiful, with her big brown eyes and overly generous smile, but the combo was a knock-out punch to the gut. Miss Evie had mentioned her great-niece quite a bit, saying how she was just like Evie had been in her youth, after she'd asked him to go steady with her for the hundredth time. Miss Evie had been quite the town character. Many of the townsfolk had thought she was too over the top, but he'd always liked her quick-hearted wit, booming laugh, and zest for life. She had thumbed her nose at convention and never married.

He'd liked her. Nate had been the one who had discovered her in her bedroom after she'd passed in her sleep, and he'd made all the funeral arrangements. Evie had asked him to years before, as she had no family in the area. It had been the right thing to do, the only honorable thing any self-respecting man would do. He certainly was going to miss the old broad.

Nate opened his oak front door, tensing as Rufus, his hundred-and-fifty-pound Great Dane, bounded toward him in exuberant glee. *Delicate* and *agile* were not two words he would use to describe Rufus, who was more in the overzealous and horrendously clumsy category. He'd once overturned all the shelves in the pantry while attempting to reach the biscuits Nate had stashed on the top shelf.

"What's up, bud?" Nate ruffled the fur between Rufus's ears and was rewarded with a thick, sloppy wet tongue.

"Go do your business, but leave the squirrels alone."

Rufus woofed in response and barreled past him. Nate stood at the front door, waiting for Rufus, who had this look of *finally* on his face as he emptied a long stream of urine into a nearby bush.

Nate leaned against the doorframe, yawning as Rufus greeted every bush and shrub in the yard. Nate shot his gaze up to the second floor of Miss Evie's and the light that still shone in the window like a beacon. He was going to have quite the bruise on his left arm from where she'd nailed him with the golf iron. Abby was no shrinking violet, he'd give her that. She was more like one of the mythic Furies sent down to avenge wronged women and eviscerate men.

All in a luscious little package that had stunned him, delaying his responses. Otherwise, she never would have gotten a hit in. She was a good foot shorter than he was, with the top of her head barely reaching his shoulder, but she was a power-packed dynamo with curves that made his mouth water.

Nate wondered how long Abby planned to stay. Most people didn't get past their first winter in the mountains. Living up here took a certain type of gumption that most people just didn't have. He'd have to keep an eye on his new neighbor, especially once the weather headed south. Up here in the higher elevations, once the snow started, it could be days before you made it out. They should hopefully have some time yet before the weather turned, but once September hit, it could be sixty and sunny in the morning then twenty and snowing by evening.

When her light darkened, and the house seemed to blend with the night, he felt like he had done his civic duty for the day.

"Rufus, come on. Let's get some dinner." He whistled for the pup, who raced toward him like a horse in the Kentucky Derby. His midnight fur blended in with the dark night as he clomped up the porch and darted inside toward the kitchen.

Nate's own stomach growled at the thought of food as he followed Rufus, who plopped his butt on the floor and waited next to his food bowl. There was a part of Nate that hungered for his entirely-too-sexy-for-her-own-good neighbor.

He really didn't need or want the complication in his life, but then again, there was nothing wrong with being a little neighborly.

Chapter Two

From *Old Man Turner's Journal:*
Actions speak louder than words.

The following morning began much the same as every day
did for Nate. Since the weather was still nice, he and Rufus
went for a six-mile run up to the banks of Echo Springs Lake,
which the town was named after, and back down to his house.
When he couldn't get a run in outside, he used a treadmill in his
basement. By the time they climbed the steps of the porch, the
sun was just beginning to crest the horizon. It was a routine he
had established years ago when he'd first started with the Denver
Police. He ran not because he liked it, but so he could chase after
suspects when it was warranted. People would be surprised how
often it happened during an arrest, like the suspect thought they
could actually get away.

Nate wasted little time inside, feeding Rufus, getting in a brief
shower, and suiting up for the day. Unlike when he'd been a
traffic cop in Denver, here his uniform consisted of jeans and an
ever-widening variety of flannel shirts, with his utility belt

complete with gun holster for his police-issued Glock and set of handcuffs. He clipped his badge onto the front pocket of his flannel after retrieving his handgun from the gun safe that was stored in the front hall closet.

After letting Rufus out to do his business a final time, Nate headed out, catching a glimpse of his new neighbor as she opened the front door. She looked fresh and enticing in the early morning light, in black yoga pants and a yellow sweatshirt that concealed more than it revealed. She lifted a hand in greeting when she spied him and he nodded back with a wave, then backed out of his drive.

He couldn't deny that he was attracted to Abby. She was like a new, shiny toy amidst the familiar, staid lineup of regulars. It was the curse of small towns. Everyone knew everybody and change rarely, if ever, came to the town. In his four years as Sheriff, he had been the talk of the town for the longest time. This meant that all the single women in the town had beaten a path to his doorway. The problem was he had known most of them since high school and they did not so much as cause a twitch of interest. He'd kept the bulk of his interactions with females to tourists passing through, who didn't ask him for more commitment than a night enjoying each other's company. So the fact that he'd not been able to get his new neighbor off his mind, or that he'd wondered more than once since she'd beaned him last night what she looked like naked, gave him pause. It was an interest strong enough that he couldn't help think he should pursue it and her to see where it led.

At least when the Chill Out Dispensary had opened up on Main Street he had been dethroned as the most interesting topic in town. That had been the subject of three town hall meetings and quite the scandal. Nate didn't necessarily care that marijuana was legal now. All it did was add to the list of things he and his officers had to watch out for on patrol. In the three years since the dispensary had opened, Nate had issued a hefty number of driving under the influence of marijuana citations.

Just because it was legal didn't mean everyone should do it. And the morons who thought they could get behind the wheel of a car while on it, pissed him off. It was as bad as driving drunk, and could end up being just as fatal.

But people also thought they could do things like hike and climb on the substance, so he and his deputies were constantly on the lookout at the nearby trails and camping sites.

At least the sibling owners of the dispensary, Maureen and Joe Shilling, were decent, law abiding citizens.

On his way to the station, Nate stopped at the Emporium Diner. It was out of his way, but it was a town institution and had the best breakfast sandwiches on the planet. The 1950s style diner with its original Formica countertop and black and white checkered tile floor was stored with memories. He'd had his first date here with Shirley Carmichael after the winter formal his freshman year.

He had also experienced his first breakup when later that same year, Shirley had dumped him for his arch nemesis.

"Sheriff? Want the usual?" Valerie Buchanon asked. The sweet redhead had been two years behind him in school and had taken over operations of the diner from her parents.

"Yes. And add a large coffee to that. To go."

"That I can do," she said, typing it into the cash register.

He sat at one of the barstools as he waited. "How are your parents?"

"They are living it up in Fort Myers. Dad's bowling league just won the championship."

"Give them my best when you talk to them," he said.

Valerie moved behind the counter in a fast and efficient manner. Within five minutes she was handing him a to-go bag and coffee. The enticing aroma made his stomach growl.

"I definitely will. I put a few cinnamon donut holes in there for you too," she said with a smile.

"You're the best," he said, sliding a few ones into the glass tip jar at the register before taking his breakfast with him back out to his car.

The diner was only five blocks from the station. The old brick building had stood for longer than he had been alive. He parked in the back and headed in through the rear entrance. Nate nodded in greeting to the deputies he passed on the way to his office.

In his office, he went through the messages that had been left for him overnight and the day's agenda while he ate his breakfast. It was a miracle that he was able to eat the better portion of his breakfast sandwich before being interrupted.

"Sheriff?"

He glanced up at the knock on the door. Jack McNair, the town's prosecuting attorney, stood at his office door, a file folder in his hand. A handful of years older than Nate, his dark hair was just beginning to show hints of gray. He was also someone the department regularly recruited for their annual guns and hoses boxing event. Jack might look like a suave businessman in his suit, but once in the boxing ring the man was a beast.

"What can I do for you, Jack?"

Jack approached his desk. "Sorry to disturb breakfast. I wanted to let you know that Judge Hamilton approved the warrant on the felony domestic case, and has added felony child abuse charges. We need to send a squad out to arrest him."

"I had a feeling Don would support it, given the evidence compiled from Doctor Townsend. Everyone in town knows Jed Carruthers has been abusing his wife for years."

Jack nodded. "And if the asshole had kept it to his wife, I doubt Clare would have said yes to pressing charges. The mistake he made was going after the kids this time. I would like it if you were there as the arresting officer. Not that I don't trust your deputies…"

"I understand. I want to make sure there are no fuck ups with this case just as much as you. Let me get the bullpen meeting out of the way and I'll head out with one of my deputies."

"Appreciate it, Sheriff," Jack said, handing him a copy of the warrant.

Nate took it and scanned the document. "Oh, and McNair, make sure you're training for the annual boxing event. We need you in our lineup again. Or are you getting soft?"

Jack snorted, gave him a cock-sided grin, and did a little *come at me* gesture with his hands. "Any time you want to join me in the ring for another rematch, you let me know."

"I will. You can hold your breath until then," he shot back good-naturedly.

Jack gave him the middle finger salute as he left his office. Nate sighed, gathered his notes for the upcoming bullpen meeting, and managed to shove two of the donut holes into his mouth before heading to the conference room.

His squad may have been small, as was typical of small towns, but he liked his people. The majority of them, anyway. After roll call, once the assignments were all handed out—with bitching from Denny Filbert, as per the norm—Nate drove out to the Carruthers property with Deputy O'Leary backing him up for the arrest. Filbert was an asshole with an attitude problem. At his next review, they were going to have to discuss it. There was no longer a way around it. The man was pissed that the town had passed him over for the sheriff's position four years ago, and had not let the matter go. Filbert's grudge had taken on a bitter edge and was polluting the entire atmosphere.

The Carruthers' property was on a half-acre of land. The two-story home had fallen into disrepair. The pale blue paint was cracked and peeling in places. One of the black shutters had slats broken out of the middle. Jed was a mechanic at one of the local garages, who liked his whiskey more than he did working. And it showed. His wife, Clare, had taken herself and the kids to her parents' house, which was only three miles away.

Nate knocked on the door. "Jed, this is Sheriff Barnes. I need you to open the door and come out with your hands in the air."

"Fuck off," came a slurred shout from inside.

Nate sighed. From the sounds of it, the man was already well on his way to being shit-faced. "Jed, don't make this more difficult than it needs to be. I have a warrant for your arrest. If you come with me now, peacefully, it will help your case."

Deputy O'Leary stood off to the side of the front door of the ramshackle home with its screen door torn in spots. When there was no response from Jed, Nate nodded at O'Leary, who made his way around to the back to ensure the idiot didn't try to go out the back door and escape.

"Jed, I'm going to give you to the count of five and then I'm coming in."

There was a shout from O'Leary around back. Nate took off and sprinted to the edge of the porch, just in time to watch Jed, in a pair of white boxers and nothing else, race around the corner and head toward the street.

"Halt, Jed."

Shit.

Nate charged after him on foot. This was why he ran six miles a day—so he could catch morons like Jed who thought they could outrun the police. Nate snagged him by the neck and wrestled him down to the ground. He took an elbow to the chin and swore before he had Jed pinned on the ground with his hands behind his back. Not quick enough, he thought as he slid the cuffs on Jed's wrists.

"For that stunt, I will be adding resisting arrest and assault on a police officer, Jed."

"Piss off, pig!" Jed yelled, uncowed by the fact that he was handcuffed. From the smell of him, he had started early on the Jack Daniels.

Nate shook his head and began reading Jed his Miranda rights. His chin throbbed like a son of a bitch and it wasn't yet noon. So much for having a slow and easy day.

~

ABBY SPENT her first few days in Echo Springs shopping for supplies and realizing that there were some things she would want to purchase in bulk for the coming winter. While winter was a way off yet, she knew that mountain roads became impassible during winter storms. Trepidation at the idea of being trapped here for days without the barest necessities filled her both with a sense of dread and the need to take up hoarding as a hobby. It wasn't that she was afraid, she had just never experienced it before. Any unfamiliar circumstance was bound to cause anxiety, especially when one had the undead doll army residing in her living room.

Abby hailed from the East Coast, where she was more familiar with the fast and rather efficient snow plows the New Jersey Department of Transportation had on hand whenever the weather so much as sneezed few inches of snow across the area. Her family home was located in Princeton, New Jersey, just a smidgeon too close to the churning business mill of New York City to ever be allowed to fully shut down, with a few blizzard exceptions through the years.

And while she'd been living in an off-campus apartment by Cornell University, which made it infinitely easier to handle her duties as a doctoral student, the grounds of the campus were meticulously maintained. She'd slogged through frigid, snowy days to classes, study groups, and lectures more times than she cared to count. But here in the mountains, getting a foot of snow was considered a light dusting.

Abby knew from her research on the area—you could take the girl out of the classroom but the love of research remained—that, in order to survive the winter months, she would have to stock up on everything from meat to canned goods and dry food staples. Before she went binge shopping at the closest Gundry's Bulk Superstore located a good hundred miles away on the outskirts of Denver, she ordered a large deepfreeze. Aunt Evie's model looked like it hadn't been used this century, and critters had decided to take up residence. Abby couldn't stop her involuntary shudder at the memory of the mice droppings and cockroaches she had discovered. She was having her bright, shiny new deepfreeze, one of the latest models, with computer technology temperature controls, delivered this morning by the local appliance store, Styman and Sons, Inc.

Abby had made progress on her aunt's house in the four days since she had arrived. Everything that had been coated by a filmy layer of dust was now Pine-Sol fresh. She'd set traps for field mice and tossed out everything from her aunt's pantry after spying more mice droppings. Her aunt had believed in throwing nothing away, which was why Abby was having to look into the disposal of hazardous waste chemicals from the 1980s.

Abby had skipped right over a light cleaning, preferring to attack the dirt and grime with a bucket and scrub brush. Room by room, she had removed the grime so that the house no longer had a musty rose scent lingering in the air. All of the dolls, those creepy little suckers, were in the living room, where she was cataloging them to sell to local antique shops. Aunt Evie's collection was quite impressive, with some of the dolls dating back to the early nineteenth century. Which meant that they were surely possessed and would rise up one night to kill the whole town, starting with Abby and her sexy neighbor. In getting rid of the dolls, she was saving her aunt's town. Although she did feel twinges of guilt at off-loading anything that had been her aunt's, really, what was she supposed to do with more than a hundred of those creeptacular things? As it was, when she wasn't cataloging them, she had them covered with sheets she'd found in the linen closet. This made the room appear like it contained a hundred tiny ghost specters, which meant Abby was avoiding that room unless absolutely necessary.

In addition to cleaning and preparing for winter doomsday style this week, she'd met with the head of the faculty at Echo Springs Community College, Professor Barry Stein. Professor Stein reminded her of the typical absent-minded professor with his crazy Albert Einstein style bleached white hair that seemed to defy gravity and styling of any kind. Tall and lanky, in a stiff gray tweed suit, he appeared far more comfortable in a lab working on his chemistry equations than dealing with the endless politics and paperwork that came with being in an administrative role. He had thrown her an impromptu meet and greet with the other adjunct faculty members, which consisted of burnt coffee and donut holes from the local bakery.

Abby was convinced the small gathering was Professor Barry Stein's way of attempting to keep her from running for the hills when she spied the sad state of the classrooms. Echo Springs Community College was a small, local college that offered two-year degrees in a range of subjects, from business and marketing to animal husbandry and agriculture. Classroom sizes were small, with no more than twenty students each. The building itself was the size of a small community center, with two floors and roughly ten classrooms on each level. It was a historic building dating back to the 1920s and had been the original site for Echo Springs School—grades kindergarten through senior year of high school.

Abby liked the old colonial style building with its fluorescent lighting and original hardwood flooring.

During the winter months, the school had an online campus established for each class, where she could give her lectures remotely via the Internet since inclement weather could cause issues and delays more often than not. This would keep her from becoming a complete and total recluse once winter roared into the sleepy little town.

Granted, she did have the delectable Sheriff Nate Barnes to innocuously observe throughout the long wintertime months ahead. She had already done her fair share of spying on him through her bedroom window in the evenings as he pulled his Explorer into the driveway. Thank goodness he'd not caught her. Abby told herself that she was doing what any red-blooded woman would do with a such a prime hunk of grade A beefcake on display so nearby. What was a little harmless stalking from her window seat? Wasn't it being a good neighbor to watch out for each other? Besides, when she did catch him through her window, he tended to mesmerize her and it would take the army of the undead to drag her away. The way he strode with such confidence and physical dexterity, his powerful long legs encased in jeans, left her hot and achy. He was like a big, sleek mountain lion with his swagger, and she found herself salivating over him.

Her libido hadn't just awoken but was acting like a maniacal Girl Scout, relentlessly ringing the doorbell in a desperate attempt to meet her cookie sales quota. As much as Abby's body might be staking a claim on her neighbor, she didn't have any intention of enticing Nate into her bedroom. Between her classes and finishing her dissertation, she doubted she would have much free time.

And that thought made her want to climb back into bed and pull the covers over her head.

It wasn't that she didn't enjoy her studies; she did. Abby wouldn't be able to work as much as she did if she hated the subject matter. That was why she'd changed majors in undergrad. The thought of working on one more calculus or physics problem had made her want to start practicing the art of voodoo upon her professors. It was then Abby had realized that, as much as she loved her parents and siblings, she couldn't continue in a field that bored her senseless.

Abby had hidden her affection for literature from her parents. Of course, it had been acceptable for her to read classics like *The Iliad* and Shakespeare, but she'd fallen in love with Mark Twain, Emily Dickinson, and Edgar Allan Poe, which led her down the path to Sylvia Plath, Kurt Vonnegut, Stephen King, and so many more. She would never forget the day her mother had discovered a Georgette Heyer romance hidden behind the dust jacket of *On the Origin of the Species* by Charles Darwin. She shuddered in horror at the memory.

Abby had left the scientific field shortly thereafter. To this day, her parents couldn't seem to reconcile the fact that she had her own life, her own likes, and dislikes. She'd never intended to be the rebel in the family, it had just sort of turned out that way. Once the break had come, Abby indulged her curiosity in everything, hence her newfound love affair with horror films, especially anything from the seventies and eighties.

Abby opened the door to two delivery men wearing Styman and Sons logos on their polos. Greg Styman Junior and Teddy Styman were the sons part of the company. They were both relatively attractive guys in a down-home Mayberry type of way, and were young—far, far too young.

While Abby might be nearing her twenty-ninth birthday, these two reminded her of students—fresh-faced, with that innocent wide-eyed wonder of youth that people tended to lose by their mid-twenties.

One of the things that had drawn her to the local appliance shop, instead of heading into Denver and one of those big-box stores to make her purchase, had been their willingness to haul away the old freezer free of charge. Styman and Sons would strip it and refurbish any of the old parts that weren't rusted or still viable and resell them online. It made Abby feel like she was doing something good for the environment because the whole thing wouldn't end up in a landfill.

Abby was standing on her porch, watching the two guys pull her handy-dandy new deepfreeze from the truck, when she was flattened.

She'd barely had time to issue an *umphff* before she was on her back on the ivory wooden porch, a hulking brute covered in dark black fur towering over her. She lay on her back, trying to assess the damage as a large, wet, pink tongue slobbered over her face. From this angle, she could tell there were a few parts of the roof overhang that needed to be fixed before winter arrived.

Her hands slid into the soft, short fur, attempting to move the massive beast as it said hello with an almost rabid enthusiasm. Abby would have had better luck moving one of the fourteen-footers nearby.

"Rufus, stupid mutt, get off her." Abby heard the deep baritone filled with abject horror.

Rufus, the mammoth Great Dane, listened about as well as a toddler playing with his favorite toy and, instead of moving off her, decided he really wanted to cuddle and lie on top of her. Her breath whooshed out of her again at the dog's impressive weight. He had to outweigh her by twenty pounds.

"Jesus, Rufus." Nate Barnes tugged and yanked the hulking beast of a dog off Abby's prone form. Rufus seemed to think that meant Nate wanted to play and wrestle around. They skirmished on her porch for a minute or so, until Rufus spied a rabbit and took off after the poor creature.

She was starting to push herself up, mentally assessing the damage, when Nate held out a hand to her, a mask of apology adding a deep line to his furrowed brow. "I'm so sorry. Are you all right? He's harmless, really. The lamebrain just thinks he's more of a lap dog and doesn't realize how big he is."

Abby felt a few brain cells faint as she accepted his help, placing her hand in his much longer one, noticing that the fingers were rough with calluses.

"It's okay," she said as she gained her feet, only to be shocked —and a little turned on—as he ran his hands over her, checking for injuries. As much as she tried to rationalize that it was a police-style frisking, a low burn ignited in her belly. Before she did something entirely stupid, like invite him in where he could give her body a private inspection, she batted his hands away. "No harm done. He seems like a big lover."

Nate smiled sheepishly as he retreated a step, and it did nothing to lessen his impact.

She almost sawed her tongue in half. *See? I shouldn't talk to people, ever.* Especially not after Sheriff Stud Muffin put his hands all over her. The action had short-wired and fried her brain, leading to her precarious foot-in-mouth disease.

As if he knew she had been talking about him, Rufus loped back up her porch, making a beeline directly for her or, better yet, her crotch, as he planted his wet nose there by way of greeting.

"Rufus, get off her. Jesus, I'm sorry. He's normally not like this," Nate explained, more than a little flummoxed and embarrassed as he tried to yank him off.

It was nice to know the guy was human. After their initial and rather violent meeting, she'd wondered if he was a superhero in disguise. She had hit him with the golf club with her full force and the guy had barely flinched.

Abby surmised the only way around this was to show Rufus a little love. Taking her physical well-being into her own hands, she knelt until she was eye level with the big brute, scratching Rufus behind the ears. "You're just a big ball of love, aren't you, sweetheart?"

Rufus all but collapsed at her feet, rolling onto his back in adoration and begging for a belly rub, his tongue hanging out. Abby obliged him, running her fingers through his soft fur. Nate knelt next to her.

"Really, I am sorry."

She shot him a grin. "Don't worry about it. I know it was just his way of saying hi."

"Appreciate it." The air between them thickened as they stared at each other. His gaze flicked to her lips more than once, making her throat as dry as the Sahara, and Abby's insides all but melted into a gooey pile at his rather large feet. Nate broke the spell and stood, with those incredibly long legs of his that seemed perfectly sculpted to wear jeans.

"Ma'am, where would you like us to put this?" one of the Styman sons asked as they hefted the deepfreeze up the porch stairs.

Embarrassed, she attempted to quash the sudden rush of desire, shifting her mind to the task at hand and failing as she said, much more breathily than she would have preferred, "In the basement. Here, let me show you where."

Nate helped her up again, his fingers warm against her skin, branding her, and igniting the distinct urge to shift into his innocuous touch. *See? Head case, party of one.* Just because her hormones had woken from their self-imposed drought like Rip Van Winkle and broken out the kazoos didn't mean she could jump Sheriff Stud Muffin's bones without suffering some consequences. Although, on the flip side, she had the unerring sense that she would enjoy the crash and burn. Probably a little too much.

There was a slight shift in his blue gaze. She would have missed the flash of lust darkening his eyes and the distinct male look if she had blinked. It said he knew exactly what she'd been thinking and he wasn't put off by it in the slightest.

Abby wasn't certain what she should do about that interesting tidbit. As it was, she was having a difficult enough time keeping her hands to herself.

But then the look vanished. Nate erected an invisible barrier, his expression dialed to controlled alpha. "We'll get out of your hair. Rufus, come on, you rascal, let's go home."

The black ball of fur woofed, leaped to his feet, and bounded off the porch, heading toward home.

"Abby," Nate said with a slight nod.

"See you around, Sheriff," she responded, more disappointed than she wanted to admit by his departure, and turned to the task at hand. By the time Styman and Sons had completed the deepfreeze installation and hauled the ancient one out, Nate's police cruiser was gone.

It was still early enough in the day that Abby made her first foray to the big wholesale box store, Gundry's Bulk Superstore, on the outskirts of Denver. She treated her trip like she'd just discovered the blue light special and stocked up on things that she wouldn't want to survive without this winter, like toilet paper and economy-sized packs of beans, pasta noodles, and coffee, adding beef, chicken, pork chops, and more to go into her new freezer. She was supremely proud of herself for remembering to grab a large cooler and ice to cart all the frozen goods back to the edge of civilization.

Abby had to admit she'd gone a little crazy. Into her cart went the gargantuan packs of toothpaste and deodorant as she stocked up on all the basics. She even included, on a whim, of course, precipitated by the fact that Sheriff Stud Muffin had stirred her up, a hundred-count mega box of condoms. Not that she had any intention of using them—the sexy sheriff could be seeing someone, for all she knew—but she preferred to be prepared. And he may not even think of her that way in the first place. Still, that didn't mean there weren't any other eligible date-able men in town. Colorado was infused with hunky mountain men, so even if the sheriff was unavailable, she could mingle with the locals instead of sitting home and moping about her lack of a love life.

Abby had had this romantic vision growing up, from all the romance novels she'd devoured, of being swept off her feet by a Prince Charming-type of manly man who would carry her off to his castle and be her true love. In reality, her scope and experience in the dating world had led her to believe that if she did meet a Prince Charming, he definitely wasn't going to ride in on his trusty steed to carry her off. If anything, her Prince Charming was riding a giant sloth somewhere, really confused.

Abby shook her head as she loaded her treasures into her Rover. The two-hour drive back to the sleepy little mountain town was rather uneventful. The scenic interstate drive was heart-stoppingly breathtaking. The mountains speared the sky as they broke through the tree line with their granite and slate monolithic structures, coated along the peaks with bands of white year-round glaciers. The road rose and fell with the land, with forests of pine trees that blanketed the rolling landscape.

The sun was setting behind her mountain when she finally pulled up in front of the house. In the short time she'd been here, Abby had begun to think of the blue and white Victorian as hers, uglier-than-sin gargoyles or not. She'd named them Fred and

Ken, just to keep things interesting. Considering she had yet to meet any of her other neighbors farther down the lane, it kept her from feeling like a hermit. Although she did sometimes wonder if she would eventually descend into madness like some of her favorite literary geniuses, what with her propensity for quantifying sentience to inanimate objects.

Hefting a box from her trunk, she started carting her load inside. Nate and his trusty sidekick, Rufus, spotted her from their front yard and approached as she was hoisting a rather weighty box of supplies. Rufus loped in a friendly gait, but his body vibrated with excited energy that at any moment could over-whelm him into a frenzy, and she prayed he wouldn't knock her down again. She had bruises forming from this morning's enthu-siastic introduction.

"Can I lend you a hand with that?" Nate asked, standing next to the back door of her Rover, whereupon he glanced inside and spied the box of condoms sitting on what she had deemed the next load. It was as if his gaze had been a heat-seeking missile and had selected the one item from her shopping bender she didn't want the man to find.

Where was the zombie apocalypse when a girl needed it?

"Um, sure, if you could take this box." She indicated the one in her hands and held it out toward him. Nate's bemused glance said it all as he reached to remove it from her grasp, like he was trying to contain his laughter at spying the mega-sized condom box. It made her want to take her nine-iron to him again to make him forget he ever saw them.

Why oh why had she bought those?

Just because her hormones were finally back online, it wasn't like she had sex often enough to warrant a box that size. Hell, it had been so long she worried that the next man she did do the horizontal tango with would spread her legs and a plume of dust would emit from her nether regions like she was the Crypt Keeper. Essentially, she was a dried-up old maid at twenty-eight. Most of the men she'd dated had hightailed it out of the relationship the moment they realized they couldn't hold a candle to the likes of her obsession with fictional heroes in the works of Shakespeare and Austen and... the list could go on.

The man must think she was an idiot, considering she was constantly blushing and stammering around him. If the ground would only open up and swallow her when she needed it to, she'd be ever so grateful.

Nate hid his smile, the smart man, and relieved her of the box. She hefted the next carton, mortified but there was no point in rearranging it and, with his aid, carted all her goodies inside. Rufus followed them as they hoisted the cooler filled with her stockpile of frozen meat.

Rufus made himself at home, seeming to know where things were as he headed into the bathroom and started drinking from the toilet while they carried the cooler to the basement.

"Stocking up a bit?" Nate asked as they set the cooler down next to the deepfreeze.

Abby shrugged, flipping the lid up to reveal packages of steaks, chicken breasts, pork chops, ground beef, bacon, sausage, turkey. Staring at the mountain of meat, she had to admit she was a little obsessive when it came to being prepared. "Well, I did some research before accepting the position at Echo Springs Community College, and it said that roads can be impassible during the winter."

"They can, but we do try to stay on top of road clearing. When it snows, the skiers come out in full force and head into the mountain resorts. All those travelers are the life-blood of this town, as they stop at the gas stations, restaurants, and shops. Without that, this town would go belly up in a New York minute. When the snows hit, the Styman boys stop working the appliance store and clear the streets, along with a few more of the locals. They work together to keep the city's roads as clear as possible."

"Good to know. But we aren't in the city." Which was something that wasn't lost on her.

"No, we're not. It can get a bit dicey out here. I tend to stay in town more and sleep at the station, but it's good that you're stocking up. Make sure you've got yourself some long underwear and some firewood."

She blushed at the underwear comment and wanted to kick herself. *What are you, a teenager?* Just because Sheriff Stud Muffin's topic made her wonder whether he was a boxers or briefs kind of man, and that she'd love to find out which he preferred, was no reason for Abby to act like an unschooled virgin.

Wait a second... "Firewood? Why would I need firewood?"

It wasn't something she had considered she would even need. Where did she get some? Would she have to cut the wood herself? Abby could see herself trying to heft an ax to chop wood. Coordination was not her strong suit. More likely than not, she'd end up hacking the wood to bits, all while taking off a few of her limbs. It wouldn't be pretty. Besides, knowing her, she'd leave the ax outside for the psycho killer to find and use to attack her in her home. She could imagine the headline:

Evie Callier's great-niece hacked to death because she didn't listen to her parents. Murder weapon apparently belonged to the victim, army of dolls suspected, news at eleven.

Jesus, she needed to get a grip.

Nate regarded her, his modest expression calling her a hundred times a fool for not being better prepared for life in the mountains, and said, "In case you lose power during a storm. It can get mighty cold up in these hills, especially when we are being pummeled with blizzard conditions. It doesn't happen all the time, but in these older homes, power can get knocked out and be out for days."

"What about a backup generator? Would that suffice?" Because if so, she'd turn right back around and head back to Gundry's Bulk Superstore for one. The thought of being without power during a blizzard chilled her, and for a millisecond, she considered hightailing it back East. Until she remembered that back East would mean having to deal with her parents' disapproval nearly twenty-four seven. She'd already visited that amusement park fun house, thank you very much, and didn't want to return.

"Yes and no. Most are gas-operated, although there are newer models that are solar but come with a heftier price tag, and if you run out of fuel…"

"You run out of electricity. Does anyone sell firewood in town?" She'd start looking tonight online for a backup generator. The thought of having only a fireplace for warmth made her shudder involuntarily. With her luck, that would be when all the creepy dolls decided to rise up en masse and strike.

"Check with Styman's. I'm not sure what their stock is this time of year, but if you'd like some help, I'd be happy to get you started."

She unloaded the last of the meat into the freezer, and shut the lid. "That would be nice, if it's not too much trouble. Thank you."

"It's no problem at all. After you." He gestured at the wooden stairs.

Nate trailed her up the steps; she could feel his gaze boring into her back as they entered the kitchen. Abby restrained from fanning her face at the jolt of heat that hummed in her system whenever he was near. Surprisingly, Evie had updated the room in the last decade, adding stainless steel appliances and dark cherry wood cabinetry. Unlike the rest of her home, which had been maintained with the original fixtures. Abby liked the small, eat-in kitchen with its cheery blue mosaic tile backsplash and soothing, slate blue walls. It was homey and inviting, the kind of place which made a person want to cook vats of soup bubbling in a crockpot, and sit at the table with a cup of coffee while nature raged outside.

Hearing a deep snore, she found Rufus sprawled beneath the oaken dinette table a shade or so lighter than the cabinetry, perfectly content, and fast asleep.

Nate stroked a hand over his five o'clock shadow beard, contemplating her like she was a deer that would spook if he moved too quickly. Shivers erupted in her at the slight scraping sound of his beard and it was akin to pouring liquid fire into her limbs. How would it feel whispering over her skin? The sensual imagery nearly made her groan aloud. Figured she would lust after her new neighbor.

Then he said, "I work the next two days, but could help you chop firewood this weekend. If you'll be around, of course?"

The question lingered in the air, almost as if he was fishing. She'd be a fool to pass up the chance to watch Sheriff Stud Muffin chop firewood. Maybe she should sell tickets. Women would line up twenty deep to view the spectacle of the rugged lawman being all alpha manly-man. Then again, she preferred to keep the show private. "I will be home and would appreciate the help."

"Then it's a date. Rufus, come on, let's let Abby have her evening."

A date? Had she tempted him with the supersized box of condoms? Did she want to tempt him? Her body did, all but banging cymbals in victory. But, did she?

Rufus glanced longingly in her direction as he stood and stretched, like he'd prefer to stay here. From one of the big boxes, she withdrew and opened a gigantic container of dog bones. She'd added them to her cart at the last minute. She was a sucker for animals and hoped that maybe if she had treats for him, she could avoid being flattened again. She extracted a bone. Rufus, upon spying the biscuit, pranced around the kitchen, his tail thumping against the cabinets in his exuberant delight.

"Here you go, sweetheart, you can come visit me anytime." He eagerly took the biscuit from her hand, staring at her with adoration while he scarfed the large bone down in a few bites. She gave him a scratch behind the ears.

"Come on, boy, stop flirting and I'll get dinner on for us," Nate said, shaking his head. Rufus bounded to the door with a *woof* at the mention of dinner.

Abby escorted them to the front door, trailing behind the

impressive beast and his dog. Holding the oak front door open, she murmured, "Thanks for your help."

Nate responded with a friendly nod and banked embers simmering in his gaze. Was the flame she spied in their depths hot enough to incinerate her resolve to maintain distance? He held her gaze, as if attempting to discern the innermost workings of her soul. "I'll stop by this weekend to help you with the firewood."

"Appreciate it."

She watched them leave, with Rufus darting after a chipmunk and Nate hollering at him to "get your ass back here," followed by "I guess you don't want dinner," at which Rufus corrected his course midstride into the forest and charged headlong toward the house.

What was she going to do about the big lug? And his dog?

Chapter Three

From Old Man Turner's Journal:
New beginnings always come with a little risk.

Nate fixed himself a steak on the stove and cracked open a beer as Rufus powered through a full bowl of Dog Chow like a dieter on a bender. As meat sizzled on the stovetop, filling his kitchen with the enticing aroma, he contemplated his beer bottle and his new next-door neighbor.

Abby was chock full of contradictions. On one hand, she was rather brave to move to a small blip on the map in mountain country on her own. On the other, she was seriously under-prepared for living here. It left him wondering how much he should interfere. She appeared to welcome his help. From the way Evie had talked about Abby, in many ways, Nate felt like he already knew her. Putting a face to all the stories Evie had regaled him with whenever he stopped in to make sure she was getting along fine was unique. He doubted Abby realized that he knew all about her upbringing back East and how staid it had been, or how proud Evie had been of her when she had rebelled against her parents' wishes and followed her own star.

That took gumption and guts, which would come in handy when winter arrived. And as for putting a face to all of Evie's stories, he had to revise his initial assessment of her doe eyes. He'd first believed they were a light brown, but now that he'd looked closer, he knew a verdant green shaded those hazel eyes.

The memory of the deep shade of red she'd blushed when he spied the jumbo pack of condoms made him chuckle. Her response had been rather cute and had gotten him thinking about sex and his neighbor. Lots of sex with his neighbor. Olympic, marathon sessions with the everlasting box of condoms nearby. He wondered if her skin flushed that same rosy shade during sex. She stirred him in ways he'd not expected.

Sliding the steak onto a plate, he froze. Was she seeing someone? Did she have a significant other, some slick city guy who would blaze into Nate's town in a sports car shaped like a penis?

The last time Evie had mentioned Abby, she'd mentioned Abby had despaired in her latest letter about being too different to find anyone. Evie had laughed and told him it was because her grandniece was like her in temperament and didn't suffer fools lightly. Had that status changed? He didn't mind a little competition, but he also didn't share or tend to poach on territory that had already been claimed. Was that why she'd bought the industrial size box of condoms, for marathon sex filled weekends with some jerkoff with a house in the Hamptons?

Nate knew he'd never be able to compete with a city slicker. That didn't mean he wouldn't rise to the challenge and discover if there was a boyfriend waiting in the wings. If not, well, he and his hormones would cross that bridge then.

Attempting to divert his thoughts away from Abby, he plowed through his steak, needing the fuel to start work on the renovations upstairs. The house was in the middle of a forced transition. Currently, he lived on the first-floor proper while he spent his free time away from upholding law and order and was remodeling the second floor. Plans and blueprints, sawdust and drywall occupied most nights. All in an effort to expand the master bedroom, merge it with the small closet-sized room next to it, and convert the bathroom into a modern bath suite, while adding a second bathroom. Nate was of the belief that if you built it, what you wanted would come. It was like giving a sign to the universe that you were ready for it in your life.

At thirty-three he found he wanted more, wanted a place that was his, which was why he'd purchased Old Man Turner's place a few years back and had begun remodeling it little by little. The house had needed a ton of work when he'd bought it, which was how he'd been able to afford it on the cheap. He'd begun with the exterior, the roof, porch and overhang. He'd replaced all the windows two years ago with more energy efficient glass instead of the ancient single paned windows that had leaked like a sinking ship.

After college, he'd tried the city thing in Denver for a few years and hated every blasted minute of it. The only reason he'd moved there had been for his college girlfriend, because he'd convinced himself it was what he wanted, when he'd just been toeing the line to be with Stacy. During his first year in Denver, Nate had worked construction while he trained at the police academy. He never wanted for work in a town that was expanding at exponential rates. But he'd detested the grind and faster-than-light-speed pace. He'd worked as a traffic cop for a handful of years and, after his relationship with Stacy imploded, had made his way back to where he'd gotten his start: Echo Springs, Colorado, population 2,141, including Abby.

He tossed a grateful Rufus his scraps, which were snatched midair and swallowed in a heartbeat. "Let's go get to work, boy."

Rufus woofed in agreement as Nate set his dishes in the sink to wash in the morning and headed up the stairs. He glanced out his bedroom window and noticed Abby sitting near the window, staring at a computer and wearing sexy-as-hell librarian-style glasses. He rubbed a hand over his stomach. She did something to him. He hadn't been interested in a woman in quite a while. That didn't mean he was a monk, by any means, but he hadn't considered a woman relationship material since Stacy, really, and that was years ago. Problem was, he didn't know if Abby was the type to stick or not. Based on the stories Evie had told him, she'd been of the belief that Abby was destined to work at a prestigious college. The nearest one to their little town was a good hundred miles away. It made the potential with his new neighbor plummet.

Then again, for all he knew, a few sweaty bouts between the sheets might be all that was needed. In his mind's eye, he was already whipping up a fantasy of his neighbor wearing her sexy-as-hell glasses and nothing else. Turning from the window, lest he be caught spying like a peeping Tom and freak her out, he slid his safety goggles on and face mask over his mouth and nostrils, switched on his stereo, and hoisted the sledgehammer. If he could get the rest of this wall torn down tonight, he could start on ripping up the flooring tomorrow and building the frame for the new walls by this weekend. After he helped his sexy neighbor first, of course.

Rufus was already sprawled in the far corner, snoring loud enough to wake the dead, and Nate swung the sledge. A plume of dust filled the air and hunks of drywall rained onto the floor. He liked the mindless, physical exertion behind construction. Some days, he enjoyed it more than his police work, which out here in the boonies was usually no more than a few drunk drivers, trespassing on private property, speeding tickets and an inordinate amount of paperwork. Although, he preferred it much more than the close calls he'd had in Denver. That was even with the recent rash of break-ins. While he was a bit miffed that they didn't have a suspect yet, he was confident he and his team would uncover who was behind the thefts. In a town like Echo Springs, nothing stayed hidden for long.

And there was the one call he almost hadn't walked away from, which had made him reprioritize his life. He liked the slower pace of police work here in his hometown, nestled against the backdrop of mountains, where he knew the people and their problems. Life here was simpler, less frenetic, and this was the only place he saw himself ever wanting to live. The old sheriff, who'd known him as a rapscallion teen, had hired him and become his mentor, showing him the true meaning behind their motto, To Serve and Protect. When Sheriff Randall retired, he'd ensured that Nate was promoted and took over his position.

Nate swung in time to the beat of the hard rock music as chunks of wall and splintered wood fell into a heap of rubble, uncovering a hidden bookshelf that had been built into the wall and then drywalled over. *Idiots.* Who would do something like that? It was a shame, really, that he hadn't known about the shelf before demolishing half of it. As he reached the midway point, where the bedroom and bathroom walls met, he swung the hammer, and a leather-bound book fell amidst the debris. Setting the sledgehammer down, handle up, he picked up the book, wiping the film of dust away with his hands, and flipped through it. The first entry was dated 1941.

Taking a breather, snatching up a bottle of water from the cooler he kept up there, he sat next to Rufus on the floor. It wasn't a book, but a journal of sorts, hand-written cursive scrawled in black upon the yellowed pages. He read:

It was the summer of 1941, and I can still remember the unseasonably scorching heat rolling across the plains and into the mountains that June. My parents' farm was suffering, with low yields on their wheat and hay crops, and had fallen on hard times. To help them out, I returned from college and took work that summer in the nearby mountain town of Echo Springs, serving burgers and milkshakes. Tourists flocked to the small town with their Chevrolets.

I remember the day my world changed irrevocably. Temperatures neared triple digits by ten in the morning. Most of the tourists had opted for availing themselves of their hotel pools and local lakes to battle the sweltering air. I had just taken a break from the oppressive heat in the kitchen as the midafter-

noon lull took over the diner, when she walked in and altered the course of my life forever.

Evelyn Callier sashayed in wearing a red shirtwaist dress with white polka dots. The dress hugged her pinup-girl curves. Her long blonde tresses were curled soft and invitingly over her round shoulders. While the rest of the diner's guests had wilted in the heat, Evelyn looked as fresh as a mountain spring.

When she sat on a barstool, the Formica countertop between us, I felt like the sun had finally entered my life. Her silver eyes had a devil-may-care air, framed by long sooty lashes.

I approached and found my tongue stuck to the roof of my mouth. I couldn't help but stare, as she was the most beautiful creature I'd ever seen. My mouth moved in an attempt to form words and ask her for her order. I knew I must look like a guppy tossed onto dry land as I stood there, frozen, my mouth open with no sound coming out.

"Hello. How do you do? Can I trouble you for a chocolate milkshake?" The heavenly angel's voice was suffused with mischief and gumption. She knew the effect her appearance had on me as she smiled slyly, a pouty smirk on her lips painted the identical ruby red as her dress.

Her words spurred me into action. "Yes, miss. Coming right up."

I'm not sure precisely what transpired next. Much of it is still hazy. Part of the flooring was still slick from Carl's piss-poor mopping job. My foot slipped as I turned, and I hit my head on the counter as I fell.

I came to with my head pillowed in her lap. Her gregarious silver eyes were dampened with concern, and a circle of patrons and diner workers had formed around me. She volunteered to go with me to the doctor's office three doors down. I had a cut on my head that needed stitches. My angel held my hand through all of it. She drove me home in her '39 Dodge coupe and helped my mother get me out of the car. In addition to the cut, I had a concussion and was supremely thankful that the drive was over before I gave in to the need to upchuck with my stomach rolling and pitching from my injuries.

My mother asked her to stay for dinner. That was something I have always remembered about my mother. Even when we didn't have much, and there were plenty of lean years, she always managed to make a nice dinner.

"Thank you, I really must be getting home, Mrs. Turner, before my

mother worries," Evie refused. I worried instantly that I would never see her again. That the farm with its sheep nearby grazing and their house were lacking in some way.

"Thank you for bringing my Bill home. It was a pleasure to meet you, Evelyn. You be safe on those roads," my mother said.

"I will. Feel better, Bill." She'd given me a sly, gamine grin, and rocked my world at its foundation. I didn't know it then, but later I would judge the epochs in my life by Evie's appearance in it.

I nodded, sure in the knowledge that I would do whatever it took to keep her in my life. I said, "Thank you, Evie."

After that initial meeting, Evie and I were inseparable that summer. Any time I had off from the diner or the farm, I spent with her. Looking back, they were without a doubt, the purest, most enjoyable days of my life. There was an innocence borne of youth and that short-sighted, idyllic notion that nothing would ever change. It was an insulated time and precious, though we didn't realize it then.

Nate sat, his back resting against the wall, stunned. Old Man Turner and Evie had been an item? This was the first he had ever heard of it. This town wasn't known for keeping its residents' secrets, it was where gossip fodder was traded at the supermarket. Turner died more than a decade ago, and this house had sat vacant until Nate returned to Echo Springs four years ago. Growing up, he had always believed Turner was just a recluse after his wife and oldest child died in a car accident, but if he and Evie were an item, why hadn't they gotten hitched?

He read a little further.

I remember the day I asked Evie on our first date. I was finishing up a shift at the diner a week after my fall and saw her exiting a dress shop on Main Street with a box in her hands. With my nerves battering my stomach like a startled swarm of bats, I rushed outside and hurried across the street.

"Evelyn," I said, although really, in my exuberance not to let her disappear from my life again, it came out as more of a shout. And I got a few stares in my direction for my trouble. But the only one that mattered was Evie.

She turned, a smile played over her lips as she spotted me. "Bill, it's nice to see you again. How's your head feeling?"

"Much better. There's only one of you now."

Evie laughed, her joy melodious and deep. "That's good to know."

"Mind if I walk you to your car?" I asked. Just being near her made my heart pound and turned my palms slick with sweat.

"That would be lovely."

"How are you liking Echo Springs?" I asked, trying to learn more about my angel.

"It is quite different from Boston. But I find myself enjoying it here more than I thought I would. And I thank you, for walking me to my car," she replied. Her gaze was hidden behind a pair of sunglasses but I noticed the way the corners of her mouth were curved up.

I glanced at her coupe, wishing I had more time with her. I don't know how, but I found my courage and said, "Next week is the Founders' Day Fair. Would you like to go with me?"

Evie tilted her head to the side and her smile grew wider. "I would like that very much, Bill. What time can I pick you up?" she teased.

I wasn't worried about my pride, that I did not have a vehicle of my own and borrowed my parents' to get to work. Evie had said yes to going out with me and that was all that mattered. After seeing her off, I headed back to the diner where I had parked my mother's car that day and drove home like I was floating on a cloud.

I knew even then how monumental it was that she said yes. That she was going to change my life in ways I had not even begun to comprehend.

And I'm writing this story, our story, more for myself as a catharsis on many levels. It's my hope that maybe one day, if anyone should read this journal who needs a little help in the romance department, they will find the courage and fortitude to woo the love of their life. My first rule: a man without a plan isn't ready to date.

Nate shook his head, bookmarked his place, and set the journal down. Was that what he was? A man without a plan? He went back to work with the sledgehammer. He was remodeling the upper floor for himself, although in the back of his mind he'd begun to think about continuity and family. As someone who'd grown up without a father, and with a mother who was more concerned with scoring her next hit, Nate had strived to better himself so that he wasn't just Sheila Barnes' son, whom everyone in town felt sorry for.

With his mom passing away last year, and his sister living in Los Angeles, Nate had begun to feel a bit like an orphan. It was probably why the former sheriff had taken such an interest, acting more like a father figure than his superior. But at thirty-three, Nate found himself wanting more out of life. It was one of the reasons he'd adopted Rufus.

Maybe he should try some of the old man's suggestions from his romance manifesto on his neighbor, especially considering every time he was in her vicinity, he wanted to trade places with Rufus in her affections and have her delicate fingers rubbing his belly—along with a few other choice spots. While he wasn't certain he wanted the complication, especially on the off chance that she fled come spring, he had to admit he found himself thinking about her and conjuring up fantasies about her lush little body non-stop.

Chapter Four

From Old Man Turner's Journal:
Start as you mean to go on.

A bby opened a bleary eye at the incessant knocking originating from the front door. The clock on her night-stand declared it was just after eight in the morning. On a Satur-day, no less. When the knocking didn't stop but increased in pace, she slid out of bed with a grimace, grabbed her robe and put her glasses on as she headed downstairs.

First order of business for today, kill whoever was at the door. Second, make coffee. Abby was not a fan of mornings. In fact, it was better just to leave her be until she'd had, at the very mini-mum, one cup of coffee—two were better, three were optimal. Did she have a problem where coffee was concerned? Probably. Did she care? Not in the slightest.

Who the hell was at her door at this hour? She was thinking maybe she should have grabbed her nine-iron until she heard a deep rumbling woof. Rufus, which meant it was Sheriff Stud Muffin banging on her door at this ungodly hour. It would be bad form to kill the sheriff, wouldn't it? Running a hand over her hair, wishing like hell she had thought to run a brush through it, she unlocked and opened the door. Rufus' hulking form barreled in, prancing around her entryway with his *hello, I'm so excited to see you* flair, while his owner stood in the doorway with a bemused expression, sexy as sin in dark jeans and a button-up royal blue flannel shirt, the sleeves rolled up to display his muscular forearms. It should be a crime that he looked so fresh and alert, tackling the early morning the way he appeared to do everything—with the utter assurance that the world bent before him. Abby cringed internally because she knew, when it came to mornings, she always looked like something the cat dragged in, and bemoaned her haggard appearance. Especially considering a part of her brain pushed past wakefulness into aroused as she stared at the way the flannel clung to his broad shoulders and licked her lips. Who knew flannel could be sexy?

"Morning?" Nate's baritone voice resonated as if calibrated to the right dissonance and frequency to spark every cell in her body to stand at attention.

"Morning," she croaked, her voice crackling from lack of moisture, making her sound more like a frog than the well-put-together woman she wanted to appear to be. Who the hell was she kidding? Part of the reason she was here, instead of hiring someone to handle her aunt's estate, was to get a handle on her life and decide what she wanted. It was why she was dipping into her inheritance for the next few months. She had to figure out the right direction, meaning deciding on the university where she wanted to teach and potentially conduct research at after graduation. Both were huge decisions in the scheme of her life, with potentially cataclysmic ripple effects if she selected the wrong one. Perhaps she'd been part of her parents' world of academia for too long. And while there was a part of her that didn't want to choose, and would much rather burrow into reality here, she couldn't forget that this wasn't home—this was a stopover.

He quirked a lopsided grin in her direction and asked, "Did you forget our date?"

Abby's brain misfired completely. Date? They didn't have a date, did they? "What date?"

Date? When did Nate ask her on a date? She would have remembered that little detail. Surely, she wouldn't forget Sheriff Stud Muffin asking her out. Her brain scrambled to recall their conversations, but it mingled with the romance novel she'd indulged in last night as her body whimpered for coffee.

Nate tilted his head to the side and gave her a perplexed stare. "Our firewood date, remember? Or am I that easy to forget?"

Her body simply went into overdrive at his flirting, with her ovaries doing a victory dance and the distinct urge rising to satisfy her oral craving for caffeine by latching her mouth onto various parts of his body. She stuttered, actually stuttered, flames heating her cheeks which she was certain must be fire engine red by now, and said, "N-n-n-no, I-I-I didn't forget. Come on in while I make some coffee."

"Late night?" he asked, wiping his hiking boots on the front porch mat before entering. His energy suffused the small space of her foyer. A woman would have to be dead not to feel it and last she checked, she was among the living. Then again, perhaps her undead army of dolls in the next room had rid her of the mortal coil overnight, which could account for her lack of brain power this morning. Nate engendered a primal, biological response in Abby. It was like her DNA recognized his masculinity as a prime directive to procreate for continuation of the species. The potency was so intense that if he wasn't standing two feet away, observing her intently with what she was certain was his law enforcement brain that cataloged crime scenes, she would have been fanning herself. As it was, she was already planning on a cold shower or two after he left in order to diffuse the sudden onslaught of need flowing in her veins.

"Something like that." She did her best to sound cool and

suave, but her reply came out flustered and breathless. This was why she did her best not to interact with other people until she was sufficiently caffeinated. Abby couldn't be trusted not to say or do dumb things without it. Mortified, not only because he was seeing her once again in her pajamas, but because he must think she was the biggest moron on the planet, she turned on her heel and headed toward the kitchen with Nate two steps behind her. It unnerved the very fiber of her being having him so near.

Abby withdrew the coffee carafe from its maker, and Nate laid a hand over hers. She almost dropped the glass pot at his touch and gripped the handle tighter. Tingles permeated her system from his slight, and rather innocent, touch. They ricocheted through her body like pinballs as she glanced up. His light blue stare was a sucker punch to her midsection. Abby didn't want to read into the care and compassion in those blue depths.

"Why don't you go get dressed and I'll put the coffee on? How do you like it?" Nate asked, and Abby couldn't seem to muster an intelligent response.

"Um…" Brain cells were imploding at his touch. How did she like her coffee? *Hot and dark and filled to the brim…* "Strong enough to power the city of Denver."

"Extra strong. Got it. I can take it from here if you want to get ready," he offered, concern dotting his brow as he took over. Did the man even have a flaw? Nate was drop dead gorgeous, had a dog who clearly worshiped him, lived to protect the small town, and then took the time out of his schedule to help his scatterbrained neighbor with a basic task. So not only was he a hunk, but he had a deep-in-the-bone goodness about him. A man for whom things like honor and trust were an inherent part of his makeup. It was an intoxicating combination. Her un-caffeinated brain went from super sleepy to craving to see Sheriff Stud Muffin naked.

Rattled, aroused, and all before a cup of Joe… suffice to say Abby needed to get a grip. For all she knew about him, which was a big fat lot of nothing, Nate was the Grand Master in control of the undead doll army residing in the living room and the moment she caved to his potent yumminess, he would use the demon doll brigade to trap her like the psycho chick in *Misery*.

But oh, was she ready—her body, anyway, if the melty sensation in her core was any indication. Abby wondered if it was possible to climax just by having Sheriff Stud Muffin look at her. As much as she'd love to discover that one, before she did something marginally stupid, say, take a bite out of him, or plant her face in his chest and inhale his manly aroma, she needed a breather away from him to collect her thoughts and sanity. "Okay, thanks. I'll be right back down."

She twisted to leave, desperate to avoid doing any untimely, unsolicited groping, and then Rufus decided to say hello and shoved his nose in her crotch. Abby knew it was harmless, but it made her exit laughable at best. Groaning internally as she wished for the army of undead dolls to attack and save her from the mortification, she pushed Rufus away. It was like attempting to move a boulder, and rather delighted him as he danced around her tiny kitchen, considering her actions more play than discipline.

Abby hightailed it away from the kitchen and the seductive temptation that was Nate Barnes, with Rufus shadowing her. And then he trailed her up the stairs to her room. Before she could utter the command for the rascal to wait outside, he barged past her and leapt onto her bed where he sprawled out, stretching his mammoth body the length of the queen-sized mattress with his head on one of the pillows. Rufus grinned at her, his expression one of sublime bliss.

"You're an easy one to please, aren't you? Don't get yourself too comfortable." Rolling her eyes at the turn of events, Abby prayed that her hormones would get back with the regularly scheduled program, erect a safe emotional and physical difference from the man and mutt, and settle down to an acceptable level. And didn't it just smart that she sounded just like her parents? Wasn't that what she was trying to avoid by spending time in Echo Springs? She shut the bedroom door and dressed in more acceptable gear for the rustic outdoors while Rufus lay on her bed with a *this is the life* look across his face.

Abby dressed in record time, opting for the hiking boots she'd picked up at Gundry's on a whim. If she was going to be forced to do the outdoors thing, she'd at least do it comfortably. When she was as ready for the day as possible, now fully dressed and groomed—she wasn't going to think about the bedhead disaster her hair had been—she headed downstairs, following the heady scent of coffee, Rufus a step behind her.

Abby entered the kitchen and all but melted on the spot. Nate, in all his flanneled glory, stood at her stove wielding a spatula like he belonged there. The thoughtful man had not only fixed her coffee, but had taken it upon himself to make breakfast. Her ovaries sighed. She couldn't want him. She wasn't even sure she would be here past this semester. Nate slid an omelet onto a plate. It made her mouth water, and not just for the food.

"Here, you'll need fuel for today." He handed her the plate.

"Um, thanks." She accepted the plate from his hands and was more than a little flummoxed. He'd made her breakfast. Abby couldn't recall a man ever making her breakfast before. And seeing him at her aunt's stainless-steel stove like he was perfectly at home there was incredibly sexy.

"Coffee's ready." He pointed to a steaming granite-colored mug that he'd already placed on the table for her.

There had to be something wrong with the man—like, he must have a small package. Her gaze inadvertently drifted to the package in question. She almost choked on her first sip of coffee as she sat. Yep, nothing wrong with the size. Maybe it was crooked or something. Abby mainlined her first cup of coffee like a college kid doing a keg stand. By her second cup, caffeine buzzed her system and began to make her feel normal.

Nate joined her at the pine table with a plate and coffee mug. "Have you checked your aunt's storage shed for an ax?"

Around a bite of eggs, she swallowed and gave him a sheepish glance. "Do I lose brownie points if I say no?"

"No. I have a few on hand, but we may want to take a look at what's inside. If you have any, I can examine what shape they are in and whether they need to be sharpened. I know Evie had the Styman boys tending her lawn fairly regularly, so I'm not positive what is in her shed."

It made sense. Abby knew that to survive up here she'd have to venture down avenues of the outdoorsman lifestyle that she had only ever read about in books like *The Call of the Wild*. She knew she would soon encounter the question of whether she was a city girl or a country girl. Considering the number of horror films that took place in the middle of nowhere, she leaned toward city girl, but for the time being, she was here in the wilds of Colorado and doing the country thing, even if the designation was purely temporary. Nate, on the other hand, was all rough mountain man who had her tangled up in her underwear.

She finally replied, "I admit I haven't had a chance to touch the outside of the house. There's been enough inside for me to wade through."

"Like creepy dolls?" He gave her a half smirk, merriment dancing in his cornflower gaze.

"Precisely. One never knows when one will have to fend off an army of undead dolls."

"Undead army?"

She shrugged. "I have a thing for horror movies."

"Really?"

"Yes, all the classic stuff, of course. *Nosferatu* and *Creature From the Black Lagoon*. But, for me, the real heyday was in the seventies and early eighties with all the campy horror films."

Nate regarded her with interest in his gaze, unlike her family who stared at her like she'd mysteriously grown a pair of antlers. He questioned, "What do you like about them?"

No one had asked her that before. Her family was so strait-laced that her horror film obsession left them gaping at her like she was ready for a straitjacket. "Um, I would say I like how predictable they are, and the lengths a director will go to try and scare the audience. It's the bad acting and the fact that the killer doesn't die easily, if at all. And it spices up things a bit."

"My favorite are the zombie films from that era," Nate murmured. A grin broke out across her face, and they shared a smile of understanding.

Abby fought the urge to ask him more about himself. A part of her wanted to field him twenty questions, uncover what made him tick, and peel back his layers to reveal the man underneath. He fascinated her, made her desire to toss all her rules and staid reactions of noninvolvement out the window, and try him on for size. But she couldn't be interested in Nate. In all likelihood, she would be gone by Christmas, or the end of the spring term. It would be wrong to start something she wasn't certain she could finish.

It didn't matter that her ovaries wanted to move right past getting to know you to doing the hanky panky. Those little bastards were puckering up and batting their lashes in Nate's direction.

She sighed and ran a mantra through her brain on repeat.

Work, good. Sexing up lawman neighbor, bad.

Speaking of which, she still had lesson plans to finish compiling for this week and needed to get this firewood show on the road. Finished with breakfast, Abby stood, picking up her empty plate and heading over to the sink. She laid it in the sink basin, thinking she had to unload the dishes from the dishwasher at some point today too. Then she turned and bumped into Nate.

It happened rather comically, like in the movies, where everything stalled into slow motion. His coffee mug launched backward and doused his chest with its remaining contents. "Shit, I'm sorry," she said. "Here, let me help you." Mortified beyond belief, she grabbed her kitchen towel and started mopping up the liquid staining his plaid shirt.

"I can get it. And I guess, in the scheme of things, we're even for Rufus turning you into a mat," he said with a teasing note in his voice.

Then his large hands covered hers, stalling their frantic movements to sop up any remaining liquid, suddenly making her realize that she had her hands plastered against some rather well-formed pectorals. His pecs. And, sweet heavens, what pecs. At his name, Rufus decided to join in on the fun and sprang up from his napping spot under the dinette. He nosed them apart so that he was wedged between them, prancing in his exuberance.

"Yeah, I guess so." She regretfully withdrew her hands from his chest. "I feel so bad. Let me at least wash it for you. I have to do some laundry later today anyhow."

"Appreciate it." Nate unbuttoned his shirt, revealing miles of taut male muscles, the kind that made smart women do really dumb things. Her ovaries, those little bastards, were cheering like tweens at a boy-band concert. While he was lean, he wasn't soft in the slightest, with ropes of steely muscles covering his broad shoulders. And he had the sexiest damn arms.

Before Abby's brain connected with the rest of her body, she planted a hand on his chest, surprised that her palm didn't incinerate on contact.

"Need something, Abby?" Nate asked, his voice deeper, more full bodied, like a bottle of whiskey that had been aged well and just uncorked.

And then she glanced at his face, which was no longer filled with amusement but awash with hooded desire. His light blue gaze darkened as he studied her like a mountain lion about to pounce on its prey. What if she let him? Gave in to the need he had awakened within her body? Would it be so bad? Part of her decision to come here was that she needed to know if there was more to life than constantly working all the time. She wanted to find the fun and joy in life that seemed to be absent. When the flat disks of his nipples hardened into points under her gaze,

Abby backpedaled, withdrawing her hand, until her rear hit the lip of the kitchen sink.

"No, um, sorry. Let me take that, and I will toss it in the wash, then I'll meet you outside."

Abby would welcome evisceration from her aunt's undead doll army right about now. Heat blazed in her cheeks. Nate's intense gaze homed in on her lips, like he was debating internally whether to make a move, and her pulse accelerated. She almost wished he would take the decision out of her hands, because it would alleviate her guilt about manhandling him in her aunt's kitchen. She wanted him but couldn't seem to force herself to reach out and take the next step. Well, more than she already had, anyway. When he handed her the drenched shirt instead, she couldn't ignore the disappointment that rose in her breast. His fingers brushed hers, and the livewire connection shook her to her foundation.

"Well, you let me know if you do… need something from me." His baritone resonated in her chest and then he retreated a few steps, breaking the spell his nearness had created.

"Will do. I'll meet you outside in a minute." So that she could take a nice cold shower before the army of dolls attacked. The last thing she wanted to be when those creepy little suckers launched their assault was horny. And it would give her a breather so that she didn't jump her neighbor's bones. The little fact that he'd seemed on board with her frisking him like he was carrying a concealed weapon had not gone unnoticed.

Abby clenched his wet shirt in her hands as she escaped the kitchen. She heard her back-door open, Rufus barking enthusiastically as the duo headed into her backyard. It was a rather odd occurrence, but her disappointment that things had not progressed with Nate was quite profound. The thought of getting an all-access pass to explore his stellar physique sent whirls of desire through her veins and made her want to toss her good common sense out the window.

She smelled his shirt, a combination of rugged man with

hints of cypress and sandalwood spliced with the coffee soaking part of the material, before dropping the garment into the washing machine. And then it hit her. She had to survive him being shirtless as he helped her cut firewood.

Abby wouldn't have to worry about an army of undead dolls when the likelihood of spontaneous combustion from sexual frustration was much more probable at this point.

Chapter Five

From Old Man Turner's Journal:
Don't interrogate your date.

Nate stood on Abby's back porch inhaling chill mountain air, attempting to douse the incessant blaze her innocuous touch had ignited. Where her palm had pressed against his chest burned like a brand. Nor had he failed to notice that she was as mesmerized as he was by the intoxicating energy present whenever they were in each other's vicinity.

Instinctively, he knew he could have pressed his advantage and now be happily availing himself of her body's supple charms. And for the life of him, he wasn't certain what had stopped him from taking that step. There was one part of his anatomy that was downright pissed that he wasn't doing the horizontal tango with Abby.

He rubbed a hand over his belly in an effort to quell his lust. Perhaps it was because he genuinely liked her. Even her obsession with her aunt's doll collection and love affair with horror films— instead of being disturbing, with Abby, it was rather adorable.

Who would have believed bright pink pajamas and bedhead would send his hormones into overdrive? When she had opened the door, he had wanted to take her right back up to bed and see if he could muss her hair up even more.

After a few calming breaths had settled some of the most potent edges of his raging lust, Nate loped down the stairs. Rufus was sniffing every bush and shrub in Abby's yard. Nate had already erected a wood-chopping station between his house and hers before he'd knocked on her door this morning. He'd had a few boxelders come down on his property that he had already stripped of their branches—for kindling—and chopped into fireplace sized logs. Today's lesson was all about showing her how to swing an ax.

What he really needed was to go dunk himself in the nearby stream. He picked up his ax, setting a block of wood up on a stump, positioned his body and swung. Maybe if he worked up a sweat this way, it would eliminate the need cascading through his body. He spent the next five minutes focused on chopping wood while listening to Rufus root around in the bushes.

Nearby, an eagle screeched, disturbing the stillness and quiet to be found away from the main hub of town. This was part of what he loved about living on the outskirts of Echo Springs; the solitude and peace. This place rejuvenated him, helped center him, unlike cities such as Denver, which made him feel like he was disconnected and frantic. There was no comparison between the two for him.

He felt more than saw eyes on him. Still holding the ax, he swiveled. Abby stood ten feet away and stared with a slack-jawed expression, her luscious mouth forming an O. Desire clouded her expressive face, and the brunt of lust he had worked to expel roared back to life. The attraction between them palpable, as if it were a living, breathing entity. Abby broke the connection, shook herself out of her stupor, and cleared her throat.

"What would you like me to do?" she asked, her voice a husky alto, and his blood simmered.

If he told Abby the truth, let his fervent desire be known, the rosy blush infusing her cheeks would darken in indignation and she'd likely run screaming for the hills. One item Nate needed to square away was whether she was seeing someone. If he was going to use Old Man Turner's manifesto to woo her into his bed, he wanted to make damn sure there were no other contenders. If there was one thing Nate refused to be, it was one of many in a woman's bed. Regardless of whether a full relationship developed between them or not, he didn't share the woman he was sleeping with, with another man.

"Have you ever swung an ax before?" He eyed her skeptically. Maybe this was a bad idea and he should just complete the task for her. Only, this was a way to get in her space and get to know her better, potentially further whatever the connection was between them.

She slid her hands in the pockets of her skinny jeans. Those suckers hugged every blessed curve of her legs, and it took all his brain power to stay focused on the task at hand instead of fantasizing about how those legs would feel in his hands and wrapped around his waist.

"No, I can't say that I have," she admitted.

"Okay, you want to grip the base with your hands spread, like this." He demonstrated his hold. "And then, when you swing, put some torque behind it by using gravity to help, like this."

He positioned a piece of wood on the block and illustrated the proper way to chop it. Nate performed the action a second time for good measure.

"Questions?" He swiveled back toward Abby and came up short. Her eyes were wide and saturated with hunger. Her hands were clenched at her sides like she was just barely keeping them to herself as she watched him chop wood.

"Abby?" he said, battling his own lust as it thundered to the forefront with a vengeance.

"Umm, I don't think so."

"Then here, why don't you try?" He held the ax out to her

while she chewed on her plump bottom lip. Nate should just say to hell with it and sate his lust. It was clear she wanted him.

Abby straightened her shoulders, then approached and said, "Anything else I should know?"

"Just take your time until you feel you have it gripped properly. The last thing you want to do is drop the ax in mid-swing."

"Okay. I can do this," she said, more to herself than to him. She accepted the ax from his hands, flexing her fingers around the handle. She hoisted the blade back above her head and was about to swing when he stopped her.

"Hold up." He approached cautiously, not wanting her to bean him with the sharp edge. She jerked and repositioned the ax so that it wasn't over her head.

"What did I do wrong?"

"Not wrong, but here, if you put your grip here and here"— he moved her hands a bit farther apart—"that should make it a little more stable."

"But then how do I—"

"Swing? Here." He moved behind her, slid his arms around her, which was something he had yearned to do since meeting her, and placed his hands over hers. He performed the movement, taking her through the correct way to swing it a few times until he felt she'd understood. As it was, her lush compact body pressed intimately to his was making his eyes cross. She was all curves and gentle warmth. Her pulse at her wrists thumped a mile a minute, telling him with more than words that she was as affected by their close proximity as he was. He had to move, and soon, otherwise he wouldn't be able to hide his desire for her. Although, she wasn't shoving him off.

"Got it?" he asked into her ear. His mouth hovered near the delicate skin of her neck. Christ, he wanted a taste of her.

"Mmmhmm," she murmured, and it sounded like a breathy sigh.

It caused a part of his anatomy to stand at attention. "Good. Why don't you try it a few times on your own?"

He released her, retreating a few steps, inhaling the pine scented air to clear his senses. Nate didn't have any other option. Need hammered his system, causing him to rethink this strategic get-to-know-you session. Her succulent, petite body made him want to defy conventional rules and entice her into a different type of physical activity.

"Once you have it down, you can show your boyfriend, or what have you." He realized he was fishing, but damn it, he didn't care.

"I don't have one, so that won't be an issue."

"Why not?" he asked. As it was, watching her concentrate as she swung the ax with a determined scowl on her face was jumbling up his insides.

"Um, I've been busy working on my dissertation and haven't really had the time."

"I see." His inner caveman all but bellowed in triumph and staked his claim on her. Excitement hummed in his veins. The seduction started now.

"How was that?" She stood back, wiping her brow with her sleeve, her cheeks flushed from exertion.

"Good. Now, let's chop some wood. Oh, and Abby? I'm glad you're not seeing anyone."

ABBY HUFFED as she hefted the ax for what seemed like the hundredth time. Sweat poured down her back. And if her hot-as-hell neighbor distracted her a bit, she did her best to hide it. He was happy she was single, which meant that, since he was asking, he most likely was single as well. Between the innuendo, sexual frustration, and physical exertion, Abby was just proud of the fact that she could still lift the ax. She was using muscles that she hadn't even known she had and wondered whether she'd be able to lift her arms to make dinner tonight.

Rufus snored nearby on her back porch. He was totally at home at her house.

"How often did you and Rufus visit my aunt?" she asked, setting the ax down to take a breather.

Nate wiped his brow with his forearm, and her ovaries applauded at the shifting, rippling muscles. Sheriff Stud Muffin was slick with sweat, his body glistened in the early morning sunlight, and she fought to keep her tongue from hanging out. It should be a crime for any one man to be this attractive. Her libido wasn't just back, it was turbo charged.

"Usually about once a week after I moved in. After I adopted that furball three years ago, Evie watched him for me when he was a puppy." He shrugged his massive shoulders, making every sinewy muscle flex, and Abby wondered if she was going to experience the vapors and faint like so many of the heroines in early literature. At least it would give her a reference point of experience.

And his statement completely explained why Rufus gave the impression he was right at home at her place. That little puzzle piece finally made sense.

"Are you working on your dissertation on your computer each night?" he said, taking a seat on the stump and lifting a water bottle to his lips.

"You're watching me, spying on me?" Her insides went all melty while her brain said, *Cue the campy horror music.* She truly didn't know whether to be offended and put off or thrilled. Her brain was acting like the UN, declaring a cease-fire until more information could be gathered.

"No, it's nothing like that. I usually get home after dark and have noticed you at the window a time or two."

"Oh." She wasn't certain how she felt about that.

"Abby, it's my job to notice things. It sort of comes with the 'to protect and serve' territory. And normally, by the time I make it home, yours is the only light on on this street, so yeah, I look up." He gave her a half grin infused with banked fires, and the tiny lines around his eyes deepened.

"So then I can stop thinking you're a deranged sociopath with nefarious intentions and worry more about bears invading my trash cans. Good to know," she teased him.

Abby conceded the point, moved to pick her ax up, and bent over near him just as Nate leaned forward to stand. Their craniums connected with a dull *thwack*. The odd angle of the strike knocked her backward onto her spine. Stunned, she gazed at a sunny blue sky with her head ringing like a fire alarm.

"Son of a bitch! Are you all right?" Nate exclaimed and leaned over her, his gaze roaming over her body from head to toe in an effort to assess if there was any physical damage.

One moment, he stood at a bent angle, hovering above her, and the next, a bullet in the form of Rufus collided with his backside. The impact of dog and man shoved two hundred pounds of steely muscle on top of her. The air whooshed from her lungs, and she found herself staring into light blue eyes not two inches from her face.

"Rufus," Nate said, exasperated.

The dog decided he was super thrilled with the two of them on the ground and piled on top of Nate's back. It was one thing to have just Nate wedged on top of her, but with the two of them combined, she was having trouble breathing.

Abby didn't know if it was her overexcited hormones or the fact that she couldn't manage to stay upright around the man, but she snickered. And then hooted outright. Tears of mirth streamed down her face as Rufus happily tried to insert his face between them and swipe both of their faces with his tongue. The great big belly laughs made her abs hurt. Nate's body quaked as he succumbed and guffawed.

Rufus finally flopped off Nate and sprawled next to them in the grass, which sent them further into hysterics, laughing like loons at their predicament. Then Rufus, the big goofball, spied a chipmunk racing across the yard and scampering up a nearby pine tree. In a flash, he charged after the poor little beastie, leaving them alone. In all the commotion, Nate's hips had become wedged between her legs. As their laughter died down to the two of them grinning at each other like fools, heat stirred in her belly.

Her fingers inadvertently curled into his hot, chiseled chest muscles. She noticed each pinprick of energy as it swirled in the very air they breathed. The way the sunlight hit his striking face. The sudden spark of desire as it flared to life behind his gaze, deepening the blue to nearly black. His smile faltered as the air electrified between them. Abby knew she should push him away, knew that was the right thing to do, the proper thing to do, but hell, all two hundred pounds of mountain man was all snug against her, and for the life of her, she couldn't seem to find the energy required to push him away.

Instead, she pulled him closer, her gaze intent upon his lips shrouded by dark stubble.

Before she second-guessed herself, Abby lifted her mouth nearer until his warm breath washed over her face. Then Nate's large hands framed her head, his long fingers slid into her hair, and he extinguished the remaining gap between them on a muttered curse.

In all her life, nothing had prepared Abby for being kissed by Sheriff Nate Barnes. He didn't just press his lips against hers and call it a day. Oh no, that would have been easy to walk away from. He consumed her. His mouth focused on her lips as he plundered, and she surrendered to the devastating tide, letting him sweep her away on a current of seductive desire. It was the steadfast way he cradled her head within his big hands, holding her mouth steady as he plumbed the depths of her soul with a single kiss, that altered the very fabric of her existence.

He had magic in his lips, she realized as they claimed hers. Abby moaned against the delicious onslaught, passion escalating as his kiss drove every other thought from her brain. She slid her arms around his expansive chest and tugged him closer until his body was fused to hers like a second skin. She wrapped her legs around his waist, wanting, needing, to get nearer. And still he kissed her. He kissed her like a soldier returning from the front lines who had been without a woman in years. He kissed her as if she was his reason for being, for existing, as if he couldn't get enough of her.

It was the best damn kiss of her life.

Abby's hands had a mind of their own. She caressed the miles of hard muscles spanning his back, enjoying the way they bunched and moved beneath her touch. A part of her wanted her top off so she could enjoy the feel of his naked flesh pressed intimately against hers and yet she didn't want to move him away to accomplish it. She wanted to feel every taut muscle. She played with the dimples on his lower back, running her fingers along the edge of his jeans before finally traveling below his belt and cupping his jean-clad ass. Shifting her grip to accommodate the smartphone in his back pocket, Abby tugged him closer until they were plastered against one another. Desire fanned the flames and she undulated her hips against the firm ridge of his erection.

He growled into her mouth and took their kiss deeper.

Her world centered on Nate and his glorious wonderful mouth as he drank in her moans and added a few of his own as her hands squeezed his firm buttocks. What she wanted, heaven help her, was Nate naked and inside her. She was about to break the kiss and suggest just that—well, as soon as he finished sucking on her bottom lip.

A cell phone rang rather loudly—loud enough that Nate broke their kiss. She whimpered at the loss of his spectacular lips on hers. He held himself up on one elbow and grabbed the phone from his back pocket.

He checked the caller ID and mumbled, with consternation dotting his visage, "Shit, I gotta take this."

Nate didn't move from his position on top of her as he pressed the answer button and put the phone to his ear.

"Sheriff Barnes," he said, caressing her with his eyes and all but stripping her naked. It turned her insides into a writhing mass of lava that heated every corner of her being. Oh yeah, she wanted to spend the afternoon inside with him, not worrying about her dissertation or finishing her syllabi for her classes next week.

"When?" His gaze sharpened, and he looked up, beyond where they lay.

"Give me fifteen minutes. No one goes in until I arrive, understand? Good. See you in a few." He ended the call, and his gaze drifted back to her with regret masking his features.

"I really hate to do this…"

"But you have to go," she finished for him.

He nodded and said, "Duty calls. I can finish the stack up for you tomorrow if you wouldn't mind letting Rufus stay with you today." He withdrew and stood, leaving her feeling bereft without his weight and heat, before he offered her a hand, which she graciously accepted. Nate hauled her to her feet.

"Sure, when will you be back?"

He had morphed from sexy neighbor amid a torrid, earth-shattering make-out session into a take-no-prisoners sheriff so swiftly that the change in his demeanor was startling. It was difficult for her system to process when her body was a livewire of liquidy, fiery goo from his kiss.

He ran a hand through his hair, his gaze already distant as he replied, "I'm not sure. I'm sorry, but there's a chance it could be late."

"No problem, I would enjoy the company. Rufus can stay the night."

Rufus sauntered back over to them upon hearing his name and plopped his butt on the ground as they talked.

"What do you say, sweetheart, want to stay at my place?" She directed her gaze toward Rufus, trying like hell not to be disappointed that Nate had to leave. Rufus woofed and cavorted in excitement, his tail wagging like mad. She was a moron. The disruption was Nate's job. It wasn't like he had interrupted their little tongue-hockey session on purpose.

"Here." He removed a key from his keyring and handed it to her. "So you can get his bowls or any of his food. I will try to get back at a reasonable hour, but if I can't…"

"I've got it covered. Give me your phone, Sheriff," Abby said, clutching the key, determined to push past the sexual frustration and be a responsible adult.

He gave her a wary look, one of his dark brows raised in question.

"I'll put my number in it. Call me if something happens and he can just spend the night," she explained, thinking she sounded pathetic. *Oh, zombie horde, where are you when I need you?*

He handed her his cell, his long fingers brushing hers, sending a volt of electricity through her veins. She entered her phone number, saving her information under her name before handing the device back.

Remorse blanketed his features, and he said, "Ah, sorry to cut and run like this after everything, but—"

"I understand you have to go. Be safe."

The heated stare he gave her, regret swimming in its depths, as if he was attempting to imprint the way she appeared in this moment to memory, turned her knees to jelly. And then he left her standing in the yard space between their homes, his stride imbued with purpose and determination as he marched away. She kept her gaze trained on him and his retreat until he entered his house. Hot damn, the man had one hell of a behind. Her fingers flexed as she recalled the feel of them in her hands. She fanned her face. When his front door shut behind him and she was left with only Rufus for company, she picked up the wood area as best she could, stacking what they had chopped into a neat pile. She needed to burn off the excess sexual energy smothering her system that currently had no outlet.

A few minutes later, Nate strode out his front door looking every inch a law enforcement officer. Even the firm set to his rugged shoulders screamed law and order. He shot her a lingering, panty-melting glance as he climbed into his Explorer and switched on the flashing red and blue lights.

Rooted to the spot from his heated attention, Abby knew they weren't finished. Nate's hungry stare had told her he intended on resuming their tête-à-tête when he returned. And Abby had every intention of indulging him. She didn't budge until he zoomed away at Mach speed, out to catch the bad guy. Dammit, but it was just about the sexiest thing she'd ever witnessed, him going all dominant and in control that way. It reminded her of the way he'd dominated their kiss, which made her groan.

She needed to think about something other than sex and her hot neighbor, as tantalizing as it was to imagine.

Blowing out a deep breath, she sighed and glanced down at Rufus, who had parked himself beside her when Nate left. "How about some lunch, sweetheart?"

Rufus gave an enthusiastic woof and trailed her to her back door. She had found dog bowls stowed under the kitchen sink and had picked up some kibble for a just-in-case scenario yesterday when she was in town.

And for Abby, on today's lunch menu: wine and a plate of brownies, just as soon as she finished baking them. Nate had her so twisted up on the inside, she worried that she would implode from all the excess energy—and it had only been a kiss.

But it had been the mother lode of kisses.

Chapter Six

From Old Man Turner's Journal:
Don't forget the flowers. Good for any occasion. Bring tokens of your affection
to show you care.

Nate drove away from Abby feeling like he was going to crawl out of his skin at any moment. The way her body had enveloped and surrounded his, her hands digging into his ass as the inferno raged between them… he'd damn near come in his pants like an unschooled teen.

And her taste, vanilla and sunshine, was something that would live with him. He craved her now. She was in his blood.

If the call hadn't come through when it had, he wasn't sure they would have stopped, and he'd likely now be buried inside her welcoming heat. He gritted his teeth as his body, already on a sexual edge, revved back to life at the thought of feeling her writhing beneath him again.

Next time, he'd be more prepared.

He took a few deep steadying breaths as he drove, attempting to regain his composure before he arrived at the scene. The last thing he wanted to do was exit his police cruiser sporting wood. In a small town like Echo Springs, that would be something the townsfolk discussed at the local diner for the next twenty years.

He drove with precision as he wove in and out of traffic on his way to the crime scene. This was the third break-in over the last month. Being a small tourist stop—if you blinked while driving along Interstate 70, you'd miss it—they didn't experience high crime rates. So a rash of break-ins was certainly cause for concern. It made him wonder if some of Denver's criminal element were heading farther afield and targeting Echo Springs.

He parked the Explorer in front of James and Angela Beaumont's place, a blue Victorian two-story with a wraparound porch. The couple operated the tourist shop Get Your Rocks Off, over on Main Street, and did a more than decent amount of business. They were in their early fifties, and their two kids, Sally and Owen, attended Echo Springs High School and worked in the store after school.

Their house was in what was considered the better part of town, which was half a mile from the bad section. Some things in this town never changed. Stately Victorians lined the street in various shades and colors. Nate remembered riding his bike into this neighborhood as a kid and wondering about the rich people who lived there.

Neighbors peeked from behind curtains, curious about the police presence. Nate's two deputies were already at the scene when he stepped from his vehicle and headed up the drive. They stood on the porch, flanking the distressed couple seated on a porch swing. Deputy Denny Filbert was a man in his mid-fifties who was not aging well, based on his sagging jowls, comb-over, and the paunch that bulged against his uniform dress shirt so that a glimpse of his white undershirt was always visible. Deputy Greg O'Leary was a young hot rod in his twenties, just back from his stint in the army and always up for action. He had all the young women in town mooning after him.

Angela dabbed at the corners of her sienna eyes, the

haunted, dazed expression on her youthful face that Nate had witnessed one too many times on victims. Then there was her husband, James, whose large, stalwart frame vibrated with a fiercely protective anger as he kept an arm around his wife.

"James, Angela, I wish I was seeing you under better circumstances."

James glared. "So do we, Sheriff. I'm just glad we discovered the break-in, and not our kids." His statement brought a fresh bout of tears to Angela's eyes and her lower lip trembled.

Nate wished he could take away their pain. They were displaying textbook grief symptoms often shown by victims of a crime. Attempting to soften the impact, he withdrew a notebook and pen from his breast pocket and sat across from them on a white wicker loveseat, trying to make it appear like they were just having a conversation. Then he proceeded with his line of questioning and asked, "Can you tell me what happened?"

He clicked the pen to begin noting his observations and the victims' comments.

"There's not much to tell. We left with the kids this morning to open the store. Angela and I had some errands to run, buying runs to make into Denver, and left right after we dropped Sally and Owen off to man the store about eight thirty or so this morning."

"Did you lock the house when you left?" he asked.

"We always do. And I know you're probably thinking we forgot and that's how the burglar made it into the house." James's anger was clear in his reply.

Nate shot him a glance of what he hoped was calm understanding. "I wasn't thinking that at all, James. I just need to make sure I have the entire picture for the report."

James nodded, comprehending Nate's reasoning. "Do you think it's the same person who hit those other two homes?"

"That's not out of the realm of possibility. We're going to dust for prints, take some pictures of the damage, and so on. What I need you to do for me is make a list of all the valuables missing. Write down what you've already noticed is missing, and then you can compile a full list later. It doesn't have to be today. In fact, I would suggest the four of you stay at the inn on Main Street for a couple nights." Nate signaled O'Leary, who handed James a small notepad and pen.

"I can do that; there were a few items I know are gone. I was already planning to have the four of us stay at the inn while I have a security system installed and get this place cleaned up."

"Give us a few days to inspect the evidence before you do any of that. I agree that you should have a security system installed. I know you want to resume your lives and have everything in order. I don't blame you. If it were me, I'd want the same. However, my job is to make sure that we have every shred of evidence, not just to catch the thief, but enough to convict them. I can't do that if my evidence from this scene is compromised."

"We understand," James murmured, never breaking contact with his wife even as he jotted items down on the notepad. Nate gave them time as James scribbled down their missing possessions.

"Anything you notice was missing right away?" Nate asked.

"The safe where we store extra cash for the store was missing. We like to keep a few extra hundred just in case the bank is closed and we need more cash for the store. I didn't see much more than that, but it's enough."

"My jewelry too." Angela sniffed. "The pieces that were my mom's, the pearl brooch and diamond earrings."

"I know, Ang, it will be all right," James murmured, then handed Nate the list.

"Good, this is a place for us to start. Why don't you go get yourself settled at the inn, and I'll contact you when you can come collect personal items you might need."

"Sounds fine. Thank you, Sheriff."

Nate left them on the porch as James gathered Angela and herded her into their SUV. He headed inside their home and began a room-by-room assessment. Whoever the hell the thief was, he had no qualms about trashing the place he burgled. Broken glass from lamps lying at crooked angles on the floor crunched beneath his boots. Cushions were strewn about as if the perp was searching for something. The television stand in the living room was empty. He gingerly stepped around broken items, cataloging his first impressions. O'Leary snapped pictures of the crime scene. Filbert dusted for prints. And Nate surveyed the points of entry for clues to the perpetrator's, or perpetrators', style. He snapped photos of gashes in the frame of the back door and on the door itself. He wanted to check them against the pictures from the two prior break-ins to be certain, but he believed the gouge marks were similar. The gouges in the wood looked like a crow bar or similar tool had been used on the latch. He zoomed the digital camera to get intricate details of the markings. He wanted to line them up alongside one another and compare them.

Even though he didn't have the complete list of stolen items, they had a starting point. Nate still had a few contacts in Denver whom he utilized for cases like this, including his buddy and counselor, Miles Keaton, in addition to a few undercover officers who watched for stolen merchandise to pop up at one of the many pawn shops. With any luck, they would get a hit. Granted, their chances would be much better once they had the entire list.

Nate and his deputies spent the next few hours cataloging every scuff and broken item, and collecting forensic evidence. He would send it all to a lab in Denver. There was a mountain of evidence and prints. They'd have to get a sample from the Beaumonts. So far, they'd found lots of fingerprints and DNA but they would have to test the family to rule out what belonged to them. But he had the sneaking suspicion, if this held up like the other two break-ins, there wouldn't be any belonging to the perp—only to the family. It was like he was a goddamn professional.

Nate wouldn't put it out of the realm of possibility that this could be crime organizations in Denver sending their people outside the city. The break-ins were too clean. It left him unsettled, like there was something crucial he was missing on this case.

By evening he was ensconced at the station, writing his report and examining the evidence they did have for similarities. It became clear as the night wore on that he wouldn't make it back home.

He located Abby in his contacts—seeing her name there gave him a pleasant jolt—and gave her a ring.

"Hello?" The sweet melody of her voice came through his receiver. In the background, he heard Rufus woofing.

"Abby, it's Nate."

"Ah, hi." He could practically hear her blushing through the phone from her breathless response. Nate knew it was because of their kiss, the one that had been on instant replay in the back of his mind today as he'd investigated. The one that caused desire to come rampaging to the forefront. He wished he could address it now. They would, just not while he was in the office. Nate did his best to keep his private life away from the office.

"Hey, listen, I hate to ask, but this case has me chained to my desk for the foreseeable future," he said, looking at the pictures and the case file spread over his wooden bureau.

"And you want me to watch Rufus overnight?" she asked.

"If you don't mind keeping him, I'll get him in the morning. If it's not too much trouble." He took a swig of coffee that had long ago lost any warmth.

"No trouble at all. That's right, sweetie, you get to stay with me."

Nate wished she'd said that to him instead of Rufus. It was criminally unfair, in his esteem, that his dog got to have a sleepover with her before he did. "I'll be by in the morning and can finish the firewood for you."

"Um, that would be nice," she said, her voice a husky whisper that churned the unrequited need in his belly.

"Gotta go," he said, wanting to crawl through the phone to pick up where they left off. "Pleasant dreams."

"Yep, you too."

He ended the call. It was a sad day when you became jealous of your own damn dog because he got to sleep with the woman you were developing a bit of an obsession with first.

At the knock on his office door, he swiveled in his chair. Deputy O'Leary stood at attention like he was still in the military. "Yes, O'Leary?"

"I checked into that angle we discussed," he replied.

"Come in and shut the door behind you," Nate ordered, compartmentalizing his lustful thoughts about his neighbor, tabling them for later.

~

NATE WOKE up Sunday morning to the sound of his cell phone ringing. Squinting at the glare of fluorescent lighting, he reached for it, grimacing at the knot at the back of his neck the size of Alaska. His boots were propped up on his desk as he reclined in his office chair.

"Sheriff Barnes," he said as he answered, wishing like hell for a fresh cup of coffee.

"Well, don't you sound all official."

A grin spread over his lips and he said, "At least I help catch the bad guys. How's it hanging, Miles?"

"A little to the right these days," Miles said with a laugh in his voice.

"To what do I owe the pleasure of your call?" he asked. Miles was one of his oldest friends. They'd gone to high school and college together at the University of Boulder and had even pledged the same fraternity, where they'd met two other knuckle-heads, Jacob and Sam. The four of them had been friends ever since.

"For one, I'll be heading your way next weekend for my mom's retirement party. Two, I might be in the market for a new job here soon if the brass around here has their way. Let me know if you hear something through the grapevine."

"Thinking of moving back to our old stomping grounds?"

"Yes, with Dad gone and Mom getting older, I'd rather be closer. She won't move. I've already had the conversation with her where she explained to me in rather explicit detail why she would never move to Denver."

Nate chuckled. Miles's mom had a stubborn streak a mile wide and Nate could just imagine the earful she was giving her son any time he brought up trying to move her. Miles would have to dynamite her out of her home.

"That's right, the party's next weekend," Nate said. Maybe he could entice Abby to attend the event with him. His brain wasn't firing on all cylinders. A move like that was dating territory, and a far cry from merely scratching an itch. Which begged the question, what did he want from Abby?

"Unless there's a murder in town, I expect you there, old chap."

"I wouldn't miss it. Buzz me when you get in, we can grab some beers and catch up." Hopefully by then, Nate would be have figured out exactly what he did want from Abby.

"Will do," Miles said as he hung up.

Nate rubbed the sleep from his eyes and went in search of fresh coffee. It would be great to see Miles. They didn't have the opportunity much since he'd moved back to their hometown. Miles worked as an attorney at a corporate practice in Denver. He wondered if Jacob and Sam would make the trip in for Ella Keaton's retirement party. It would be good to have the gang back together, even just for an afternoon.

After infusing his body with a modicum of caffeine and checking on any leads on the trio of break-ins only to come up empty-handed, Nate headed home for some rest and relaxation. He pulled into his driveway, and the woman who had reserved a starring role in his dreams, both sleeping and waking, was there. Abby had arranged some patio furniture on the wraparound porch. She was curled up on the white wicker couch with Rufus, who took up two-thirds of the thing and had a blissful look on his face. In fact, Rufus was so comfortable, he glanced with a raised brow at Nate and then laid his head back down on her lap, the lucky son of a bitch. Abby had her computer and those librarian-style glasses perched on her nose as she typed. Lust simmered underneath the surface as he exited his Explorer.

She had no idea how beautiful she was, and that was one of the things he liked most about her. She didn't fawn and simper in front of a mirror, or wear so much make-up it was lacquered on, but was unconventionally beautiful, with pearlescent skin and thick eyebrows that had been scrunched in concentration as he drove up his drive.

Her gaze swiveled toward him, and there was a hint of a smile on her plump lips, while a blush shadowed her cheeks. If she knew the fantasies he'd had last night with her in the starring role, she'd likely run for the hills. Or perhaps not, she seemed just as confounded by the intensity of their attraction to one another.

"Hi," she said, putting her laptop on the nearby matching wicker table.

He climbed the stairs and said, "Hey, thanks for watching Rufus for me last night."

At his name, Rufus's ears perked up, and he rolled in Abby's lap like he had claimed her as his personal property. Rufus even gave him a look like, *She's mine, and there ain't nothing you can do about it.* In all his years, he'd never thought he would have to challenge his dog for a woman's affections, because Abby seemed perfectly content to scratch Rufus behind the ears and on the belly.

"He was the perfect gentleman. Granted, I might need a bigger bed the next time he stays."

Rufus gave him a grin like, *Yep, I totally got there first.* Ignoring his smirking pup, Nate handed her a bouquet of flowers he'd picked up at the market on his way home.

"As a thank-you for watching the knucklehead," he explained.

Abby smiled, a bit flustered, and took the bouquet from his hands. "Thank you. Oh crap, is that what I think it is?"

Then she gasped and wheezed. She dropped the flowers and stumbled as she stood.

He gripped her biceps as she paled and wavered. "What the hell? Abby, what's happening?"

"Daisies, allergic," she gasped as her breaths were becoming more and more labored. "Need EpiPen... in purse... in kitchen."

"Stay here, I'll get it." Shit! Abby was displaying symptoms of going into anaphylactic shock. Nate called dispatch as he strode to her kitchen and withdrew the device from her purse. He carried both back with him. They'd need her information at the clinic.

"9-1-1, this is Sherry. What's your emergency?"

"Sherry, this is Sheriff Barnes, badge number two-nine-four-five. I have a female, twenty-eight, suffering from anaphylactic shock, and need medical assistance. Address is 314 Creekside Drive."

"Yes, Sheriff, let me put you on hold for just a minute while I contact ambulance services."

He hurried back outside and discovered Abby lying on the porch, her breathing labored and blood leaking from her forehead. Rufus whimpered as he lay by her side. Christ, she must have hit her head when she fell. One issue at a time. First, he had to get the allergic reaction under control, then he could worry about the blood. He knelt, removed the safety cap on the EpiPen, placed it on her thigh and inserted the shot to get her body the much-needed epinephrine to start combating the attack.

"Sheriff, the ambulance will be there in twenty minutes."

"Shit, she doesn't have that kind of time. I'll get her to the hospital myself. If you could call this into Echo Springs Hospital and let them know I'm en route with a critical patient..."

"Right away, Sheriff."

He hung up, shoved his phone in his pocket. "Come on, Rufus. Get inside."

He opened Abby's front door and ushered a whimpering Rufus in. He reassured him as he danced frantically about. "I know, boy, I'll be back with her as soon as I can."

Then he hoisted her into his arms, purse and all, and raced to his Explorer. Nate loaded her into the passenger seat, buckled her in and her head lolled to the side, blood seeping from the cut near her temple. Shit! No time to get his med kit out and patch her up, it would have to wait until he got her to the clinic. Slamming the door, he all but flew around the side and vaulted into his seat.

"Stay with me, Abby."

Turning his lights on, he drove like he was Marty McFly trying to outrun Libyans, all while applying pressure with just his hand to the wound on her head. They made it to Echo Springs Hospital in less time than it would have taken the ambulance to reach them. He parked directly in front of the emergency entrance, where Doctor Jonah Townsend and a bevy of nurses were waiting for them with a stretcher.

"Sheriff, what do we have?"

"Doc, female, twenty-eight, severe allergy to daisies. I administered epinephrine at her home, but she seems to be responding poorly to the medicine. Her breathing has been labored, she's clammy and warm to the touch, and her pulse is erratic and she's not responding. She also has a contusion on her forehead that was caused when she fainted."

"Those things, for what they cost, are a low dose, and from the severity of her attack, looks like she's going to need a bit more. Not to worry, that dose you administered kept her alive. We'll get her fixed up. And head wounds tend to bleed like the dickens. Any other known allergies?"

"Shit, I don't know," Nate said, rattled now that his adrenaline had no outlet.

"It's fine, Sheriff, we'll take it from here."

The doc started issuing orders like a general on a battlefield as they wheeled Abby on a gurney into emergency. Nate needed something constructive to do to take his mind off his fear for her. Following the gurney, he strode inside to the registration desk with her purse. After he'd given the nurse all of Abby's pertinent information, along with explicit instructions that they were to send the bills to him for anything her insurance company wouldn't cover, Kathy with registration, whom he'd also gone to high school with, directed him to a restroom where he could wash the blood from his hands. Abby's blood. Then with nothing to do but wait he took a seat in the waiting room, her purse on his lap as he called himself every name in the book.

Nice going, idiot, you bring a girl flowers, hoping to possibly have her invite you in, maybe pick up where you left off yesterday, and injure her instead. This incident didn't bode well for their relationship—he'd almost killed her with the very first romantic gesture he'd made. He'd wanted to do something nice for her since she had been more than accommodating in watching Rufus, and Old Man Turner's journal had mentioned taking the woman you want to woo flowers.

Maybe he needed to read that thing more thoroughly. And maybe he needed to have his head examined if he was taking dating advice from a dead guy.

Chapter Seven

From Old Man Turner's Journal:
Be sure to be a gentleman and ask permission for things like a kiss.

"How do you feel?" Nate asked, pushing Abby in a wheelchair out to his waiting vehicle. The sun was shining overhead as they exited the sterile hospital. She blinked at the bright glare.

"I'm fine, really. Sleepy from all the medicine, but all I need is some rest," she assured him, her words a bit slurred.

When she started to stand on her own, her limbs visibly trembling, he sprang into action and said, "Here, let me help you—"

She feebly batted at his hands. "I can do it. I'm not helpless, you know."

"Non-negotiable." Nate had inadvertently caused her harm. There was no way he would allow her to further injure herself because of misplaced pride. He hoisted her into his arms, not missing how much he enjoyed having her in them, and gently deposited her on the passenger's front seat. When Abby blearily tried to put her seatbelt on, he moved her hands out of the way with the gentlest care.

"Abby, let me," he pleaded.

She rolled her sleepy eyes, then gave him a groggy stare with her head cocked to one side before blowing out a breath as her whole body turned fluid under his hands. "Fine, have it your way." She yawned as she settled back in her seat.

At her surrender, his gut finally unclenched, and he buckled her in.

One of the nurses took the wheelchair back into the hospital so he could focus on getting Abby home and taking care of her after his blunder. He walked around to the driver's side, feeling as if he was on a razor's edge. Regardless of whether it had been unintentional or not, he had still hurt her. The consequences could have been fatal if he'd been slower to act. Nate waited until they were on the road before he said, "I'm sorry, Abby. I didn't know that you were allergic to those flowers, or I never would have brought them for you."

Around another yawn, she said, "I know that. It's not a big deal. I'm fine. It's not the first time I've had a reaction."

It was the one and only time under his watch. "Any other allergies I should know about?" *So that I don't inadvertently kill her later.*

"Ivy and shellfish."

"Good to know."

Abby was drifting to sleep, burrowing into the passenger seat with her knees up to her chest, as he pulled into the driveway. Not wanting to wake her after the morning she'd experienced because of his clumsy blunder, he gently lifted her from the seat. Her arms slid around his neck and she buried her face in his shoulder. That little action hit him in the chest, and he held her tighter as he carried her from his car, along with her purse and medicine, into her house. Rufus, his usual exuberance diminished and as somber as the day they discovered Miss Evie after she had passed away, followed them up to her bedroom.

Nate pulled back the covers and gently laid Abby on the bed. He removed her shoes then helped her remove her shirt and jeans that were splattered with blood from her head wound. Desire burned in his system at uncovering the supple lines of her form in nothing but a black bra and matching bikini panties, but he drew the comforter up over her.

As much as he wanted her, now wasn't the time. He stroked a hand over her silky hair. Even in a weakened state, Abby fought to stand on her own. He respected the hell out of her for that, especially knowing she'd had a life full of ease, financially at least. As much as he worried about how enamored he had become in such a relatively short time, Nate couldn't think of anyone or anything he wanted more than Abby. Maybe it was the fact that her aunt had infused his visits with stories about Abby's childhood that to his own upbringing in a trailer at the edge of town, had seemed foreign and exotic. Abby was this warm, welcoming woman with a heart as big as the nearby fourteen-footers, who seemed to defy her cold upbringing.

Reluctantly, he withdrew his hand, grimacing at the bandage on her forehead, and she snuggled deeper under the covers. He scooped up her blood-stained clothes. The least he could do was wash them and make sure she didn't have to worry about anything today. Then he'd clean the porch off and get rid of the flowers that were still lying there, waiting to cause Abby more harm.

"Stay with her, boy, and let me know if she needs anything, okay?" he said to Rufus, who understood his meaning and curled up on the rug next to her bed. "Good boy."

With her jeans and shirt balled in his hands, he headed into the bathroom. Maybe he could soak them and attempt to remove the bloodstains. If not, he'd pay to replace the lost clothing. It was his fault, after all. He ran the faucet on the ivory pedestal sink, pulling the stopper up so that the basin would fill, but the stopper wouldn't seal, leaving an eighth of an inch of space for the water to drain through.

Well, he could fix that while she slept as well.

Instead of using the sink, he filled the claw-footed ivory tub with cold water, letting her clothes soak a bit. Abby had added color to the otherwise functional but drab bathroom. Her fluffy purple bathrobe made him shake his head as his body responded in a purely male way as he imagined her wearing only that, so he could take it off her.

Christ, she was making him revert to a teenager with his first crush. Before he did something embarrassing, like smell her robe, he grabbed some white vinegar from the kitchen and added it to the cold water. Then he headed back downstairs into her kitchen, where he put together a chicken tortilla soup in her crockpot. It was one of the few recipes he knew how to do that wasn't grilling meat or nuking a frozen dinner. He set the temperature on high, hoping the soup would be ready by the time she woke up. It was hearty, and in his mind, the protein would help her body heal. He let the crock pot do its thing and cook while he headed out back and started chopping the rest of the wood for her.

Was he going overboard? Probably. But it was his way of making amends. He didn't want her to suffer any more than she had already. As he chopped wood, he couldn't help but remember how, not three feet from where he now stood, he'd experienced one of the hottest kisses of his life. The world had fallen away, and her mouth had been the sole focus of his universe. Her little mewls had fueled his desire to a fever pitch. He craved having her lush little body writhing beneath his again.

Over the next two hours, he chopped the remainder of the firewood that would at least see her through the first part of winter. Who knew how long she would last in Echo Springs? Then again, he hadn't asked her what her plans were, and other than a "for the time being" response from Abby the night she'd arrived, he didn't know whether she was planning for the long haul or not.

When he finished stacking the cut wood, he power-washed her front porch, removing the hazardous flowers and hopefully any lingering pollen. Then he retrieved his toolbox from the second floor of his house. Being as silent as he could, not wanting to disturb her sleep, he went back to the upstairs bathroom. Pulling her shirt and jeans from their soak, he saw that the bloodstains had hardly diminished. He planned to try rubbing some salt on the stains after he fixed the sink, see if that would have any effect.

The sink was an issue. He did discover the problem, but ended up having to take the entire lever apart and reassemble the sink to get it in proper working order. Nate had just finished reconstructing the sink when a bleary-eyed Abby, her bedhead hair poufing around her face, now wearing her pink pajamas, entered the room.

"What the hell are you doing?" she asked, her hands on her hips, framing her curves. Her hazel eyes scanned his tools spread over the ivory tile floor.

"I was fixing your sink."

She inhaled a deep breath, vexation in her gaze, before she said, "Look, I know you feel bad about this morning, and I appreciate the effort and thought behind it, but please don't go running around my house fixing things without asking me first."

"Abby, the stopper wasn't working at all, and now it does. I just wanted to do something nice for you."

She crossed her arms in front of her chest, and from the irate look on her face, it was probably to keep from strangling him. Nate was just happy that nine-iron of hers wasn't in the vicinity.

"Nate, how would you feel if I marched into your home and started doing things without asking you first? It's not that I don't appreciate it, but you have to understand I moved out here to get away from my overbearing, yet well-meaning family," Abby said, exasperation clouding her voice.

He winced. When she put it that way… Shit, he'd let his guilt eat at him. Wasn't that something Stacy had always accused him of? He hadn't meant for it to come off as overbearing.

"I'm sorry, for everything, then. It's not that I don't think you're perfectly capable of handling it yourself. I just assumed, after this morning, you'd be feeling poorly and not up to the task, so I took care of a few things for you." He stood, feeling a bit contrite.

"What did you do?" She punctuated her words by gesturing with her hands.

He stared down at her irritated glare. Instead of guilt, her scowl revved the ever-present desire he harbored for her, and it flared to life. Why she aroused him with fury blazing in her eyes, her hair a mess, and a bandage covering the right portion of her forehead, he had no idea, but she did. Not to mention, Nate wasn't going to apologize for being nice and lending a hand—he had needed to make amends. "The rest of the firewood, cleaned the front porch and made dinner."

"Why, oh, why did you do that?" she asked, exasperation coloring her words. Her scowl just did it for him.

"Isn't it obvious?" Before she could argue her point further, he corralled her against the wooden door and kissed her.

Her sharp little moan ignited a firestorm in his blood. Nate needed her like he required air to breathe. He didn't seduce, he invaded. He wanted to kiss her like no other man ever would. He growled into her mouth when she wrapped her arms around his neck, pulling him closer. He explored her lips, spurred on by the pleasured mewls she emitted. He took her under again and again as an inferno of desire raged between them. Abby's mouth was pure carnal bliss. He could suck on her lower lip for hours. But there was so much more of her that Nate yearned to taste.

Abby lifted her right leg up to his waist, attempting to get closer. He was totally onboard with that plan. He wanted to climb inside her, extinguish any remaining distance until he was surrounded in her sweetness. His hands caressed the backs of her thighs, hoisting her body up until her legs wrapped around his waist, and he pressed his hips against her center. At the intimate contact, he moaned into her mouth, his eyes nearly rolling back in his head at the delicious torture as she undulated her hips against his erection.

Nate couldn't get enough of her. Abby was just as hot for his touch, groaning against his lips. Her delicate hands slid into his hair, holding his mouth prisoner against hers as she thrust her tongue inside his mouth, dueling with his. He snaked his hand beneath the hem of her pajama top; the sexy pink fabric was a flimsy barrier. Beneath, her skin was soft as cashmere.

Nate moaned, humming in the back of his throat when he discovered she wasn't wearing a bra under the shirt. Cupping a heavy, silken globe, he rasped his thumb over her areola until it pebbled into a taut point. Christ, he had to taste her. He broke their kiss and dipped his head as he hoisted her shirt. Abby was stunning. He gazed at her creamy flesh, his arousal spiking. He groaned deep in his throat as he enveloped the pert bud into his mouth.

Abby's head fell back against the door as he feasted on her breasts, kneading the mounds as he learned their shape, their size, just how soft her flesh was on the underside of each boob. The lust-infused sound she emitted as he suctioned the nipple into his mouth nearly drove him out of his skin, his body craving to sink into hers. Nate bit down then laved the peak, curling his tongue about the distended flesh.

Her fingers gripped his hair tighter and she gyrated her hips against his pelvis. Nate's eyes almost crossed at the torrent of need blasting his system. He released her breast and carried her across the hall to her bedroom. He kicked the bedroom door shut behind them when he didn't spot Rufus. The last thing he wanted was his lovable furball interrupting. Nate tenderly laid her on her bed and then followed her down. He ached to slide inside her. His knuckles rasped over the swollen, dark rouge nub, and her pupils dilated as desire overrode her gaze. Then Abby's hands went to the buttons on his shirt as he claimed her mouth in another torrid duel of lips, teeth, and tongues. With his help, her hands slid his shirt off his shoulders. They both moaned at the exquisite sensation of being skin to skin. The sensual contact ignited a maelstrom of fiery need. Nate plundered her mouth, reveling in the feel of her hands caressing his sides and sliding around to his back.

And then his damn phone in his back pocket rang. Damn phone had interrupted them yesterday too. Why did his work have to come between them? Again? He wanted to toss the offending device into the nearest creek bed. He could ignore the summons, stay precisely where he was, and planned on doing just that when the ringing continued. Duty called. Nate regretfully released her mouth and said, "I have to check this."

He shifted slightly, staring down at what was surely every man's fantasy: a gorgeous, topless woman, her hair mussed from his fingers, lips swollen from his kiss, and a desire to welcome him into her bed with open arms. Even the small bandage on her forehead didn't diminish how damn sexy she was.

He stared at his screen. It took a moment for him to refocus his lust-filled gaze and register who was calling.

"Unfortunately, it's the station," he said. "I have to answer." Cursing up a blue streak in his mind, Nate rolled off her succulent form into a sitting position. He'd never be able to concentrate with her bounty wrapped around him.

"Sheriff Barnes," he said as he answered, the phone at his ear, wincing as his erection strained against his pants.

"Sheriff, it's Kate."

"Deputy, what can I do for you?"

Abby slid from the bed, padding quietly across the floor, and retrieved her shirt from where they'd tossed it on their route to her bed. He wanted to whimper when she slipped the top back on and covered herself.

"I wanted to inform you that forensics finished their analysis of the evidence."

"And?" He liked Kate, but Christ Almighty, there were times when he didn't want to play twenty questions with her.

"It was as you suspected, no prints other than the family, just like the first two."

That did not bode well for solving this case, dammit. He issued his orders. "All right, let James and Angela know they can return home tomorrow. We need them to compile that list of missing items as soon as possible. Understood?"

"Got it, Sheriff."

"Need anything else?"

"Nope, I've got the graveyard shift tonight."

"Got it. I put a call in to highway patrol yesterday. Let me know if the state boys return my call. Otherwise, I'll see you in the morning," Nate said.

"Night, Sheriff."

"Deputy," he said and ended the call.

"Everything okay at the station?" Abby eyeballed him sitting on her bed. From her stance, they weren't going to proceed any further this evening or pick back up where they'd left off. He shook his head. It was a bleeding shame that the job seemed to disturb them at the most inopportune times. Granted, if she wanted to be in a relationship with him, interruptions like these came with the territory.

When the hell had his interest in Abby morphed from purely physical into something more? Because he did want more. Just how much left him off-kilter, like his world had become a Tilt-A-Whirl.

He needed to shift topics and escape the confines of her room. Otherwise, his body would override his level head, and he'd figure out how to entice her back beneath him. He stood up. "Yep. How about some dinner?"

"Dinner would be great." She waited for him near the door as he walked toward her.

"After you," he said, opening the door for her, and they headed down to the kitchen. Rufus lay sprawled near the back door and perked up when Abby filled his bowls.

Dinner was a pleasant affair, during which Nate apologized

again for overstepping any boundaries. "Abby, I didn't mean to wrangle control of things. If it would make you feel better, I can go back upstairs and break the sink so you can fix it."

She laughed and then blushed. "No, please don't do that. It's the steroids. They tend to make me cranky and over-react. Sorry about that. I hate taking them just for that reason, among other things. I know you were just looking out for me after everything and I appreciate it, really."

Instead of making him feel satisfied that they had cleared the air, his confusion about the next steps to take between them deepened. He and Rufus left a short time after dinner. The last thing he wanted to do was crowd her. And he had to decide whether pursuing more with Abby was the smart choice.

Because this was much more than just scratching an itch.

Chapter Eight

From Old Man Turner's Journal:
Drink in moderation.

Abby spent the next week immersing herself in her classes by day. At night, she made progress on her dissertation, *Romantic Literature, and Its Impact on Women's Roles in Modern Society*. In the back of her mind, Nate was always present, even though she studiously attempted to forget about him. He crept into her thoughts at the most inopportune times. And she'd had to swear off reading romance novels altogether. The last one she'd read about a sexy time traveling Scottish highlander, when she pictured the dashing hero, it had been Nate's image she'd projected. The man even had the nerve to appear as the starring role in her dreams. She'd woken up achy and needy, and reaching for him.

Abby didn't care for how much he had taken up residence in her mind, among other places. She obsessed over him. Their relationship had progressed too quickly. She barely knew him. Which meant the likelihood of her undead doll army rising up to slaughter everyone in the event that she did the horizontal tango with Nate was significantly high. Instead of feeding her desire to see him naked, Abby had decided to avoid temptation altogether, succinctly ducking for cover and dodging any potential interactions with him this past week. Living next door to him made it so much more difficult to eschew interaction. It forced Abby to try and act like a ninja, all stealthy, checking out her windows before she left. The problem was, she didn't have a stealthy bone in her body. Her ninja skills were hampered by the fact that she moved with all the grace of someone wearing one of those tyrannosaurus rex costumes that had become all the rage lately, and she wiped out more than once. Her knees were bruised from her last fall.

It wasn't that Abby didn't want to see him. She did, and that was the problem. Whenever her thoughts drifted in his direction, she would end up fanning herself because the imagery would inevitably turn to scorching hot, pulse-pounding sex. Her id and ego were both on the same page in their desire to boink her sexy neighbor. This left her questioning her decision to avoid him. Why was she studiously avoiding a man she had the hots for and obviously wanted? Nate had certainly made no bones about his interest. While he hadn't been around this week, she wondered if that was her doing. Abby's biggest concern was starting something she would end up leaving in a few months. Was that a recipe for disaster? And was she putting too much stock into it? Shouldn't she just count her lucky stars, have awesome, toe-curling sex for a few months and then head off to whatever destination her career would take her?

Except, she'd never been one of those women who could sleep with a man and not develop feelings for him. Where her body went, inevitably her heart became involved as well. She had to face the fact that she was a hopeless romantic and sex for the sake of sex had never interested her. In her humble opinion, Sheriff Stud Muffin was too damn mouth-wateringly handsome for his own damn good. Not to mention, he'd been gone a lot, probably out catching bad guys and putting them in handcuffs.

Abby groaned and thunked her head against the desk. Her hormones were out of control, overriding her good intentions at every turn, and offering suggestions for why she should throw caution to the wind and seduce Nate. It wasn't like her subconscious hadn't given her a plethora of fantasies she should indulge in, including using the tools of his profession in the bedroom. Most people didn't get excited at the mere thought of handcuffs but Abby? Oh yeah, she'd had a number of dreams this week involving her sexy neighbor and handcuffs.

This was the problem: she would think about him and it eventually led down a rabbit hole where she imagined seeing him naked. Which inevitably left Abby having to fan herself at the most inopportune times as she imagined what she would do with such a fine specimen of manhood laid bare before her as if he were her own personal amusement park. That was why she had to throw the brakes on their potential almost-romance. He occupied far too much real estate in her mind and they hadn't even done the deed.

Except, she missed him.

Gah! How did that happen? Abby didn't get attached. But somehow the big guy had wriggled inside, and she missed his direct stare, missed his laugh, the way he wore a pair of jeans, and even missed his ginormous furball sidekick, Rufus. She'd noticed Nate out in the yard, or the lights on upstairs in his house late at night, and wondered what he was doing. And wishing it was her.

It was pretty clear he had been avoiding her, too, this week. Other than when he'd finished the firewood for her last Sunday, and except for the few times she had spied him out in his yard with Rufus, he'd surreptitiously evaded running into her. Not that she blamed him. Abby was acutely embarrassed at her overreaction to him fixing her sink. Most women would practically kill to have their husbands or boyfriends tackle home improvement projects. What had she done? Bitten the man's head off. In her defense, the steroids did make her cranky. They tended to mess with her emotions, putting them on a rollercoaster which made her seem bipolar. In fact, yesterday she'd left the community college and burst into tears in her car for no reason. And she wasn't expecting her period for another two weeks. It was the damn steroids. Luckily, she had only two more days on those suckers. Otherwise, she'd go stark raving mad.

Abby helped herself to a fresh cup of coffee in the professors' lounge and sat at one of the tables to prepare for her next class. Echo Springs, for all its charm, like Main Street with its historic buildings with their 1950s style storefronts, was most likely a stopover place for her. She already had top-notch universities courting her for potential research and grant work once she completed her dissertation. She couldn't do any of that from Echo Springs.

The door to the lounge opened and in strode Tessa Roe, the graphic arts instructor, wearing a formfitting black tee with some video game image splashed across it, green cargo pants, and black Converse shoes. The woman was gorgeous in a cyber-punk, kick-butt way.

"Hey, it's Abigail, right?" Tessa said as she poured herself a cup of coffee.

"Abby's easier," she replied and smiled. Tessa had this chaotic energy, kind of like when you went to a carnival, and couldn't stand still.

"Sounds more like you. Abigail is someone's grandma. You're Evie Callier's niece, right?" Tessa sat across from her and Abby noticed her bright, royal blue nail polish.

"Yeah, I am."

"And you're living in that big house by yourself?"

Abby shrugged. That big house had quickly begun to feel like home. And she didn't mind being alone, she had a nice view. She said, "It's not too bad. It's quiet, so I'm getting the chance to finish my dissertation."

"Yeah, I'd heard about that. Something about Shakespeare or something like that?"

"In a roundabout way, yes. And you design comic books in your spare time?" Abby quipped.

"Graphic novels, but yes. I wouldn't want to be doing anything else. I'm sure you know what I mean. The latest one is about a vampire who seeks revenge on his sire. Very cool stuff."

"I'm sure it is. I'd like to read it when it's done." Abby smiled to cover the inescapable sinking sensation in her core. That's what had been missing with her dissertation: passion and excitement. No wonder she considered it a chore lately, the subject matter didn't thrill her like it once had. That didn't mean she didn't love literature, but academics as a whole had become rather staid and boring. She enjoyed the classes she taught here, and the students, but the thrill of discovery and excitement were sadly absent these days. Mayhap that was why her parents weren't supportive—because she wasn't satisfied any longer, and it showed. Or perhaps she was just burned out from a lifetime spent working excessive hours without any time away.

While she'd been working on her dissertation, she had avoided dating or being uber social by telling herself she would get to do those things later. That she was working toward a goal which most people weren't capable of sacrificing themselves for. But had she sacrificed too much? Had it become more about suffering and her unintentional cross to bear?

Abby had been mourning her life, not living it. She'd watch couples, women, and families through the windows of the libraries and wish she could be out there experiencing the street fair, trying delicacies from food trucks, hell, just existing outside during the day and soaking up some good old-fashioned vitamin D.

"I get advanced copies and would be happy to give you one. Oh shoot!" Tessa said, glancing at her watch, and collecting her items from the table. "Hey, I gotta run to class, but if you aren't doing anything tomorrow night, you should come down to Smitty's Pub. My sis bartends and gives me a discount. Plus, it's really the only place to go in town on a Friday night if you want to avoid all the teens and young college crowd at Papa Beau's Pizza. And, if you are looking for some eye candy, there are some super fine male specimens who play pool on the weekends and are a hoot to watch."

"That sounds like fun. Count me in." Although Abby already had one stud muffin she had no idea what to do with, and she didn't need another one. But part of her goal with moving here was to discover if she would allow herself to start living. That started now. She'd been doing the same thing at her aunt's that she'd done at Cornell, used her home as a buffer and a reason not to go out. No more. She would grab the bull of life by the horns and ride it.

"Great. See you there." Tessa left the lounge in the same way she entered, like a whirlwind of tornadic activity.

Abby could use the break in her routine. She would allow herself to experience that crazy thing called life. Because let's face it, when you were counting down the days until the undead doll army struck, a girl needed to get away. And maybe a girls' night out would get both her mind and her loins away from pining over her sexy neighbor.

The alarm on her phone beeped, and she collected her belongings to head in to class. If only life were as simple as the stories in her books.

NATE WORKED as if the hounds of hell were nipping at his heels this week. He was in a constant state of sexual need, remembering with crystal clarity the way it felt to have Abby beneath him. Instead of doing what he wanted, which was march himself across his lawn and satiate his ever-present desire for Abby until they were both so satisfied they couldn't move, he worked.

He and his deputies exhausted every lead, whether viable or not, on the three break-ins. It was frustrating work when they continued to come up empty-handed. Then, at night, he came home only to see Abby studiously sitting by the window, working, and making him yearn to cross the distance they had placed between themselves.

Instead of slaking his lust, he channeled his energy into more of the demolition and remodel of his second floor. Intermittently, during his breaks, he continued reading Old Man Turner's journal, hoping it would provide him with a path forward with Abby.

He had finished ripping out the walls and removed the old bathroom fixtures. He had the new tub and toilet standing by in the corner and would get those installed after a much-needed break.

Nate relaxed on the floor beside Rufus, chugging some water, and read:

As I mentioned in the previous entry, from the moment Evie and I met, we were inseparable. After Evie played Florence Nightingale, I asked her out. I've never been so nervous. I can still remember the smile she gave me when I stuttered, "Would you go to the town fair with me?"

Since I didn't have a vehicle at the time, the night of our first date, she picked me up in her car. I'll admit that I was filled with anxiety, and in my insecurity wondered if she thought less of me because of my lack of transportation. But she never made me feel like I was less because of it. I think that was part of her charm. She had the unique ability to look beyond the surface value to the true grit of a person. And in the end, that night, she never made a jibe at my expense over my lack of vehicle. Her parents were fairly well-to-do. They had moved to Echo Springs while her father, a rather well-known geologist, studied rock formations and carbon-dated the area.

THE NIGHT WAS MAGICAL. *We walked hand in hand. The temperatures were warm but had dipped into a more reasonable, pleasant warmth. The stars twinkled in the cloudless sky. The high school field had been transformed into an amusement park with rides and games. I can still remember* the way her sky-blue dress hugged her curves. And the way her hair was perfectly coiffed and curled.

"What would you like to do first?" I asked, standing a bit taller that night because I knew the prettiest girl was with me.

"How's your aim?" She quirked a blonde brow in my direction and tugged me over to a booth.

"Fair to middling. Why, see something you want?" If she had asked me to rope the moon for her, I would have figured out a way to accomplish it.

"I have a thing for pandas," she admitted with a playful smile.

"One panda, coming right up." I paid the man, who handed me three baseballs to knock the bottle towers down. It took me more than three tries. But Evie, her effervescence and enthusiasm, made winning that stuffed panda for her worth it.

We ate hot dogs and cotton candy.

"So, Bill Turner, what do you want to be when you grow up?" she asked, her hand clasped in mine while we walked.

"My parents want me to take over the farm."

"And that's not what you want?" she asked.

"No. I'm good with numbers. They just seem to make sense to me when not much else does. I'd like to be an accountant." It was something I thought would take me far away from farming and the life I had known.

"Isn't that a rather boring profession?" she teased.

I shrugged and replied, "Perhaps for some. But I know it's something I can make a decent living at that doesn't depend on the weather." Because, for as long as I could remember, my parents' farm had been struggling. That was something I didn't want to do for the entirety of my life. "What about you?"

Her smile lit up and her eyes gleamed. "I want to travel the world, and paint it."

"What about getting married and raising a family?"

"What about it? I can want those things, too, but I don't have to be defined by them as the only accomplishments I can achieve or want. I would expect you to understand not wanting to be defined by your upbringing." Her eyes flashed with the passion of her convictions and I knew, right there and then, I wanted to marry her. That I wanted to be the one to take her around the world. But the words, the conviction behind them, stuck in my throat.

I cleared my throat and said, "Well, before you head off on your globe-trotting adventure, you must ride the Ferris wheel with me."

By the end of the night, it felt like Evie and I had known each other our whole lives. It wasn't only our first date, but it was also the night that she kissed me for the first time.

She laughed, that deep, throaty, full-bodied laugh of hers that spoke of her zest for living, as I steered her over to the line for the ride. We rode the Ferris wheel as the sun set behind the mountains. My arm was stretched out behind her on the seat, and she cuddled up against me. In that moment, she looked at me as we stopped at the top, with the entire town spread out before us, and leaned in and kissed me. I had worried about whether she would allow a kiss, since it was our first date. But I'd never wanted anything more than to taste her lips. She took the decision out of my hands, and I was so very grateful. I think that was the moment I knew Evie was different for me than all the other girls I had dated.

And I knew from that first taste as I cupped her chin that I would marry her.

For the remainder of the summer and fall, Evie and I were inseparable. We fought, and made up. We hiked and swam in the lake. And we fell in love to the point where my day wasn't complete without seeing her, touching her, kissing her. But our necking up by the lake didn't advance beyond that until a fall day in September. I will never forget it. The memory is one that carried me through dark days ahead, but I'm getting ahead of the story here. It was during an early winter snowstorm on one of our afternoon picnics that we had to take shelter in one of the hunting cabins. It was there Evie and I made love for the first time. I will never forget how beautiful she was or how hot the flame burned between us.

The winter squall blew up on us as we descended in her car from the mountain lake. The car slipped and slid as I drove us down the precarious mountainside, praying we would make it in one piece.

"I'm sorry I didn't listen to you when you said we should leave," Evie said. "Are you mad at me?"

"I'll be mad later. Right now, I'm trying not to kill us."

I maneuvered us about halfway down and spied one of the small hunting cabins. Praying it was vacant, I steered the vehicle toward it.

"It's not safe to go any further. I fear we need to stop until the brunt of the storm has cleared and the roads made visible."

"I trust you, Bill," Evie said.

The car slid to a halt ten feet from the cabin. We grabbed the blanket and uneaten picnic lunch in the wicker basket in the back seat and made a mad dash for the comfort of the cabin.

Inside the small wooden structure, I started a fire in the fireplace while Evie made a small nest on the floor with the blanket. Once the fire was cheerily pumping out heat and filled the room with a soft golden glow, I joined her on the blanket. She snuggled up against my shoulder and a feeling of peace, of rightness, infused me. I tipped her chin up and claimed her lips as surely as she had laid claim to my heart.

It wasn't planned but then, the best events in life usually never are. The kiss morphed into a potent desire and need that consumed us both. It was our first time, and I'm sure no one has lost their virginity in a more precious manner. We laughed, we loved tenderly, and we raged as the spark ignited into a flame that singed the very fabric of my being. Buried deep inside her, connected to her in a way as ancient as time immemorial, I knew in that instant, staring down at her, her hair strewn out upon the blanket, her impassioned gaze staring up at me in wonder, she was the only woman for me. We loved with the purity of youth, the innocence of discovery, and the certainty that our love would last forever.

After that night, I knew I wanted to spend the rest of my life with Evie. She was the woman for me. And looking back on the way she loved me, I know she was just as in love with me as I was with her.

Then the Japanese attacked Pearl Harbor. That event altered the course of our lives irrevocably. When the news flooded into our sleepy little town, I did what I knew in my heart to be right and enlisted in the Army.

I'll never forget the night I told Evie.

I ducked as she chucked a vase filled with the roses I'd brought her on our last date. It shattered as it hit the wall.

"I can't believe you would do this without telling me. Go down to the office and tell them that you take it back," she yelled, angry tears streaming from her goddess eyes.

Cautiously, I approached and tugged her stiff form into my arms. I didn't want to leave her, but I knew deep in my soul I had to fight, not just for my country but for Evie. I couldn't be a decent man if I chose to sit this one out.

"Evie, you know it's the right thing to do. Look at me. We can't let the Japanese Empire or Hitler and his armies continue to threaten the freedom of people on this planet. I wouldn't be worthy of your love if I didn't go."

"But you'll never come back." She shook in my arms and buried her face in my chest. Her tears soaked my shirt.

I knew that was a possibility. That was the stark reality of war. Men died, sometimes horrible painful demises, but I couldn't run from this war. In my soul, I knew that it would catch up to us eventually, even in our sleepy little mountain town, and I wanted it to be on my terms.

"I'll always come back to you, Evie. I love you. Whether in this life or the next, I will always be with you."

She gripped me tighter, and I decided to ask her something I'd been planning to at Christmas, but love and war had altered my timeline a bit.

"You can't know that. What if you're careless? What if—"

I cupped her cheeks and turned her face up to mine. "Evie, what if I fell off a cliff tomorrow? There are no certainties on when our time on this earth is over. What I do know is that I love you more than life itself, and Evelyn Callier, I would die the happiest man on Earth if you would do me the honor of becoming my wife. Let me take your name into war with me and sleep each night dreaming of my return to you."

Her tears started anew and she nodded. "Yes, oh Bill, I just don't want you to leave me. I have this horrible feeling I'll never see you again."

I wish I could say that her fears were unfounded, but as the weeks and months passed with the US becoming embroiled in war on two fronts, our world changed, and not entirely for the better.

Evie decided that she couldn't sit at home doing nothing, and enlisted as a nurse. I couldn't have been prouder of her than I was that day. I knew she had reservations about joining, but she also said that she couldn't just sit home and wait for me to return without going mad.

I WILL ALWAYS REGRET that I didn't make her marry me before I left *for basic training. She said she wanted to wait until I returned, to give me an incentive to make my way back to her. We made love the night before I had to ship out for basic training, and Evie had never looked lovelier.*

I will never forget the way she looked the next morning as I boarded the bus and left our sleepy little mountain town. When you truly fall in love with no reservations, giving the other person all of yourself, it is truly the greatest gift that life can bestow.

Little did I know that it would be the last time I would see her beautiful face for more than twenty years. If I had known, well, there's a reason the sages say that hindsight is a fickle bitch, and I'd like to think I would have changed my mind, but then there would be so much more of my life that I would have missed out on, like my girls, and I wouldn't trade them for all the tea in China. But I digress... I had finished basic training and was preparing to ship out for Europe when I received a letter from Evie.

'My dearest Bill, It's hard to believe that it has been months since we last saw one another. I go to sleep every night with your name on my lips and a prayer that you will return to me unharmed. And every morning, I wake knowing that somewhere in the world you are watching the same sunrise. It makes the miles between us that much easier to bear, especially now. I have the happiest news. This fall, our child will arrive. Amidst all the terror and horrors of war, we created life. I am thrilled that I have a piece of you inside me. It makes the days and nights we are apart easier to bear somehow. I love you so much, Bill Turner, and live for the day I will become your wife and we are together again, raising our child. Always Yours, Evie'

She was pregnant with our child. I will never forget that day, and just how happy it made me to know that should I die on some distant shore far from home, there would be a piece of me, a piece of the love Evie and I shared, that would survive.

I left the shores of my country carrying her name and that of our unborn babe on my lips, completely unprepared for how much you lose in war.

Nate closed the journal, stunned to his core. He'd read a whole lot more than he had initially intended, and he had an early start. It fascinated him that Bill and Evie had loved each other. He wondered about the child they'd had. Did Abby know? How had the gossip mongers of this town kept the child a secret?

It was unlike them. He'd read more tomorrow night if he had a chance.

"Come on, Rufus. Let's go to bed."

Rufus stood and stretched, yawning himself. Then he glanced at him with what Nate had come to recognize as his, *dude, I gotta take a leak, help a brother out*, look.

"One last trip outside to do your business." At the mention of outside, Rufus woofed, then barreled down the stairs. Nate trailed after Rufus's excited form. The dog stood at the front door with his nose on the seam between the door and frame, like he could already smell the freedom of cool mountain air. Nate took pity on him, opened the front door, and Rufus darted past him onto the lawn to relieve his bladder. As he stood on the porch, waiting for Rufus to finish his nightly bush ablutions, Nate hazarded a glance up at the golden light emanating from Abby's bedroom. And there she was, dark hair piled on top of her head in one of those fluffy updos, black-rimmed glasses perched on her pert nose, the unearthly glow from her computer illuminating her frame.

Nate hated to admit it, but he yearned for her. Desire churned and made his gut twist, but it was more than simple passion. He genuinely liked her, craved to learn more about her. She was clearly more intelligent than he, but her stellar brain only made her a sexier package.

And then she glanced out her window and stared directly at him. Their gazes held for a long moment across the distance. He knew she felt it too, this pull and quixotic magnetism. Abby gave him a small smile and a wave before turning away from the window and shutting off her light.

"Rufus." He whistled for the knucklehead, who raced past him into the house. Nate headed inside, knowing deep down that he and Abby weren't finished with one another. Not by a long shot.

Chapter Nine

From Old Man Turner's Journal:
Pick your battles.

Nate spent the majority of his Friday at the station filling out paperwork. A few of the Beaumonts' stolen goods had been discovered at Gold Star Pawn Shop in Denver. It was the best lead they'd had since the case began. The pawn shop had a partial license plate from a silver Chevy Tahoe on the store surveillance. Unfortunately, the interior video was corrupted so they didn't have an image of the perp. And the information used on the forms was phony.

Nate had discussed the case with the State Police, who were now on the lookout for the silver Tahoe. He couldn't remember if there was an Echo Springs resident who owned a Tahoe, but both Filbert and O'Leary were out searching for the vehicle.

It felt good, talking to the state boys, getting a lucky break with the pawn shop, and retracing his steps in each of his break-in cases. They were getting somewhere on this case. He knew it would be only a matter of time before the thief, or thieves, struck again. But this time, they were ready. At each crime scene, the valuables stolen had been easily fenced goods, like gold bracelets and rings, along with whatever cash was present.

They'd also stolen some of the more valuable artwork, china, and silverware, so he started checking in with some of the local and not-so-local antique stores to see if they'd had anyone bringing those items in. There was no rock so big or small he didn't plan to look under to catch this asshat.

At the end of Nate's shift, his buddy Miles sauntered into the station, looking slick and duded up in his fancy dark gray pinstripe tailored suit. His blond hair was snipped short, just a touch longer than a buzz cut, and his eyes were weary, but who the fuck wasn't tired these days?

"Look what the cat dragged in," Nate teased, unable to stop the friendly grin from spreading across his face as he stood and moved around his desk. It had been too damn long since they'd seen once another. "Some high city slicker out to dazzle us country folk."

Miles flashed a smile, and said, "Ah, Sheriff, does the city council really let you come into work looking like that?"

Nearly the same height, in their college days girls had always asked if they were brothers. While they may not be by blood, they were in the way that mattered. Nate clapped him on the back in a bro hug and laughingly said, "We're not big-city slick like you. Good to see you, Miles."

"You could be if you wanted to, Nate. It's been too long." Miles let go and Nate noticed strain on his face.

"You know I left that life a while back and have no desire to go back to it. I like my life in Echo Springs just fine."

"I understand, really, but it would be nice to see you more than every few months. Ready to go, or are you still working?" Miles asked.

"Nah, I can leave." There was always work for him to do at the station, even without the rash of burglaries. It was more that he took necessary breaks so he could go back refreshed. Otherwise he would come to hate the job and burn out. It happened all too often.

"Good, 'cause Jacob and Sam are meeting us at Smitty's."

"I was wondering if those two were going to make it to your mom's retirement party," Nate murmured. The gang was all back together. Suddenly he was looking forward to the evening more than he had when Miles contacted him last weekend. He'd thought to entice Abby into a date but put it on hold. A night away from watching his sexy neighbor at her window was precisely the ticket he needed to get himself back on an even keel.

"Under pain of death was the only way I was letting those idiots fail to show. I figured we could all crash at your place."

Which would hamper any plans for seducing Abby, putting them on the back-burner. "Yeah, well, we might have to camp out in the living room, but we'll manage."

They headed out of the station. Nate took one look at Miles's car and shook his head. "Since when did you get a penismobile?"

"That little beauty is a 911 Porsche, and women tend to love her. Respect the machine."

"Yeah, and it's totally inappropriate for driving in the mountains." That thing would end up going over a cliff if Miles wasn't careful. At least Sam wasn't the one driving it. With that dude's need for speed, adrenaline junky lifestyle, he'd inadvertently drive the thing up the Silverton pass at Mach speed just to say he conquered it, and would end up in the morgue.

"Okay, Grandma. I promise to be careful. Besides, it's just a rental for the weekend. I'm not sure I'm ready for a long-term commitment with the likes of her."

Nate rolled his eyes as he stowed his badge and gun in his glove box and locked it. The last place he would take a firearm was into a bar. "Whatever, man, just follow me over. I'm sure you remember the way, or do I need to draw you a map?"

"Please, bitch, this thing can outrace that bucket of bolts in no time. A map?" Miles snorted and gave him a derisive glance.

"You do realize, if you speed, I will have to ticket you, Counselor."

"Bite me, dickwad. Let's get over to Smitty's before Jacob and Sam drink all the beer and decimate the female population."

～

SMITTY'S WAS an old-fashioned pub where the locals went after a long work day and as an excuse to escape the confines of their houses in winter. The place had a rustic, cowboy feel to it, with a long wall-bar in dark ebony wood that ran the length of one wall and matching barstools lining it. It was the hottest place in town for the over-twenty-one crowd on a Friday and Saturday.

The main area had tables, where people met for dinner. Smitty's served traditional pub fare like burgers, hot dogs, pizza, and wings, but for a pub, it was good. The after-work happy hour crowd had arrived, and a few people called out greetings as Nate and Miles entered. Except it was the two knuckleheads at one of the tables farthest back, near the bank of pool tables, whom Nate was interested in most.

He'd recognize Jacob's towering six-and-a-half-foot frame anywhere. In college, his teammates had dubbed him *The Beast* for his ability to annihilate an opponent on the football field. Little did people realize that, despite his size, he was the pacifist of the group. His black hair had gotten longer but he had tamed it into a ponytail, of all things.

And then there was Sam Bonds, blond-haired, blue-eyed thrill seeker. When scaling mountains and jumping off cliffs hadn't been enough for him, he became a stunt double in Hollywood, performing death-defying feats that made the blockbuster action stars look like movie gold.

"Nate," Sam and Jacob said in unison as they sidled up to the table.

"Jacob, Sam, how's it hanging?"

After a few bro hugs, they all sat on their barstools and shot the breeze until their waitress, Cybil, sauntered over. Nate liked her. She had a good head on her shoulders. She and her sister Tessa had been part of the community for more than a decade now after tragedy had made them plant roots here. Cybil was a tall, long-legged brunette who didn't hide her body in the slightest. And she had quite the form, decked out in skinny jeans and a red, form-fitting top that displayed her ample cleavage. Her long hair had been pulled back into a high ponytail and trailed down to her mid-back. Cybil knew she was a beautiful woman and didn't apologize for it.

"What can I get you fellas?" she asked. Jacob and Sam practically had their tongues hanging out of their mouths. And Miles, well, Nate didn't know what he was, because Nate had never seen that look cross his face before.

Since the rest of the brigade appeared astonished by her beauty, Nate took the lead and spoke up. He said, "We'll start with a pitcher, unless city living has pansied you guys up and you want fruity girl drinks."

"Dude, I jump out of moving cars for a living. Don't mind him, sweetheart, his mom dropped him on his head a lot as an infant. We don't like to bring it up much but in certain situations." Sam gave her his Mr. Hollywood smile, which Nate knew from experience tended to dazzle women into agreeing to anything Sam wanted.

Cybil admonished Sam with an unimpressed glance, one fine-boned hand at her waist, and said, "Honey, I'm used to guys waving their dicks around in here to see who has the biggest bravado, and usually, the loudest in the bunch has the smallest package."

Jacob hollered with peals of laughter. Nate chuckled, having been on the receiving end of Cybil's take-no-prisoners attitude before. It was comical watching Sam's smile fall, like he couldn't believe a woman wasn't fluttering around him over his profession. Then there was Miles, who sat in stony silence, his eyes haunted as he stared at her. Nate would have to ask him later what that was all about.

"You boys want anything to eat?" Cybil asked.

"Yeah, two extra-large pies, the works," Nate said, since the three knuckleheads seemed incapable of carrying on a conversation with her present.

"Sure thing, I'll put the order in and I'll be right back with your pitcher." Cybil sashayed back toward the bar, and his buddy Miles's gaze followed her with what Nate could only describe as hunger. Now wasn't the time, but there was a story there.

"Jacob, tell me. What's new in the computer tech world?" Nate asked, relaxing on the stool and settling into a rhythm.

"Well, you remember that stock I told you all to invest in on that start up firm that I thought had a great product? Wait until you see how much it's earned. And it's only the beginning."

The four of them fell into a pattern as the years receded and wiped away the stain of responsibility and distance between them. They discussed what was new in their lives, rehashed old college war stories and, in the end, discussed their favorite topic: women, of course. Sam always had a story. Jacob made Nate wonder if he planned on becoming a monk. And Miles was supremely private about his love life. However, every time Cybil came within ten feet of their table, Miles would tense and his face would get this weird look.

When Sam and Jacob started playing pool, with Nate and Miles on deck to play the winner, Cybil stopped by with a refill on their pitcher.

"I see your sister arrived." Nate nodded toward the bar area where Tessa, in her alternative goth style black dress, sat holding court. It was then that he spied a brunette he hadn't expected to see this evening. Abby was seated on a bar stool in a form-fitting forest green dress that ended mid-thigh. And she was sitting next to the one asshole in town he hated, Alex Dotson. He'd been a smarmy prick in high school and hadn't grown out of that phase.

Abby glanced over her shoulder and spotted him. She held

up a fruity pastel pink cocktail in a *cheers* gesture and then shifted her attention back to her group.

"And she didn't come alone," Cybil said with a snort. "She brought most of the Echo Springs Community College faculty. In fact, one of them lives next to you. Abby Callier."

"Yes, I know her." Nate wasn't going to admit that he knew what she looked like naked from the waist up, or how she sounded as desire washed over her. Or that her lush ass seemed to fit perfectly in his hands, or that he couldn't get her out of his mind.

"Need anything else?" Cybil asked.

"No, not at this moment."

What Nate needed was the woman currently laughing at something his arch nemesis had said in her ear.

"What gives, Nate?" Miles said. "Who's Abby, and why do you look like you want to wipe the floor with Dipshit Dotson?"

"She's none of your business," Nate said with more force behind his words than he intended. He'd staked his claim on Abby and didn't want the interference.

"Oh, who are we talking about?" Sam interjected, filling his glass up again with amber beer.

Miles said, "Nate has a crush on his neighbor."

Jacob ribbed him, "Which one is she? Maybe I could take her off—"

Nate glared at the behemoth and said, "Enough, A-wad. Are you ready to lose your shirt?"

Jacob puffed up. "I don't lose at pool. You know that."

"Put your money where your mouth is, son." Challenge accepted. Game, set, and match.

Nate broke up the line of questioning regarding Abby. He wasn't ready to discuss her with anyone, let alone his caring, but dickhead, friends. That didn't mean he was happy about Abby getting too close to Alex for his comfort. He and his buds played pool, and as the night progressed, he paid more attention to Abby's group.

One thing had become definitively clear. He planned to stake his claim on Abby, tonight. She just didn't know it yet. Hunger and need clawed at him, demanded he intervene and step between her and Dotson.

But he bided his time. He would make his move before the night ended.

Chapter Ten

From Old Man Turner's Journal:
Plan for the unexpected.

A bby felt Nate's hot, sexy eyes on her all night long. The impromptu after work gathering with her fellow colleagues had been her way of avoiding said hot neighbor. But running into him at Smitty's, when Nate looked like sex on a stick in his navy flannel and jeans, had made a mockery of her attempts to avoid him. Almost as if fate was conspiring against her feeble efforts to maintain distance. Every time their gazes clashed across the crowd, heat infused her veins and her pulse fluttered in heady anticipation. The air clogged in her lungs as each glance scorched her from the inside out.

It took a herculean effort to remain focused on why she was here, instead of on Nate's intense, panty-melting smolders. They were hot enough to melt nearby glaciers. Tonight was about getting to know her colleagues, not staring at Sheriff Stud Muffin like some lovesick teen with her first crush.

But she was glad she had come to Smitty's. The bar was

packed, the people were friendly. And when they learned she was Evie Callier's great niece, they accepted her into the fold as if she was one of them, no questions asked. The dichotomy of it all, how different it was from the people she knew at her university and growing up, where she was included based on her academic accomplishments and how she might benefit the group, amazed her. The warmth and friendliness of the community sent her already jumbled emotions into further tumult.

She enjoyed chatting with Tessa in her funky retro black dress and knee-high black boots. The only color in her otherwise black funeral wear was the bright purple coloring the ends of her ebony hair in an ombre style. It was a look Abby would never be able to pull off in her wildest dreams but on Tessa, it worked. Abby met her sister, Cybil, and they hit it off well. Abby knew they could be fast friends if she stayed in Echo Springs. The rest of the faculty were nice, with Barry Stein, Jon Harrison, Ted Bailey, Jennifer Wilson, Eva Monroe, and many more in attendance this evening. Then there was Alex Dotson, professor of American History. He was attractive, with wavy blond hair that was neatly trimmed and a runner's build. Perhaps, if she had never met Nate, she might have been interested in his obvious flirting. But as flattered as she was, as Alex laid the charm and innuendo on thick, she wasn't interested in him at all.

The problem was she had met Nate first. Even with the frustrating distance between them this past week, the barriers they'd both erected, not once had she stopped thinking about him, or watching for him out her window. There was more to the sexy lawman than protecting the people of Echo Springs and she was dying of curiosity to uncover all his layers. And then there was the teensy, incontrovertible fact that she had missed his presence. That in itself gave her pause. When had she ever missed a man? Never, dammit.

Abby had feelings for Nate. She didn't know how deep they ran, but they existed, and she wasn't a woman who could turn her feelings off and on at will.

"Seriously, I need to see inside your aunt's house," Cybil said. "I was curious before she passed away and never had the chance, but I just love old places." She loaded another serving tray full of drinks before heading back into the fray. Cybil definitely had no problem stating exactly what she wanted. Maybe Abby should take a page out of her book, she thought as she shot a glance at the hunky man in question, engaged at a pool table with three guys who were all attractive, but Nate stood out among them. She nearly moaned when Nate bent over the table, angling a shot, giving her a perfect glimpse of his well-formed posterior, and remembered all too well the feel of his firm rear in her hands.

"And I would love to sit on your porch and paint," Tessa said. "It would be a magnificent experience with the view you have." Then she turned to respond to something Alex had said.

"Well, maybe the three of us could do a girls' night at my aunt's," Abby offered when Cybil returned with a tray laden with empty beer mugs and shot glasses.

"Really?" Cybil almost squealed as she set the tray on the bar. She had this vibrant energy and was almost bouncing in her excitement. Girls' night at Abby's place it was, apparently.

"Well, sure. I could cook." It had been a long time since she'd had company. Nate didn't count, and she wasn't certain why. Like he was already part of her make-up at home. But she'd not had girlfriends that were outside of her career in, well, forever. And while Tessa worked with her at the community college, the place wasn't about prestige but focused on the students' learning and growth.

"You cook?" Tessa said. "I'm so there. The only thing I can cook comes out of the microwave. Anything more complicated than pressing a button, and I'm lost. I'm great at ordering take-out, though."

"And yet, your waistline defies convention," Abby said, thinking if she ate like that, they would have to put her out to pasture with the other heifers.

Tessa shrugged. "Genetics."

"I'm with you, Abby. My sister likely was planted here by aliens, which is why we are nothing alike," Cybil said as she hoisted another full tray. Jesus, just watching Cybil maneuver back and forth, from the bar to tables and back again, was making Abby tired. And the woman did it in heels. But she was correct in that she and her sister seemed to be spawned from different parents. Where Tessa was a geeky gamer chick and graphic artist with funky clothes and colored streaks in her jet-black hair—today, they were purple—Cybil was a supermodel type in lacquered-on jeans, cowboy boots, and a frilly, fire-engine red blouse that displayed more of her ample cleavage than it hid. Her inky hair was artfully arranged in a high ponytail that stopped in the middle of her back.

"I'd love to see your aunt's place too, Abby," Alex interjected.

She turned and glanced at him to see obvious invitation swimming in his nutmeg gaze. As much as she appreciated his interest, there was only one man in this town her body and hormones seemed calibrated toward.

"Well, it's a girls-only night. You understand, don't you, Alex?"

"Sure, another time maybe."

Abby wanted to hang her head. She hadn't meant to make Alex feel bad. She just figured it was easier and better to be clear now that she wasn't interested in that sort of relationship with him. Her mind—and, okay, her heart—were consumed by Sheriff Stud Muffin. But that's because they were like two dowsing rods whenever they were near each other. She'd known he was here before she'd spied him sitting near the pool tables because she'd felt him.

While she wanted to go say hi, Abby was intimidated by his three reasonably attractive male friends. In her limited experience, men sometimes acted different when they were with their buddies. She worried her bottom lip, trying to decide if she should go over or not. Did she really want to know if Nate was a jerk in a group setting? Truthfully, no. It would be far too disappointing. So she did nothing but pine for the man. How pathetic was that? Tonight was supposed to be about fun and here she was mooning over the sheriff.

"How are you at pool?" Tessa asked, an expressive smile on her face. "I've got a hankering to play."

Abby had a feeling Tessa could convince people in hell that they didn't want ice water if she put her mind to it. Pool would put her in Nate's sphere and give her a wing-woman, so she could say hello and not be intimidated. Butterflies flitted in her chest at the prospect of being near him once more. Decision made, she said, "I can hold my own."

"Sa-weet, let's go. There's a table that just opened up. Hey, sis, can we get another round back at the pool tables?"

"Yep. Have it out to you in a few," Cybil replied, hoisting her tray, and heading toward another table.

Abby followed Tessa as she wove through the crowd. As they neared Nate's group, her breath caught in her throat and her palms started to sweat. She was acting like a schoolgirl with her first crush and not a grown damn woman.

"Abby," Nate said with a nod in that rich, deep, velvety voice of his, and it made her insides turn to jelly. His voice was like an intimate caress along her spine, making her shiver.

"Sheriff," she replied, hoping she didn't sound as breathy and high-pitched as she thought she might. But in his presence, she had this heightened awareness, as if it was just the two of them and the rest of the world didn't exist.

"What am I? Chopped liver, Nate?" Tessa interjected with a deviant smile.

"Tessa, good to see you," Nate said. His congenial attitude and warm gaze spoke of their friendship. It was only when that blue gaze shifted Abby's way that his eyes darkened with hunger. It stoked the smoldering fire inside her. How was it that a mere glance made her want to jump the man's bones?

Tessa studied and selected a pool cue like she was picking a rare diamond. "You too. Who are your friends?" she said, indicating the three men behind Nate.

"Tessa, Abby, these morons are Sam, Jacob, and Miles," Nate said, introducing each one. Miles was slick, with a polished sheen Abby recognized from a lifetime spent within a short train ride of Manhattan. He was attractive with his short, clipped dirty-blond hair. He wasn't as tall as Nate, maybe an inch or so shorter. Sam was a heart-stopper with a gregarious smile that Abby was sure charmed most women, not to mention his movie star good looks and devil-may-care smile.

"Hi, I'm Sam, and this here's Jacob. Would you take pity on him and end his monkish lifestyle?" He slung a friendly arm around the man who reminded Abby of a giant. Why wasn't this man playing professional football with his towering frame?

Jacob good-naturedly shoved Sam off. "Cut it out, A-wad." Jacob's voice reminded her of a deep organ bellow. His nearly midnight hair was pulled back at the nape of his neck, and his black beard was closely cropped. But it was his demeanor that charmed Abby. Jacob's dark eyes darted briefly to Tessa, with a stare filled with such longing it made Abby ache for him, and then his glance darted away, color shadowing his face.

"Would you ladies be interested in a game?" Sam quipped with what she was sure was his signature ladies-swoon smile.

Tessa finished racking the balls on the table next to the guys and shot Abby a glance. "Your call."

That was when Nate said, "I don't think that—"

"I think we can take them," Abby said, bristling slightly at being dismissed. "I'm in."

Nate cast her a simmering glance that she ignored. If she was going to put her money where her mouth was then she had to concentrate on the game and not Nate, otherwise she'd melt into a puddle at his feet. Abby didn't want to let her new friend Tessa down. Then there was that tiny bit of pride that wanted to prove she could be around Nate and remain unaffected by his nearness. Besides, when it came to pool, Abby could hold her own. It was all angles and geometry anyhow, one of the subjects she'd excelled in before switching to literature.

Abby and Tessa played the first round against Miles and Sam. They were good, but the ladies were better. Abby suspected at first the men thought it'd be cute to invite the women to play with them, until Tessa broke the balls with the skill of a seasoned veteran pool shark, sinking two of the stripes. After two rounds with Miles and Sam, the girls were declared the winners each time, once when Tessa sank the eight ball to win it in the first round, and again when Abby rather cockily sank it with a banked shot into the corner pocket.

"Our turn." Nate indicated Jacob, who blushed furiously every time he so much as looked at Tessa.

Abby nodded. "So it is."

She let Tessa break, because the woman seemed to know just how to strike to sink a ball to get the game moving forward. All the while, Nate's nearness kept turning her insides into a gooey mush, which made her miss a shot or two. The repartee in the group was congenial, with the men tossing friendly barbs at one another as they played.

Abby didn't miss the fact that Tessa exaggerated her movements, wiggled her hips, or leaned against the table when Jacob was about to shoot. Her methods seemed to work. When Jacob caught sight of Tessa's cleavage as she bent over during one of his shots, he not only missed the mark, but the cue ball rocketed off the table.

And through it all, Nate watched Abby with that intense gaze of his, stirring need and desire in her limbs. The air between them clogged with heat and unspoken yearning. Caught up in Nate's aura, she missed Alex trying to get her attention at the bar. She ignored Sam as he hit on Cybil, while Miles watched her with an unreadable expression.

Nate was the sole focus of her universe as she lined up her shot. Abby took aim, banked the ball into the corner pocket, and the cue ball rolled back just enough to give her a money shot with the eight ball.

"All right, Abby, you got this," Tessa said, standing by the table, her excitement palpable. It would be something if they swept the guys.

Abby nodded. Her stomach tightened in knots as she called the center pocket and lined up her shot. Feeling Nate's energy circling her like a bird of prey, she raised her glance off her shot, only to be walloped with sexual energy so potent her knees trembled.

Abby refocused on the shot, her gaze computing the angle of the shot, and positioned her body accordingly. She inhaled a few steadying breaths, letting the dull roar of the bar diminish as she struck the cue ball, watched it roll across the green, tap the eight, and then sink the eight ball in the center pocket.

The cue ball banked on the opposite wall and trundled to a stop.

Tessa tossed her head back and laughed as she did a little victory dance, then gave Abby a high five. "We make a good team, Abby. Wanna go another round?"

"I think I'm done for the night," Abby said. Better to stop before her body went up in flames from Nate's nearness.

Jacob interjected, "Nice game."

Tessa gave him a gamine grin and said, "You too. Since Abby's out, what do you say to another game, big guy, just you and me?"

"Nice to meet you guys," Abby said. "Nate, see you around."

"I'm out too," Nate said. "Early morning. Miles, you have my spare key if you all need a place."

"Later, Sheriff Do-Right." Sam saluted him.

Abby retrieved her jacket with Nate on her heels. She swiveled as they entered the parking lot and said, "You know, you really don't have to leave now. I can make it home on my own."

"Abby, you've had a few drinks, and I'm going to make sure you make it home okay. And then there's this."

One minute she was enjoying the crisp cool mountain night. The next, fire emanated from every pore of her being as Nate enveloped her in his arms and drank her startled moans with his mouth. It took Abby's stunned brain all of two seconds before she responded and plastered her body against his as he continued the delicious onslaught. The man kissed her and the rest of the world simply ceased to exist. He became her universe. Abby returned his kiss. Who needed air to breathe when pleasure swamped her veins? She wanted to crawl inside Nate, fuse together with him and remain this way for years, decades even.

Before she could slide her hand inside his flannel shirt, Nate lifted his head, his breathing labored and lust clouding his visage. He said, "I'll drive."

All she could do was nod. Her brain had melted into her toes upon first contact. She wanted this, him, with a desire bordering on manic. He helped her into his Explorer and he drove them to her house. Thank goodness. She'd never have made it. Not with desire pulsing through her with the magnitude force of a major earthquake. They didn't say a word to each other in the cab of his SUV, but then again, they didn't need to. There was no denying they wanted each other with a fascination and desire that eclipsed all rational thought.

Nate pulled the vehicle into his driveway, but before she could climb out, he was there, helping her down, his fingers threaded through hers as he pulled her toward her house. Abby's heart thumped in her chest. She knew she should cry off, but for the life of her, she couldn't think of a simple reason why. She wanted him. Wanted him like she craved air to breathe. Nate wanted her, too, and she couldn't tear herself away from him. Abby was done denying herself what she wanted.

He removed her keys from her hand and opened the door. Thank God. Her hands were shaking too much, and she would have made a fool of herself. They stepped across the threshold, Nate closed the door behind them. They were barely inside when Nate spun her into his arms. At the commanding tug, Abby went willingly, meeting him halfway as he claimed her mouth in a torrid duel.

From the moment his dog had flattened her on the porch—hell, the moment she'd clobbered him with her nine-iron—they had been heading toward this like it was an event horizon. There was no turning from the need and the hunger as it erupted like a match on dry kindling. His hands trailed down her back and cupped her rear. Abby needed little prompting, but with his help, she wrapped her body around his. The skirt of her dress bunched near her waist. And she couldn't stop kissing him. They leaned against the front door, and Abby's hands went to his navy flannel shirt. When she couldn't undo the buttons, she yanked at the material, buttons popping off and pinging against the hardwood floor.

Then her fingers were against his heated flesh. Her palms slid over his pectorals and lats. Christ, the man was ripped and hard, and oh god... He sucked her lower lip into his mouth, then growled as he helped her discard his shirt. She adored his arms and chest. God, she couldn't seem to get enough of him as he kissed her so deeply, her soul ignited into a miasma of carnal bliss.

His hands undid the zipper of her dress and he tugged the top half down until her breasts spilled into his hands. On a guttural groan, he curled his tongue around a pert bud, then enveloped the areola into his mouth and her head fell back at the exquisite arcs of pleasure bombarding her system. Her hands threaded into his hair as he feasted on her cleavage. The man had a singularly skilled tongue; he instinctively knew just how to caress and tease her flesh until she was writhing against him, needing him to fill the emptiness.

Her hands descended to his belt.

"Not here. Upstairs," he murmured around her breast. He took a few steps, carrying her, and she wriggled her hips.

"Christ, don't do that till I get us upstairs," Nate groaned, his breathing heavy.

"Not upstairs. Now. Here." Abby's hand slid between them and into his pants, where her fingers gripped his bulging erection. There was so much of him. He was incredibly hard, but the skin so soft, and it burned her like a brand.

Nate moaned, and his face darkened with lust. Desire overrode everything else between them. He managed two steps before he course-corrected and backed her up against the thick wooden doorframe leading into the living room. His hands shoved the skirt of her dress further up her waist. He slanted his mouth against hers, claiming her lips in a heated exchange that left her breathless. Her hands fumbled a bit as she unbuckled his pants, then slid the zipper down. She shoved his boxer briefs over his hips, freeing his member as he withdrew his wallet from his back pocket and removed a square foil packet. She helped him protect them both, rolling the condom down over his length. Then he ripped her panties off with a tug.

Nate guided his firm manhood into place, positioning the crown at her entrance, and then he rolled his hips, penetrating her deeply. Their twin groans of pleasure filled the air. As she kept her gaze trained on him, he began to thrust his hips, withdrawing his length and plunging deep.

Abby overflowed with his heat and canted her hips, meeting his every thrust as she took him inside. Heaven, she decided, was in his arms. His rapid-fire, short, brutal strokes made starbursts of pleasure implode in her veins. His long, languorous penetrations were meant to tease a heated response from her. Over and over, he thrust, and her hips moved in sync with his, meeting him time and time again. Nate kissed her as he used the doorframe for support. The tenor and tempo of their lovemaking increased to a fevered pitch. Her nails dug into his solid shoulders while the storm of need crested and carried them further over the precipice of ecstasy.

Nate filled her, surrounded her, shuttled her body up a cliff of heart-rending desire, only to retreat and start the pleasured madness over again. And through it all, she kept her gaze on his, seeing herself in his eyes and feeling all the defenses she had erected, all the excuses, slip away with every solid thrust of his hips.

Then the heat between them crescendoed, meant to obliterate her control. Nate gripped her tighter as his desire began to unwind. He clasped her to him, her arms wrapped around his shoulders as he buried his face in the hollow of her neck.

Abby's body unraveled. A supernova exploded in her body, rippling soundwaves of ecstasy. Her sex quaked and she trembled in his arms as she came undone.

"Abby," Nate moaned as his body went rigid and his final thrust slammed home. His frame jolted, his length pulsed, and he groaned as his climax hit.

She held on to him while the waves of ecstasy roiled through her system. After the ferocity of the storm, she sank bonelessly against him, trusting he would keep her safe. She rested her head upon his shoulder, feeling his heartbeat return to a normal pace as he held her close.

Abby opened her eyes and, in the half light from the hall spilling into the living room, spied the army of dolls. "Oh, sweet Jesus."

She hid her face in his neck, trying to stop the laughter and failing miserably. She hated those things. This just proved she had to get rid of them.

"What's wrong?" Nate murmured, placing a light kiss on her temple.

She lifted her gaze and nodded her head toward the living room. "Seems we had an audience."

"Oh, yeah." Nate gave her a sexy male grin as he looked into the living room. "I thought you were selling them."

"I was—I am. Those creepy little suckers look like they're going to attack us at any minute."

"Should I be worried about your obsession with inanimate objects and your belief that they will kill us?" Nate asked.

"Only if you know something I don't, like that they really are alive. No, I just have an overactive imagination. Habit for someone who likes to read a lot."

"Speaking of imagination, I have a few things I imagined this past week, if you're game."

Lust stirred in her belly at his suggestion. "Really? I might. What did you have in mind?"

He chuckled darkly. "I'll show you."

Nate never set her feet down, she clung to him as he headed toward the stairs. The she asked, "Wait, what about Rufus? Doesn't he need to be let out?"

"Shit. You're right." Then he stilled as the sound of multiple cars pulling into his driveway reached them. He smiled. "Miles and the guys will take care of him for the night."

At the base of the stairs, Nate cupped her chin, nudged her mouth open with his thumb, and slanted his mouth over hers. The world could have been falling into a demonic hell dimension with the damn dolls leading the way and she wouldn't have noticed. Abby had no more thoughts or concerns for Rufus or anything else, for that matter, as Nate stole her ability to think or feel anything but him.

When he broke the kiss, she said, "We'll make it up to Rufus in the morning."

"Good call," he said, and with her in his arms, he relocated them to her bedroom. It was the most erotic ascension of her life. Nate stopped every other step to kiss, fondle, lick or caress whatever came to mind.

As he laid her down gently and followed her down onto her bed, she wondered if she would survive the delicious onslaught. Then she wondered no more as Nate took her under again and again.

Chapter Eleven

From Old Man Turner's Journal:
Seduce her with every thought and deed.

N ate stretched, more rested and at peace than he had been
in ages. The ice blue covers slid down his torso, and he
reached for Abby only to encounter empty space. The whisper
soft sheets beside him held her warmth, but her delectable,
succulent form was missing. Where the hell was she? Christ, but
the woman was an addiction. He'd lost count of the number of
times he'd touched her and gone up in flames, only to come back
down to Earth and need her again.

Once was never going to be enough with Abby.

Perhaps, on some level, he had known instinctively that she
wasn't a woman you loved for just a night. Which certainly
explained why a part of him had resisted—at least at first. Abby
was a woman a man kept. She was a woman he built a foundation and life with. Reducing everything to a single night in her
arms was a fool's errand.

His gaze focused on the empty space. Abby had been a revelation. Even after the multitude number of times he'd found himself buried deep inside her, he craved to feel her there again. Feel the way she enveloped him, how her nails dug into his back or butt, how she unraveled beneath his hands and how hot he burned in hers.

She moved him in rather unexpected ways. She was intelligent and sweet, and had held her own with his friends last night. They were a hard bunch to keep up with sometimes with their ribbing. Not to mention, the woman was scarily good at pool. It had been quite the turn-on watching her concentrate and line up her shots.

Wiping the sleep from his face, Nate sat up. Where the hell had she gone? He made no bones about the fact that he wanted her again, needed her. Rays of golden light streamed in through the curtains, illuminating her bedroom. The desk near the window was piled with books and her computer. And it looked like she had left her sexy librarian style glasses by the computer keyboard. The golf club with which she had gone all *Xena: Warrior Princess* on him with that first night was propped up against the side of the desk. Nate listened for her, for movement in the old house. A smile spread across his face at the sound of cascading water emitting from the shower across the hall. He slid from the bed, uncaring of his naked state and focused on the woman currently occupying his every thought.

After grabbing a few foil packets from the box on the nightstand, he trod across the hall, opened the door, and heard her humming. Steam filled the room as he padded across the tile. He pulled the shower curtain open and she gave a little yelp.

"Mind if I join you?" he said, stepping in, loving the way the water flowed over her curves.

"N-n-no, you just startled me. I'm not used to—" She cut off what she was going to say. Her hazel eyes looked more luminous, filled with a mixture of embarrassment and desire.

A sense of possession and satisfaction infused his being.

"You're not used to having anyone spend the night? I don't

mind that. In fact, I rather like that you're not used to it." He pressed his advantage, crowding her lush body against the tile wall. Then he lowered his lips to hers and invaded her mouth.

He drank her sweet little cries as she mewled in the back of her throat. Kissing Abby was the closest to heaven Nate had ever come. It altered his world. *She* altered him. Heat and steam encapsulated them and desire inundated him. Nate wanted to leave his mark on her as he sucked and nipped at her bottom lip. He reveled in her hands threading into his hair to hold his mouth in place. Their kiss was a tangle of hungry lips and dueling tongues.

His mouth left hers—much to her dismay, given her frustrated whimper which he soon turned into a gasped moan. He smiled as he tasted her neck and the small hollow between her shoulders, grazing it with his teeth before laving it with his tongue. The tub was small for someone his size, but he managed as his mouth traveled over her shoulders, down over the slope of her breast and the slight mound of her belly, to her sex.

"Nate, I don't think—"

"Just hold on, honey, and I'll take care of the rest." He parted her thighs, lifting one leg up and over his shoulder to give him the perfect view and access. With his gaze trained on her expressive face, he swiped his tongue through her crease.

"Oh," she moaned on a strangled gasp and her head fell back against the tile.

Nate braced her hips, holding her in place while he loved her intimately. He laved and licked, flicking his tongue through her folds as she trembled and writhed against him. Her scent filled his nostrils. Her taste flooded his mouth. Her fingers threaded into his hair and held on tight. Every part of him became intimately attuned to her every nuance as he drove her body up a blistering peak until she crested and came apart in his hands.

"Nate, oh god," she wailed, her pleasured cries echoing off the tile walls.

Unable to wait any longer, he stood, lifting her sagging form into his arms, pressing her back against the wall. Her eyes were heavy lidded with desire. Her arms clasped around his neck and he wedged himself between her thighs. Lowering his mouth, he pressed his lips to hers. He could kiss this woman forever.

He fumbled with the foil packet as water sluiced over and coated their forms. Once he had protected them both, with a roll of his hips, he was sliding inside her clasping sheath with a groan. She felt like electrified silk. Time seemed to suspend itself as he loved her. There was no beginning and no end as he moved, studying her expression as he learned all the subtle nuances of her form.

He discovered what made her writhe, what made her moan, and what made her scream. Nate explored every inch of her desire until he could no longer maintain his control. Gripping her tightly, he unleashed the reins of his passion, carrying her with him into the storm.

It was quite some time before they emerged from the shower. They washed each other and loved again. Only after two world-altering orgasms did they leave the confines of the shower and bathroom. By then the water had run cold, but the happy smile on Abby's lips, the light and warmth to be found in her hazel gaze, had been worth every second. They would have stayed there longer if cold water and a hunger for sustenance hadn't driven them out.

Nate dressed in yesterday's clothes. He located his flannel shirt near the base of the stairs as they descended, and slipped it on. Not a single button remained. He shook his head. It had been more than worth it.

"I can make some eggs if you'd like," Abby offered, sexy as all get out in her fluffy robe, when they trod into the kitchen.

He caged her against the granite countertop, and murmured, "I wish I could this morning. As it is, I have those morons you met last night staying in my house, and need to make sure they didn't demolish it overnight. Especially not with the remodeling I'm doing on the second floor."

"Really? I'd like to see it. Then again, I haven't been inside your house, so I don't know what it looked like before."

He leaned forward, his mouth hovering over hers and said, "I promise you, as soon as they are gone, we can arrange that."

"I'd like that," she said with a little hitch in her voice.

His gut clenched at the sound, and his body revved back to life. His fingers toyed with her hair. Oh yeah, he wanted to see what Abby looked like in his bed. Christ, he had to leave now or he would never get out of there.

Her mouth opened and her pink tongue darted out, wetting her bottom lip. It was like waving a red flag in front of a bull. With his gaze on her, Nate kissed her. Her lips were soft and slightly swollen from their over indulgence. But he couldn't help himself, she was fast becoming an addiction. Abby plastered her body against his, her entire form surrendered against him, and his eyes crossed. He would love nothing more than to spend the entire day in bed with her—a week, even—but unfortunately, it couldn't be today.

But soon.

Regretfully, he released her luscious mouth and lifted his head. His thumb traced her lower lip, still craving every minute touch. "I hate to leave, but I have to get to the station."

"I understand. And your friends are in town, I get it."

He cupped her chin before she could withdraw from him. "They leave tomorrow. They are only in town because Miles's mom has a retirement party tonight. She was like a second mother to our group, we all know and love Mrs. Keaton, we are required to go."

She hid her disappointed gaze, lowering her face, and said, "Oh, it's not a big deal. I know that we aren't seeing each other."

Oh, we aren't, huh? He tipped her face up and held her gaze. "Oh, I think we are. In fact, I saw quite a bit of you last night, and would like nothing more than to see if your aunt's kitchen table is sturdy enough so that I can see more of you."

"Oh," she said, her breath expelling in a rush. Her pupils dilated and she bit her bottom lip.

"Come with me tonight. Be my date to Mrs. Keaton's party," he said, stroking her cheek with the back of his knuckles.

"Oh, I don't think... I hardly know anyone, and wouldn't want to impose."

"Abby, Mrs. Keaton will be fine with it. And I'd like it if you went with me."

A small smile spread over her lush lips as she nodded. "All right, what time should I be ready?"

"Five." He gave her another brief kiss to remind her that this was far more than a one-night thing and that they were seeing each other. Talk about a complication in his life but so far, he relished the challenge. If she didn't believe that they were dating, he had to step up his game. Because they were an item, and it was up to him to prove it.

Reluctantly, he released her—he had to or else they would be discovering if the kitchen table was sturdy enough. Nate inhaled a steadying breath and sauntered to the back door. Opening it, he welcomed the rush of cooler air to calm his inferno of need. He glanced over his shoulder and said, "Oh, and Abby?"

"Yes?" she said, swiveling from the counter with the coffee pot in her delicate hand.

"Wear something that's easy to remove." His gaze raked her mussed form from head down to her delicate toes.

"Okay," she said breathlessly. Then he noticed that the hand holding the coffee pot was trembling. He left with a smile on his lips and a spring in his step.

The satisfied feeling stayed with him, even as he entered his home to encounter complete chaos in his kitchen. Jacob stood at the stove, frying up a good pound of bacon. Miles sat at the kitchen table on his cell phone, jotting notes onto a yellow legal pad, and Sam, judging by the rough, pale, somewhat green tinge he exhibited, was nursing a severe hangover.

Sam spotted Nate first as he entered and shut the door

behind him. Then Rufus bounded over, his body vibrating with excitement, his big thick tail wagging.

"Dude, you and the hot neighbor chick, way to go, bro." Sam gave Nate a shit-eating grin, then winced at the movement. Yep, he had a hangover, and a bad one too by Nate's reckoning.

"And it's none of your business, dude. Find your own damn woman," Nate replied good-naturedly. Leave it to Sam to make him feel territorial. Not that they would ever poach on each other's turf, but the mere thought made Nate want to go all caveman, perhaps pee a circle around her home and mark his territory like a beast in the wild. Chuckling to himself, he doubted that would go over well with Abby.

Jacob chimed in, "So it's serious, then, you and the schoolteacher?"

Nate ignored the question as he stopped at the counter, grabbed a mug from the overhead cabinet, and poured a cup of coffee. He took a long drink of the dark brew before he responded. "I'm not sure what it is yet. I would appreciate you morons butting out until I do, especially since I sort of invited her to the party tonight." Nate shot a look at Miles as he hung up the phone. "I hope you don't mind."

Miles shook his head. "Mom won't. In fact, she'll be happy that one of us is seeing someone. Maybe you and your schoolteacher can divert attention away from the fact that Mom keeps trying to set me up with every friend of a friend's daughter she can possibly find."

Nate asked, "What about Cybil? You two seem to have some chemistry."

A pained expression crossed Miles's face before disappearing behind a mask of cool indifference. "That's not going to happen. I gotta run and start helping Mom get everything set up. I expect you all promptly at five thirty. Do not be late." Miles escaped the ribbing over Cybil, heading out the front door with a slam. The tires of his Porsche squealed as he sped away. Nate would have to remind him not to break the sound barrier, otherwise the guy would force his hand until he had no choice but to ticket him.

Jacob, wielding tongs and transferring bacon onto a plate, said, "I wonder what's going on with Miles and Cybil. Do you know anything?"

Nate held up his hands. "Don't look at me. I just work here."

"Speaking of Cybil, did you notice how hot her little sister Tessa is?" Sam interjected. "I know she's a bit off-beat with her comic books and all, but she's got this clear freak-between-the-sheets vibe that's rather enticing."

"She's not your type, Sam, and you know it," Jacob muttered, munching on bacon and transferring the plate to the kitchen table. Then he returned to the stove, frying a few eggs and adding some toast. Jacob had a legendary appetite and could out-eat all three of them. Granted, he did have half a foot and a good fifty pounds on the rest of his friends.

Sam leaned back with a smirk. "Dude, she's female. They're all my type."

Jacob snorted as he slipped fried eggs onto a plate and placed the frying pan in the sink. Carting his meal to the table, he took the chair on the opposite side from Sam, eyeing the guy like he was a recalcitrant teen. "Yeah, well, I think that one's a little too off-beat for even you."

Sam sighed, snatching bacon from the center plate. "Yeah, you're probably right. Besides, with my upcoming schedule, I won't even have a weekend free."

"Weren't you seeing that actress, what's-her-face, Kendra Lewis?" Jacob took a bite of toast.

Sam gave them a half grin and wiggled his brows. "I'm not sure seeing is the right word."

Jacob rolled his eyes. "Dude, when are you going to grow the fuck up?"

"If I can help it, never," Sam quipped with his lackadaisical sarcasm.

"Can I trust you two not to get into a fight? I have to run to the station for a bit," Nate said before he gave in to the temptation to knock their heads together. As much as he loved them, there were days…

It was Jacob who had the level head. "Yeah, I have some work to get done today anyway. I just need your Wi-Fi login and password, if you don't mind."

"Not at all. Sam?" Nate cocked a brow in his direction.

"I have to head down to Main Street and find a gift for Mrs. Keaton. While I'm at it, maybe I'll hunt down Tessa and ask her on a date," Sam teased Jacob as he stood and danced out of arm's reach on a laugh. The front door slammed shut behind him, followed by the rev of his Mustang as he peeled out of the drive. *Damn hot rod.*

"I should give him a ticket just for being a dick," Nate said. Sam was not acting like the guy he knew. His edges were sharper, his arrogance more pronounced, and Nate wondered what the hell was going on with him.

Jacob shook his head with a pensive countenance. "Like that will change him. Hollywood has corrupted him a bit."

"You think?" Nate certainly didn't care for Sam's bad attitude. He'd always been a bit wild, adventurous and confident. But that had now twisted into an egotism that left a bad taste in Nate's mouth.

Jacob shrugged. "It was his choice, man. We all make them, for better or worse."

"Do you think he needs our help?" he asked, because there was something else going on with Sam, he could feel it. His brain already attempting to put the puzzle pieces together as if it were one of his investigations.

"I do, but I don't think he'll take it. He hasn't hit it yet." Jacob stroked a hand over his beard in a thinking man gesture. It was the one the guy usually reserved for when he was deep in thought, working on his computer.

"Hit what?" Nate asked. Although, deep down, he knew in a fatalistic sense the danger he smelled around their friend.

"Bottom."

That's what Nate had been picking up—the out of control, barely holding it together, on a collision course, unstoppable energy. Needing the confirmation—because when it came to those he cared about, there was no way for him to come to an impartial conclusion like he did on the force—he asked, "And you think he will?"

"I love the guy. He's one of my brothers from another mother, but I don't think things will change for him until he hits it. And when you're living life in the fast lane like that, it all ends at some point. Mine did."

"Is that why you moved back to Colorado?"

Jacob's glance was thoughtful. "Yes and no. I could have stayed there and survived well enough, but the fact is, I missed it here. And the tax breaks for moving my little startup to Colorado weren't half bad either."

"Well, I for one am glad you're back in the state. It will be good to have you near again."

"I am too. And I'll be closer than you think. I'm building a place here in Echo Springs and moving down from Boulder. I need to get away from city life." Jacob stared at Nate, as if gauging his reaction.

"No shit? Where?" Jacob, in Echo Springs? That was a change of pace. But Nate was thrilled.

Pleased with himself, Jacob tossed Rufus a few strips of bacon and shrugged. "I purchased the McKinley property."

"Get the fuck out. That was you? Why? What brought this on?" Nate asked, delighted at the new development. Jacob was one of the best guys he knew. It would be nice having him around more. Even though Jacob could get started on a new project and go into hermit mode, it would still be nice to have him living on the outskirts of town.

"Yeah, mainly because I'm tired of the city. I have people I trust running the daily operations, letting me focus more on my tech inventions. And it's also because I want a place that's smaller, more homey."

"And closer to a comic book chick who shall remain nameless," Nate teased.

Jacob leaned back in his chair. "Tessa? Naw, man, she'd never even glance my way. I'm far too straitlaced for her."

"Uh huh." Interesting. Jacob didn't deny his attraction. Nate rifled in his junk drawer and found the login information for his Wi-Fi, then handed it to Jacob. "Here you go. Knock yourself out. I gotta run and check in at the station. Need anything?"

"I'm good. I'm glad you installed the tech I recommended to make this a smart house. There are a few add-ons you can do upstairs, if you're interested. Boosting the Wi-Fi signal and the like."

"I'll think about it. Could you let Rufus out at some point today?" The silly mutt glanced up from where he lay near Jacob's feet with a look that said, *I'm good, man. I like him. He gave me bacon. Why don't you give me bacon?*

"Later, then," Nate said and headed into the living room— pseudo temporary bedroom—and grabbed a new set of clothes. Tossing his ruined shirt on the bed, he realized he couldn't find the energy to toss it away. Not after Abby had ripped it from his body. He'd never expected her to be such a wildcat. Not that he minded one bit. The woman made him weak and made him burn all in the same breath. The mere thought of her, the memory of last night, feeling her writhe beneath him, made him want her. Again.

He hadn't been this addicted to a woman since Stacy in college, and that alone gave him pause. But Stacy had never been open and giving like Abby. In fact, Abby was the complete opposite of Stacy. Nate trusted Abby. Everything she felt or thought, she wore on her face. And her reactions were pure and unguarded. It made her a breath of fresh air in his life that he hadn't realized had gone stale.

Nate dressed in a fresh pair of jeans and a flannel shirt in burnt orange and brown. Once he was outfitted, he opened the closet in the foyer. Inside it was his gun safe. Sliding his belt on, he added the hip holster and then opened the safe. His back up Glock was inside with ammunition but his other firearm was missing. Dammit. He had been so thoroughly wound up with Abby last night, he had forgotten he'd stowed his badge and gun in his glovebox. It was a rookie mistake that he would blast one of his deputies for making. Closing and relocking the safe with a muttered curse, he grabbed his keys and headed out the door.

With a last glance at Abby's house, he climbed into his Explorer and retrieved his firearm and badge from the glovebox, ensuring the safety was on and that the clip was properly loaded before he placed it in the holster. Shoving his badge in his front breast pocket, he drove to the station. It wasn't lost on Nate that despite the short amount of time Abby had lived next door, he no longer considered it Evie's house. She'd transformed it with her presence and decluttering. But it was more than just what she had done with the house. This place—Echo Springs—suited her. Maybe she didn't realize it yet, but he wanted to prove it to her, starting tonight.

Chapter Twelve

From Old Man Turner's Journal:
Enjoy the present, because that's all that is guaranteed.

Abby spent the better part of the morning grinning like a fool, all while attempting to make progress on her dissertation and failing miserably. Who could blame her? She'd had knock-your-socks-off into the Milky Way sex with Sheriff Stud Muffin multiple times—as in, multiple orgasms. Her cheeks flamed at the memory.

Up until last night, Abby had enjoyed sex. Who didn't? But sex with Nate was on a different level entirely. It transcended and eclipsed every instance before so that there was now a clear line of demarcation in her life: before Nate and after Nate. She hated being a walking cliché; the woman who fell for a man because the sex was stupendous.

But it had been.

With a single swoop, he had usurped all her favorite heroes in literature. Who wanted a Mister Darcy or King Oberon when a girl could have a Nate Barnes? Now that she knew precisely what was beneath his rugged exterior, Abby had a few fantasies of her own she'd like to act out. She wondered if she could convince him to wear the sheriff's hat he'd left on his dashboard—and only the sheriff's hat?

By ten o'clock, Abby had given up the pretense of work altogether. It wasn't like she was getting a thing accomplished—except daydreaming about Nate, of course. Which, while it was certainly an enjoyable way to pass the time, wasn't productive in the slightest. Exasperated with her lack of concentration, she decided the only way she would make it through the day would be by calling in reinforcements. She rang up Tessa.

"Talk to me," Tessa said over the phone.

"Tessa, it's Abby."

"What's up?"

"Well, I was hoping you could help me. I need a dress for tonight and don't know where to go locally," Abby said, glancing at her nails and thinking a manicure wouldn't hurt either.

Tessa exclaimed, "Shopping excursion! Come meet me at the Emporium Diner on Main in thirty and we can go shop."

"You want to go with me?" Abby asked, indescribably excited by the prospect. It had been ages since she'd had other women to go do girly stuff with.

"Why not? I love to shop and, quite frankly, it's been ages. Not to mention, I'm having a bit of a brain freeze on the latest comic, so I can show you where all the awesome places are, not that there are many, unless we want to drive to Aspen or Telluride."

On the mountain roads that could take much more time than Abby had available. She nixed leaving Echo Springs. "No, we don't have that long. I have to be back at my house by five."

"Re-e-eeally? All right, get your tush to the diner, pronto," Tessa commanded.

"Fine, I'll meet you there. See you soon."

Abby left the house fifteen minutes later, heading for her Rover, and was brought up short. Shit. Her car was in Smitty's parking lot, where she'd left it last night. Nate's pal, Jacob, the gentle giant, was out in the front yard with Rufus. She waved and approached them. Abby braced herself as Rufus attempted to barrel her over.

"Whoa there, boy. I know she smells nice but that's no way to treat a lady," Jacob said, grabbing Rufus by the collar and forcing him to sit.

"Hi Rufus." She scratched his ears and then glanced up. "It's Jacob, right?"

"That it is, Abby. Nice of you to remember." His voice was so deep it reminded her of organ bellows mixed with a sarcophagus opening up. His black hair was pulled back into a ponytail, giving her an unobstructed view of his prominent facial features, from the high forehead to the strong, square jaw covered in a trimmed black beard. He had on gray cargo pants and a black tee shirt that said, *There are only 10 types of people in the world: Those who understand binary and those who don't.* Nerd humor on a guy who looked like he bench-pressed semi-tractor trailers as a favorite pastime was rather adorable.

"I hate to ask but is there any way you could give me a ride to my car? We left it at the pub last night and I'm supposed to meet Tessa at the diner in a bit," she asked, doubting that this town had Uber or Lyft. Hell, she doubted they even had a cab service. If Jacob couldn't take Abby, she'd call Tessa and have her come get her.

"Sure, I don't mind at all. Rufus, let's get you inside. Give me a minute to grab my keys and we'll go." Whereas Nate had this steady confidence and the instincts of a cougar, his big friend made Abby think of a giant teddy bear, and made her want to hug away the resigned loneliness she spied in his dark eyes.

"Thank you. I appreciate it so much," she said, grateful that he didn't say a word about her and Nate and their activities last night.

Jacob was true to his word. After he put Rufus indoors, he drove Abby to Smitty's Pub in his black, souped up Escalade.

"How are you liking Echo Springs?" Jacob asked.

"It's growing on me. I'm used to having all the big city amenities at my fingertips, so it is a change." But Abby didn't miss all those things. At least, not yet.

"Good to know. I've got a place I'm building here that I should be moving into by the spring, if we can get it built by then. It will be nice to know more people than just Nate." He gave her a friendly grin.

"That's great. Where are you moving from?" She returned his smile even as guilt flooded her. Because she would be gone by then.

"I'm currently up in Boulder."

"Ah, so you're another city transplant," she said.

"That I am, but I'm looking forward to the change of pace. Which one is yours?" Jacob asked, pulling into the parking lot.

"The Land Rover toward the back." She pointed toward her vehicle. Her tan Rover was one of the few vehicles parked there.

"Here you are. Need anything else?" Jacob asked with a gentle smile.

Oh, but the man was a sweetie. Far too decent a guy to be single. She needed to find him someone nice who would complement him. Then again, she wouldn't be around here to do so, and Abby was startled over how sad that made her.

"Thanks so much, Jacob. I owe you one," she murmured as she climbed out of his car.

"No problem at all, Abby. See you tonight," he said and gave her a small salute. Then he waited, apparently unwilling to drive away until she was in her Rover and had it started. She waved him off as she left the parking lot.

Nate's friends were interesting. She had enjoyed their dynamic last night. The ride to the diner took longer than anticipated, not only because she'd had to get a ride from Jacob, but because she couldn't find a parking spot. Every Echo Springs resident appeared to be in town this morning, along with a smattering of tourists.

The Emporium Diner was a throwback to another generation. Abby almost expected to see poodle skirts and black leather jackets along with a group of high school kids about to break into a rendition of *Greased Lightning*. The tables were ancient, and a bit scarred on top but that was part of the charm. But they were clean, if a bit well-worn, and added appeal to the Formica dining counter and booths.

She loved it. The Emporium advertised their old fashion soda fountain and made from scratch milkshakes. As she entered, the din and hum of patrons enjoying conversation surrounded her. The scent of freshly cooked bacon, coffee, and the hint of sugary pastries made her mouth water and her stomach growl. It smelled wonderful and she was starved—probably from all the extra exercise she'd gotten last night.

Abby spotted Tessa and Cybil in one of the back booths and headed toward them. She entered the fray and wound around a table but was brought up short.

"Well, hello there, young lady. How's your aunt's place coming along?" said a voice that sounded like sandpaper scraping over plastic.

She glanced at the table in front of her and spied Clark Biddle the Third, her aunt's former attorney. Although it was a Saturday, Clark wore slacks and a tweed suit jacket, complete with a colorful bowtie in canary yellow. His nearly nonexistent white hair was trimmed short and gave him—or at least his head —a fuzzy wuzzy appearance. The man had to be ninety, given that his frail, reed thin form looked like a strong wind would take him down, but as he'd told her on the phone weeks ago, he still practiced law three days a week and half a day on Saturday. She said, feeling a soft spot in her for the older gentleman, "Mr. Biddle. How nice to see you. My aunt's place is lovely. I'm enjoying it immensely."

"Very good, my dear. And what are your plans for the estate? If you decide to sell, I know the market around here very well and would be happy to assist you with the sale," he offered, a gleam of sharp intelligence in his gaze. While his body might be aging and frail, his mind was still strong as steel.

"I will take that into consideration if that's what I decide to do. If you'll excuse me, I'm meeting someone."

"Not at all. Lovely to run into you." He nodded and stood, laying a cash tip on the table.

"Same to you." Abby wasn't ready to decide on that front. It was there, hovering like a horde of rabid bats waiting for the signal from Nosferatu to strike. She knew she had to choose a direction for her life after her dissertation was completed and her degree in her hot little hands. But, like an ostrich who didn't want to see the approaching hurricane, she preferred to put her head in the sand and avoid it for as long as she could. She wanted to enjoy her time with Nate, at least for one full day, before reality smashed into her contented bubble.

She continued her journey to the table in the back, then she spotted Alex Dotson. Or, more accurately, he stood up from his table and blocked her forward progression. She liked Alex. He was a nice, attractive man with his golden hair and easy smile, and he didn't have a chance in hell with her. The problem was he didn't hold a candle to Nate. Nor did she think he was capable of competing—not for her affections, at least.

"Abby, you left so suddenly last night, I wondered where you had gone," Alex said, his nutmeg gaze searching her face. Abby knew what he wanted to find there and tried to keep her expression as bland and congenial as possible.

"Alex, good to see you," she said, and then almost kicked herself because after her reply, hope glimmered on his face. In his gaze was a hunger that didn't even garner a ping from her system in response. She feared that, after last night, Nate had ruined her for other men. Between the two men, there wasn't even a competition.

He gestured to the empty seat next to his and asked, "Would you like to have breakfast? If you're not busy, of course."

And that's when Tessa, bless her, saved Abby from making an

even bigger fool of herself. Tessa interrupted with a *get real* glance at him. "Never going to happen, Alex. You might as well give up now and save yourself the headache."

"Tessa." Abby blushed. She didn't want to hurt the man's feelings, she just wanted to re-direct them to someone more appropriate. That didn't mean she couldn't be friendly toward him.

"What? He'd find out sooner or later that you're dating the sheriff. May as well cut the line now." Tessa was so matter-of-fact about Abby dating the sheriff that it gave her a jolt. And Tessa had established this just from their interaction at pool last night. Nate had mentioned they were more than a booty call but to hear Tessa put them together as confirmation spilled warmth into her limbs. They were dating.

"I see. Abby, Tessa, good day to you." Alex collected his newspaper from the table and, before either of them could say anything more, departed the diner without a backward glance.

Well, crap! That didn't go the way she'd planned. Abby stammered as Tessa pulled her back toward the booth where Cybil sat, looking Cover Girl model gorgeous. "I don't know whether to thank you or yell at you," she said, feeling wretched that Alex had left the diner like that. The poor man didn't even get his breakfast. She'd have to do damage control and apologize the next time she ran into him at school.

Tessa shrugged as she scooted into the booth next to her sister, "I saved your ass back there. No thanks needed."

Cybil interjected, "Now do you see what I have to live with? No social boundaries, this one."

"I do appreciate it. I just wanted to let him down easier, is all," Abby explained, feeling like the scum of the earth.

Tessa shot her a glance with a raised brow. "So that he would sit and pine for you? That's cruel. It's better to make sure he understands that there's no hope for anything but friendship. Otherwise, all you'll do is hurt the man. He's not a bad guy, and while he can be a bit of a dickwad at times, that doesn't mean he should be tortured."

When Tessa put it that way, Abby's guilt increased exponentially to include every man she'd tried to be nice to but had never given a definitive no. Crap on a cracker! "I see your point."

Their waitress, a teenager with pink spiked hair and piercings galore, sidled up to their table. "What can I get you guys?"

"Coffee, and lots of it," Tessa said, not looking up from the menu.

Abby asked them, "What's good here?"

"The pancakes," the sisters said, almost in unison.

"Pancakes it is." The carbs wouldn't hurt Abby today. Not after all the calisthenics she'd done overnight. She handed her plastic menu to their pink-haired waitress. Her nametag read Cecily, but Abby already had dubbed her Pinky. Granted, if she changed her hair color, Abby might have to revise that.

"So spill," Tessa pounced the moment their waitress walked away to put their order in.

Abby looked between Tessa and Cybil's expectant faces. They leaned forward in their seats, obviously attempting to goad her into giving them a play by play of her night with Nate.

"I don't know what you are talking about," Abby said as heat suffused her cheeks and she had an incredibly difficult time not smiling.

"Uh huh, yep, they did it. Told ya. You get to pay for my breakfast." Tessa smirked at Cybil with a superior air. Cybil gave Abby an assessing stare to the point where she began to fidget under the directness.

Cybil nodded and said, "Yeah, she definitely has that I-just-had-an-orgasm glow about her."

Abby whipped her head around, praying that no one else had heard her comment. Then she said, "But I can't—"

Cybil cut her off. "Abby, we have to live vicariously through you since neither of us is currently seeing anyone or getting any action. The simple fact is you left with Nate last night. Then, today, you mysteriously want to go shopping. Not that we are averse to a shopping excursion. But the main reason women tend to require them immediately is because a certain man got them out of their clothes. It means you got lucky, and we need the dish."

"Please help us single women know that there is light, hope, and carnal bliss on its way for us, and spill." Tessa clasped her hands together and batted her eyes, with a *pretty please have mercy on us single women* gaze.

Still on cloud nine after last night, Abby caved with a sigh, and said, "Well, you know that whole long arm of the law phrase?"

"Yeah?" they said.

"Sheriff Stud Muffin proved last night that there's definitely a reason for it, if you know what I mean," she replied, her voice dripping with innuendo.

Cybil snorted. Tessa coughed, attempting to hide her mirth. Before Abby knew it, the three of them were laughing so hard that tears leaked from their eyes. Breakfast arrived as they finally calmed enough to take a breath.

"That good, huh? I really need to get myself back onto the market." Cybil sighed as she poured maple syrup on her flapjacks.

"It was. Each time too." She shrugged. And wasn't that a conundrum she couldn't figure out? With all the men she'd dated before, after the first two times, the fires tended to bank and diminish until it was pleasant sleeping with them, but didn't stoke the flames. But not with Nate. If anything, each time with him so far had been the same, explosive, mind-melding experience. Just thinking about it made the air in her lungs back up and heat curl in her belly.

"Each time? As in multiple orgasms?" Tessa asked, a forkful of pancakes halfway to her mouth.

Abby bit her bottom lip and nodded.

"I think you're my new hero. We simple mortals bow before you," Cybil said with a grin.

"Yeah, we'll call it *The Adventures of Nympho Girl and the Sheriff*," Tessa teased.

"Very funny." Abby blushed at the quips.

"It's no wonder you're glowing so much that you could power the town of Echo Springs. I would be, too, if I was getting a heaping of what you are. Are we to assume that this impromptu shopping trip is for a date with Sheriff Stud Muffin?" Cybil asked, looking at Abby over the rim of her coffee mug.

"Yeah. He invited me to go to Ella Keaton's retirement party with him tonight," she admitted.

"It's serious then? You and the sheriff?" Tessa cocked her head, a grin tugging at her lips.

Terror seized Abby. She wasn't ready for serious, was she? "Are you sure that means it's serious? Couldn't he just want a date to the party so that he doesn't end up going stag?"

"Honey, I hate to break it to you, but Nate and Miles have been best friends since like grade school. Miles's mom, Ella, was like a second mother to Nate, especially with all the issues Nate's mom had when he was growing up. For him to invite you to the retirement party with him is pretty huge," Cybil explained.

"But… but I thought we were just having a good time. It's not like we've even been on a date."

Tessa shrugged. "Anyone could see the attraction between you two last night. This isn't a bad thing, Abby. Who wouldn't want a hot, sexy, nice guy to be into her, and for more than just sex?"

"Seriously, you found the damn unicorn that most of us never find, so enjoy it," Cybil said with a wink.

Enjoy the moment. Enjoy him. Wasn't that part of why Abby had come to Echo Springs in the first place? To see if there was life outside of the classroom? And now that she'd found it, she was acting like a scared rabbit, ready to dart away at the first sign of something different.

"You have a point. So, who's ready to go shopping?" Abby asked. She could do this. She could have a love affair with the sexy sheriff and not get burned when her real life butted in.

"Let's do this." Tessa rubbed her hands together.

They paid for their breakfast and headed out, walking the few blocks over to Main Street. In each shop they visited, Tessa and Cybil introduced her to the shop owners. For a change, Abby had people around her because of who she was as a person and not because of who her parents were and what befriending her could do for them professionally, with the positions her parents held at Princeton. The shop owners—when they learned she was Evie Callier's niece—welcomed her as if she were a long lost relative. It was awesome.

NATE PATROLLED the streets of Echo Springs for a few hours. Saturdays along the strip tended to be busy, so he always preferred to have an officer on duty. He was filling in for Deputy Filbert, who had a lead on their B&E burglary cases to investigate with a potential witness who would only speak to him anonymously. It rubbed him the wrong way. There was something about Filbert that set Nate's teeth on edge. He couldn't quite put his finger on it. It was more than that he was just an asshole, too. Nate's friends were assholes half the time, but they never once gave him pause or made him think they were feeding him a line of bull-crap.

Well, except Sam. The conversation with Jacob that morning worried Nate. He had seen one too many live-fast thrill-seekers hit bottom. Usually, it ended with their body being scraped up off the pavement or from around a telephone pole.

As he patrolled, he spotted Sam's Mustang parked outside Smitty's Pub and pulled his SUV over. What the hell was he doing at the bar? Nate shoved his hat on, then headed inside. In the dim light, he spotted Sam on a barstool, flirting with one of the waitresses behind the bar, nursing a beer. Nate wasn't one to criticize how someone chose to live their life, but this was his friend, and it was barely three in the afternoon. That screamed problem to Nate. He'd watched his mother slide into the bottle too. Nate couldn't wait for him to hit bottom before intervening so he approached Sam.

"Little early, don't you think?" Nate said, sliding onto the barstool beside him.

Sam grinned and said, "It's never too early. What can I do you for, Sheriff?"

Fuck me.

The moron was slurring his words. His eyes were bloodshot, and the stench of alcohol saturated the guy's very pores. Attempting to remain calm and level-headed, Nate asked, "Please tell me you aren't shitfaced. Miles will go nuclear if you aren't sober at his mom's shindig."

"Just taking the edge off." Sam shrugged. A haunted look flickered in his eyes before he shook it off and took another drink.

"The edge off what, Sam?" Nate wished like hell he'd known there was an issue sooner. But that was hard to do with him living in Los Angeles, and every time they'd talked, Sam had always made it seem like he was living the high life. Now that Jacob had mentioned it, he was right; Sam hadn't hit bottom yet. And if they didn't step in right away and yank him back from the edge, he would. Nate regretted that he'd never once picked up on the trouble Sam was in when they'd talked.

Sam appeared like he was going to say something, then shook his head and said, "Don't worry about it."

"When you're acting like a drunk, I will worry about it. Let's get you some lunch and sobered up for the party."

"I don't think—"

"I wasn't suggesting, Sam. Or I can toss your ass in a cell and let you sober up that way. Have fun explaining to Ella Keaton why you weren't at her retirement party," Nate snapped, not above giving his buddy a little tough love if he needed it.

"You'd do it, too, wouldn't you? Put me behind bars." Sam glowered at him with a scowl, his face hard and unreadable.

"To save you from being an idiot? Absolutely."

"Fine, let's go." Sam angrily tossed a few bills on the bar. His shoulders were hunched but he had this *fuck off* vibe emanating from him.

Nate drove him to Papa Beau's Pizza and ordered a large pizza, loaded. The restaurant looked like a cross between a pizza joint, with its white tables and plastic menus, and a Western saloon, with its pine wooden floors and brick walls. Hanging from exposed beams in the ceiling, acting as chandeliers, were what looked like wooden wheels from ancient stage coaches that held lanterns at the edge of each spoke. They did serve beer at the saloon-style bar, but the majority of people had soda or their famous lemonade with their mile high apple pie.

"You do know I can't eat that crap, right?" Sam said gesturing at the menu. "It's bad for the physique."

"Right now, I don't give a goddamn about your physique. You need carbs, so load up, son," Nate said as a waitress set the piping-hot pizza on the table. He put two large pieces on a plate and shoved it in front of Sam. "Eat," he ordered.

Sam's demeanor didn't change, he visibly bristled at Nate's tone. The damn fool was acting like he had a burr up his butt, but he did eat. As he did, the glassy-eyed sheen present at the pub began to diminish as he loaded fuel in his belly.

"What's really going on, Sam? And no shitting me. We've known each other too long for that." It tore Nate up that he had no clue about Sam. He leaned back in his chair, waiting for Sam to respond as he chewed another bite.

Sam sipped his water, then said, "It's just the job, man. There's this director who's not happy with my stunts. You know, Tinseltown politics stuff."

"Is Hollywood the problem, or is it something deeper?" Nate

studied him. There was more that Sam was keeping close to his chest. But then again, he always had been like that, refusing to ask for help if he needed it.

"I'm... oh, what's the use? Fat lot of good it will do to talk about it. I know my problems seem small, and maybe they are. I just need some time." Sam began munching on a third slice, avoiding Nate's eyes. As much as Nate wanted to push, he also knew that if Sam didn't want to talk, the guy would clam up and refuse to come near them. Which was the last thing he wanted after seeing the distress on Sam's face. There was something wrong, and by the looks of it, it was huge. Nate backed off —for now.

"We're here if you need something. You always have a place you can go. You know that, right?" Nate said, trying to bridge the gap Sam had erected.

"Yeah, I know. Let's get out of here. I want to shower before the party."

Nate tossed a few bills on the table as they left. He didn't feel better about Sam, but sometimes there was only so much a body could do for a person. They had to want to help themselves. He and the other guys would be there when the time came, because Jacob was a hundred percent correct. Sam was in the fast lane and headed for impact. Nate just hoped there would be pieces left to pick up when it all came crashing down.

Chapter Thirteen

From Old Man Turner's Journal:
Dress to impress your date.

At five o'clock on the nose, Abby's doorbell rang. Skitters raced along her spine. She couldn't believe she was nervous. They'd already had sex multiple times and yet here she was, anxious about their date. It wasn't even a traditional first date but a group outing, with his friends and the people who obviously mattered to him.

Did that mean she mattered to him as well? The thought gave her pause as she walked across the hardwood.

As her heels clicked over the floor, she glanced into the living room at the unholy mass shrouded in white sheets. Why was it that she overwhelmed herself with worry about their date, when she clearly had other pressing matters to attend to? Like sending the undead doll army to hell before they had the opportunity to murder her in her sleep.

She was being ridiculous and she knew it. Far worse than any of the too stupid to live heroines she'd come across in books.

Steeling herself, Abby answered the front door, anticipation tingling in every nerve ending. And holy hand grenade! Nate was so damn handsome. As if by magic, he had grown more so overnight. His eyes were bluer, deeper, more enigmatic. His lips appeared fuller, spread in a sensual smirk that churned her insides into melted marshmallows. How was it even possible?

"Well, aren't you a sight?" Nate's hungry gaze raked over her like a caress from head to toe. Those dang marshmallows began a slow burn, invading every limb, tissue, and vein until she was a mass of pure, undiluted sexual need. The carnal gleam in his eyes reflected the same potent desire, as if he was already considering the multitude of ways he wanted to strip her out of her rose-colored dress, fall into bed and not surface until the first rays of sunrise dotted the horizon.

Abby was one hundred percent on board with that idea.

Her tongue was stuck to the roof of her mouth and her lips were dry as need incessantly beat inside her breast. Nate crossed the threshold separating them, stepped inside, and backed her up against the newel post at the base of the stairs. Her pulse pounded like she'd run the forty-yard dash. Abby clenched her fingers, worried that if she touched him, she would erupt in flames and they would never make it to the party.

"I like this." He traced his hands, in a feather-soft caress, from her bare shoulders, over the spaghetti straps, down the sides of her empire-waisted gown. His fingers grazed the mounds of her breasts, and he stopped his exploration at the curvature of her hips. He only had to dip those piano player fingers another half a foot or so, to where the dress ended at mid-thigh, to touch her flesh. At war with herself, she wanted him to touch her, to forgo the outside world, and remain in their own little sensual bubble, but the rational part of her brain knew they had to leave.

"You look nice too," she finally uttered in a whisper. Her breath expelled in a rush. And, boy, did he ever. Gone were his signature look of jeans and flannel shirts. Instead, he was dressed like a businessman on Wall Street, with pressed black slacks belted across his lean hips, and a royal blue button-down shirt which accentuated the solid muscle beneath with every movement, and made his eye color appear that much brighter. The finishing touch was a dark gray silk tie she wanted to wrap around her hand and use to yank him even closer so she could inhale his scent that was all spicy musk and male.

Had he put a spell on her? Because she couldn't tear herself away from him and the emotions, the need, and the heat swirling through her body like leaves on a windy fall day.

She moaned deep in the back of her throat when he cupped the back of her head, slanted his mouth over hers, and claimed her lips in a torrid duel.

Holy crap on a cracker, the man could kiss!

Abby's body was enflamed. She was certain sparks were emitting from her fingertips. Her brain stopped functioning. Who needed a brain when she had Nate's incredible mouth turning her inside out? It was as if her very reason for existing boiled down to their intense lip-lock. As for the rest of the world, Killer Clowns from outer space could be rampaging across the globe and it wouldn't matter. It only mattered that he kept his tantalizing, seductive lips working their magic on her.

Who cared what she wore? The sooner they were out of their restrictive clothing, the sooner she felt his flesh pressed intimately against hers, the better. Who cared that she'd spent hours this afternoon with Tessa and Cybil to locate the perfect outfit for tonight? Not this girl. She only cared that Nate's lips had become her new religion. The manicure and pedicure in a becoming blush mauve she'd sprung for that afternoon, and extra time pampering herself no longer mattered. It was no big deal that she'd shaved her legs, had lathered her skin with moisturizer, and had curled and styled her hair into a sophisticated up-do.

Not one bit of it counted now that he was kissing her. Abby surrendered to the heat and need, pouring her essence into the demanding, sinful and wholly erotic kiss. Her hands wrapped around his tie in a bid to keep him prisoner against her lips. She loved this man's mouth. Adored how the rest of the world simply ceased to exist the moment his lips touched hers. How even the air she breathed was infused with him. In the end, Abby realized, she could have painted her head purple and she doubted it would have concerned him overmuch.

Abby was drowning in him and she knew she should stop him. But she didn't have the desire or strength to separate herself —she'd missed him today.

"Cool it, you two, or we're going to be late. Do you want to give Miles an aneurysm?" said a voice.

Nate broke the kiss and gave her a gentle smile filled with meaning. "Hold our place," he murmured.

She inhaled a ragged breath and nodded. Nate turned, then his right hand clasped her left and threaded their fingers together, connecting them. Sam was leaning against her door frame, with his rakish good looks and his arms crossed over his chest. He wore slate-colored slacks with a mint green dress shirt and no tie. The man was handsome but his attitude was dialed to bored arrogance.

"Are we all going together?" she asked, glancing up at Nate. There was a tick in Nate's jaw that hadn't been there before as he glared at his friend.

"Ding, ding, ding, the schoolteacher wins a point. Jacob's already waiting at the truck," Sam said.

"Sam," Nate said with a warning behind his voice, his face a hard mask.

Sam held up his hands defensively. "Sorry, not trying to be a dick. See you in the car."

Then Sam walked away, down off her porch, heading out of sight and toward Nate's driveway. But the undercurrent still hung unanswered in the air. When Abby spied Nate's concerned grimace at the empty space, her heart bled for him. Nate's troubled gaze shifted back to her. "Sorry about him. He's not usually such an ass. You don't mind if they tag along with us? It's just easier, considering they're staying with me."

Going on instinct alone, she laid her free hand against his cheek, offering comfort and support. She murmured, "It's okay. What's going on, though? Are you upset with Sam about anything more than the fact that he interrupted us? Is there something I can do?"

He caught her hand upon his cheek with his and placed a kiss in the center of her palm. His gaze shifted to liquid heat, and he replied, "Yeah, you can promise me the last dance."

"Done. I'm ready if you are," Abby said, picking up her black clutch purse and nudging him forward.

After locking her front door, Nate escorted her across the expanse of velvety grass just beginning to take on its fall hue. At the Explorer, she saw Jacob had claimed the rear back passenger seat and Sam, well, the man could give lessons in being an ass. He'd parked himself in the front but Nate wasn't letting him get away with it. Abby knew she should just sit in the back. Except, whatever was happening between these two, she didn't plan on getting in the middle of it anytime soon.

"Out," Nate said as he opened the front passenger door, indicating to Sam that he needed to move.

"I called shotgun," Sam said, exasperation clouding his voice.

"Not tonight, you didn't. Back seat, both of you," Nate ordered. "And if you have a problem with it, I can always toss you in a jail cell until you cool off."

With a pithy glance, Sam exited the seat and stalked around to the back, muttering beneath his breath. There was definitely more tension here than Abby had initially guessed. She would ask Nate about it later, but for now she wanted to defuse the pressure.

"Jacob, it's nice to see you," Abby murmured after Nate helped her into her seat. It was a balancing act to climb into the elevated cab in her heels. Jacob sat in the back seat directly behind hers and she swiveled slightly.

"You too, Abby." Jacob gave her a friendly smile, making her think of a big stuffed teddy bear. The man was such a sweetie pie. She'd have to do some match-making on her end for him.

"Thanks again for your help this morning," she said.

"It's no problem at all. Gave me an excuse to run by the grocery store afterwards and pick up supplies," Jacob replied.

"Supplies for what?" she asked.

"For the sheer fact that these jugheads are eating me out of house and home," Nate commented with a wry grin.

"I see." And she did. None of them were puny men. She could only imagine how much the four of them put away. "Well, if you need extra meat, I have a freezer full."

Nate shot her a sensual glance, telling her with more than words that he remembered that all too well. Especially since they'd already availed themselves of the mega-sized box of condoms. Abby was just thankful she'd had the foresight to invest in such a wise purchase.

The ride to the party was eye-opening as Abby studied the dynamics between the three friends. There was that familiar bond which only came with knowing someone a long time, an ingrained sort of being, which was why Jacob seemed none too concerned by Sam's bad mood. She quickly noted Jacob as the peacekeeper of the crew. Nate's displeasure was of the controlled variety in comparison to Sam's rather expressive *in your face* moodiness.

"So how long have you guys known each other?" Abby asked as Nate drove.

"Since college at University of Boulder," Jacob answered for the group.

"Really? Isn't that a party school?" She raised a brow and looked at Nate, trying to imagine him on a college campus without his badge and sheriff's hat. She just couldn't.

Sam chuckled darkly and snorted. "Of course it is, which is why it was heaven on earth. Good times were had by all in this truck."

"Is that a fact?" She sent Nate an inquisitive glance, who had the good grace to glare at Sam in the rearview mirror.

"Where did you go to school Abby?" Jacob asked, neutralizing the strain between Nate and Sam as best he could.

"Well, I started at Princeton, but in my sophomore year, I changed my major from astrophysics to literature and transferred to Cornell University. I've been there ever since." She was so ready for a life outside that campus now. As much as she loved it, that place had been her insular world. Although, in the scheme of things, it wasn't a half bad place should the zombie apocalypse occur.

"And you're getting a PhD?" Jacob asked.

"Yeah, my dissertation is finally almost finished and I should graduate in the spring."

Sam rolled his eyes and said, "Why anyone would want to keep going to school is beyond me. What's the fascination with it?"

"Sam," Nate warned.

"What? I'm just asking. Fuck," Sam snapped.

Abby tried to smooth things over between them. "I like the steadiness of it. The annual progression with the start of terms, the winter and summer breaks. I enjoy expanding my scope of knowledge. It's not for everyone, but it suits me. And it's far more reliable than a career jumping out of moving vehicles."

"Whoa-a-a! Burn!" Jacob said, chuckling.

Even Nate grinned.

"It's the thrill and adrenaline rush. I love it." Sam shot her a curt glance.

"Good for you. That's no reason to sneer at what I do just because you don't understand it, and for some reason, your panties are in a twist over who knows what," Abby said. She liked Jacob, and what little she'd seen of Miles. Sam on the other hand —she wanted to knock some sense into him, and judging by Nate's expression, the feeling was mutual.

"Sorry. Didn't mean to be an ass. Perhaps you have some

college friends you could introduce me to who would help me out of my funk?" Sam teased.

Nate turned the vehicle into the parking lot and Abby was grateful that the short ride was almost over. She shook her head. "No, not really. At least, none who are looking for babysitting duty."

Jacob lost his mind laughing at her response and Sam, well, he just seemed to cave in on himself. Abby wished she could take her insensitive but honest retort back, but she had promised after breaking free and changing her major that she would never again be someone's doormat. And Sam needed to understand that he couldn't treat people poorly. People treated you the way you allowed them to. In order to soften her reproach a bit, she smiled at Sam and said, "Besides, most of my college friends drifted. Especially when I switched majors, and I had so much to catch up on with my new studies that it left little time for shenanigans."

"But that was the best part of college," Sam said, and returned with a half-hearted grin. It was something, at least. She couldn't help feeling that Sam, out of all four of their tribe, while by far and away the most successful, was also the one most scarred and broken by life. Maybe she was being fanciful or making assumptions, but there was pain in his eyes.

"Don't listen to him, Abby. Not all of us were big partiers back in the day," Jacob said, unbuckling his seatbelt and opening the truck door to disembark.

"He lies," Sam said, doing the same and climbing out of the truck only to slam the door shut behind him.

Jacob quipped, "Like hell. I studied my ass off, which is why my company's stock is out-earning the rest of the tech companies combined."

"Yeah, yeah, rub it in our faces," Sam chided.

Nate opened her door and helped her out of his Explorer. Thank God! Heels and his SUV weren't the best idea she'd ever had. Then again, she'd let Tessa and Cybil dress her, and Nate seemed to appreciate it, so who was she to say?

Nate held her hand as they walked into Springs Tavern Ballroom, which sat next to Springs Tavern Bar, just off one of the side streets from Main. Both red brick buildings were on the town's historic registry and had a Victorian-era flair to their interior décor. The ballroom looked like something one would have found on the Titanic, or where one might have expected to see Teddy Roosevelt, smoking a cigar and holding a crystal glass with a liberal splash of brandy in it, sitting at one of the round tables lining the walls, leaving the center dance floor open. Dark woods glimmered in golden candlelight. Giant crystal chandeliers hung from the ceiling, their sparkling lights glistening.

A sumptuous buffet had been erected along the far wall. There were bars at the four corners of the ballroom, with guests mingling around them, in order to quench their thirst. From the size of the crowd already in attendance, it looked like the entire town had been invited. As they entered the fray, she spotted Miles next to a rather tall, willowy woman—almost as tall as he was—in a simple black cocktail dress, her blonde hair becomingly dusted with silver highlights, greeting guests.

Nate escorted Abby through the line procession, over to them. Jacob and Sam trailed behind while Sam muttered something about getting to the bar.

"Nate," Ella Keaton exclaimed, her face transforming into joy at spying him, and she beamed. "So good of you to come."

Nate released Abby long enough to give her a generous hug. "Ella, congratulations! You certainly deserve it."

"Oh, posh. I'm just glad I had the chance to work as long as I did. And who is this lovely creature you've brought with you?" She turned her vibrant turquoise gaze, the color of the water in the Bahamas, toward Abby, curiosity blazing in their depths.

"Ella, I'd like to introduce you to Abby. She's Evie Callier's great-niece," Nate said with a hint of pride in his voice.

Delight raced across Ella's beautiful face and she replied, "I'll be damned. Is that right?"

Abby knew exactly from whom Miles had inherited his eyes

when she looked at Ella. She held out her hand. "Yes, it is. It's nice to meet you. Congratulations."

Ella took her outstretched palm, warmth radiating from her as she clasped their hands together and said, "Oh, and I'm very glad to meet you. I have some stories about your great-aunt, if you are ever interested."

Here was acceptance and friendliness that Abby found every time she turned around in Echo Springs. It was so very different from her life back east. That wasn't to say people weren't nice, but it took far longer to be accepted, people were a mite more suspicious. But not here. The welcome mat was never retracted. And it made Abby wonder if maybe her problem hadn't been her lack, but that she hadn't been in the right location. She craved the community and family, the warmth of familiarity that spanned generations. Abby replied, "Absolutely. We corresponded up until her passing, but I hadn't seen her in years."

"Well, I will have Miles give you my address, and you come for a visit anytime," Ella offered and gave her hand a quick squeeze, leaving Abby a bit dazed.

"That would be wonderful, thank you," Abby replied to Ella's offer. She would take her up on it, too, before she left Echo Springs.

"Thanks for coming, Abby," Miles said, and surprised her with a quick hug. The man smelled amazing. Not as good as Nate, but he had that unique, manly, urbanite scent with an understated cologne which, when a woman caught it, acted like a tether, drawing a girl in. It made Abby wonder why he, out of all of Nate's friends, wasn't in a relationship. Where Jacob was a sweetie, Miles was solid, with a city sheen on him.

"Nate," Miles said, shaking his buddy's hand. There was a friendly bond between them that seemed more solid than the others had.

"Go on with you now and have a drink. Get Nate to take you out on the dance floor," Ella ordered, shooing them on with her hands.

"Yes ma'am, I will," Nate said with a wink and then moved them along past Miles and Ella. Abby heard Jacob and Sam making a fuss over Ella and smiled. That was what she wanted in her life; what had been missing—the human connections and bonds which made life so much more enjoyable. It wasn't that her family were cold people, they just tended to place accomplishments as the most important measure of a person, instead of their hearts. In Abby's mind, that was backwards.

It was one of the reasons why she adored literature and reading as much as she did. In her opinion, doing so gave so much more back than the words on the page. Books opened doorways into others' lives, other thoughts and methods of existing, and Abby believed reading a lot made a person more capable of empathy.

They moved deeper into the ballroom. Abby spied Tessa and Cybil, who waved them over to a table. Tessa wore a fire engine-red dress that hugged her voluptuous curves. The purple streaks that had been in her hair just that morning were now absent and her locks were pure, glamorous ebony. Abby thought her own two-inch heels were killer, but spying the four-inch spiked heeled stilettos Tessa wore put her to shame. Cybil, not to be outdone by her younger sibling, was radiant in a mint green sheath dress. The voluminous waves of her dark hair spilled in loose curls down her back.

When they reached the table, Nate, with a friendly smile on his handsome face, his left hand resting on Abby's lower back, asked, "Tessa, Cybil, how are you?"

"Not as good as you, apparently," Tessa replied with what could only be described as a saucy, know-it-all glance. Cybil nudged her sister's shoulder at her blatant comment. Tessa glanced reproachfully at Cybil, and said, "What?"

Abby's face flamed in embarrassment. How could Tessa rat her out like that? Would Nate be upset with her? These were people who had known him a lot longer than she had.

Cybil took pity on her and said, "Don't mind Tessa, she's just pissy because her characters are misbehaving again."

"Is that the case?" Nate asked, glancing between them. Abby wished for a murderous zombie horde to invade, removing the focus from her and the oodles of sex she had experienced with Nate. Although, Nate didn't appear perturbed that everyone seemed to know they were an item like she'd been worried he would. Instead, the man appeared downright pleased as punch.

What did that mean? Was she in over her head with him already? And were they something more than just spectacular, knock-your-socks off sex? The man already claimed the majority of her thoughts when she wasn't working. Keeping him from them while she worked had become a job in and of itself. Abby couldn't get ahead of herself with Nate, even though a part of her wanted to, wanted to take everything he had to offer and roll around in the joy of it. He just seemed so happy, damn him. Like he was proud he'd made such an impact on her that she'd spilled the details to her new girlfriends.

Nate flashed her a wicked grin, power-packed with meaning, causing her knees to tremble, and murmured in her ear, "What can I get you to drink?"

"White wine would be wonderful. Thank you," she replied as he released her. His hand caressed her lower back as he withdrew it, and she yearned to lean into him. Nate cocked his head and asked, "Ladies, what about you?"

"Just bring us one of whatever Abby's drinking. Thanks, Sheriff," Cybil said.

"Fair enough, I'll be right back," Nate replied and sauntered over to the nearest bar, leaving them alone at the table.

"How could you say that?" Abby asked Tessa.

Tessa winced. "Sorry, I sometimes forget that not everyone is as open as I am about things. Cybil's used to it by now. I promise to keep my trap shut in the future. Do you forgive me?"

"Yeah, it's just that everyone seems to know that, you know…" Abby could feel the damn blush spreading up her neck and into her face. She wasn't ashamed—far from it, considering she wanted to do it again tonight—but she also didn't want to flaunt her bedroom activities in front of the whole town.

"That you're getting your freak on with the sheriff?" Cybil blurted with a bemused expression.

"Yeah, why is that? Is it that obvious? I told you two about it, but everyone else seems to know and—"

"Honey," Cybil said, sliding an arm around her shoulders. "It's because when Sheriff Stud Muffin looks at you, it's in his eyes. They simply smolder."

"Really?" Abby thought they did, too, but had told herself she was seeing things and not to believe in it, not to trust in it. Their relationship had escalated so quickly, and their lovemaking was so fierce, she was having a hard time trusting her feelings —and his.

"Dude, if a guy looked at me that way, we'd never leave the house unless it was on fire," Tessa said. "And you look at him the same way."

"Oh, well then. That's settled," Abby said, although it wasn't, not by a long shot. Because their coming together was still new to them so they were in the heady, couldn't keep their hands to themselves phase. Those never lasted. It was the infatuation stage. It would pass, wouldn't it? Perhaps, but she'd never felt anything remotely this intense with any other man. And there had been a period about two years ago when she'd become a dating whirlwind and signed up for those online dating sites, then gone on too numerous to count first dates. Funny how not one of them had been inspiring enough to warrant a second date; what with the guys who had suggested they go back to their place and did Abby mind that he had a roommate—aka his mother—living with him, or the ones who'd asked her if she'd found Jesus Christ as her lord and savior. With all the mama's boys and being told she was going to hell for her obsession with horror films, she'd assumed it was just her. That invariably she had something wrong with her because she couldn't seem to find a guy who was at least halfway normal, nice, gainfully employed, and didn't want to convert her to his religion, cult or otherwise.

And that was why being with Nate had knocked her off her center of gravity, like she was one of the spinning tops from her childhood and, instead of spinning upright, was wobbling back and forth, upending her balance.

Jacob and Sam joined them at their table, helping Nate with the drinks. Abby chugged her first few swallows. Sam turned on the charm with Tessa and Cybil. Neither of her new friends were wallflowers and doled it out as much as Sam dished it. Jacob didn't talk much—granted, they did grab dinner from the ginormous buffet. There was fried chicken, ham, roasted new potatoes, puff pastries, and mini quiches. Abby smiled at the pigs in a blanket, although they seemed to be a crowd favorite. There were multitudes of salads, spinach, and romaine, with vegetables, pasta salads, fruit salads and more.

The air was congenial and friendly at the table. But Abby did wonder about Jacob. He was super sweet and she caught his gaze flicking to Tessa when she wasn't looking. He turned away before Tessa caught him, but Abby's gaze met his and he had the grace to blush. Tessa hadn't mentioned an interest in Jacob, but maybe Abby could nudge her in that direction.

As dinner began to wind down, Miles stood up from the center table near his mom. "May I have your attention?" he said to the crowd and the ballroom quieted.

"First, I'd like to thank you all for coming tonight. I know it means the world to my mom. Second, I want to raise my glass to my mother, Ella Keaton. Mom, you taught me from an early age the meaning of hard work, not from words but your deeds. I watched you and dad carve out a business with tenacity and determination. Then, when dad passed, you chose a new dream with the same vibrancy and enthusiasm you've displayed my whole life and I couldn't be prouder. So I raise my glass to you, Mom, congratulations on your retirement. If I know you, you will conquer it the same way you do everything. I love you. Cheers!"

"Cheers!" The crowd toasted Ella. Abby wiped at the few tears that had escaped. Had she ever known love like that? Ever had someone so solidly in her corner? Yes—Aunt Evie, from the moment they'd first exchanged letters. Regrets that she hadn't spent more time with Evie and visited her more often assailed Abby. But perhaps, in living here, in Evie's home and her town, she was being given the familial bond her aunt knew she'd done without.

Then the band started up and Abby let her maudlin thoughts drift away. Now was not the time to brood. She'd do enough of that later when the time came to make her decision about this place.

"Come dance with me," Nate murmured into her ear and held his hand out. Abby shivered and turned her gaze toward his, and her breath stuttered. Everything he felt was naked and on display. With trembling fingers, she slid her hand into his and he towed her onto the dance floor. The band was playing a fast, country, boot-stomping number. Nate twirled her into his arms, pulled her tight, and then began to move them around the dance floor. Surprisingly, he wasn't a half-bad dancer. It shouldn't surprise her really. The man was physically adept and danced as he did everything else, with complete confidence. He showed her the steps and led her around the floor.

He spun her out, then tugged her in a with a pivot, and she laughed up at him. Abby knew she was grinning like a fool and didn't care. Her breath caught at the expression on his face as he pulled her close. The song shifted into a slow ballad and her smile slipped as she gazed into his eyes.

She'd gone into this with him with her eyes wide open but she couldn't fall for him. Except that her heart hadn't gotten the memo, it seemed. Which was stupid of her when she wasn't supposed to be here past the fall semester. The rest of the world dimmed around them. Couples swayed on the floor. Nate caressed her cheek with his knuckles, tipped her chin up and kissed her. It was tender, his lips moving against hers, gently seducing, a bubbling cauldron of heat beneath the surface that, with a single nudge, would explode into a five-alarm fire. Abby leaned into him, aware with every fiber of her being that she was walking a tenuous line.

Abby's heart plummeted into her toes when he lifted his head. *Oh, brother!*

She was already sunk. She just hadn't realized it until now. Oh hell, the undead doll army certainly was coming for her at any moment. They were likely already amassing to strike. And she'd just figured out she wasn't the plucky survivor but the in over her head heroine who was always the first to be eviscerated. Instead of freaking out, and running from her emotions as she normally did in times of existential crisis, Abby chose to ignore the whisperings of her heart. She wasn't a skilled practitioner when it came to dealing with her feelings. Her parents weren't necessarily the warmest people on the planet. They had doled out compliments for academic achievements, not hugs, passing that way of living to her two siblings. And that was part of why Abby had left the east coast—because she'd wondered if she even had a heart. But right now, she didn't want to analyze or doubt the emotions overflowing like a groundswell in her chest. Tonight, she wanted to revel in being the sole focal point of Nate's world.

Chapter Fourteen

From Old Man Turner's Journal:
On your date, have dinner (not coffee or drinks). And make sure to take her
somewhere special, where the two of you can get to know each other without
pressure or interference.

Abby's feet ached when she finally sat in the passenger seat
of Nate's Explorer at the end of the evening. Her head
buzzed a little bit from the wine she'd drunk. She couldn't
remember ever having danced as much as she had tonight, and
while dancing with Nate had been the best part of the evening,
she'd also been partnered with each of his friends—including
Sam, who was charming when he didn't have a burr up his butt.
She'd laughed and smiled more tonight than she had in months.
She'd even taken a turn around the dance floor with good old
Clark Biddle the Third.

Everyone accepted her as one of them, no questions asked,
no tests of her intellect. She was a descendant of one of the
townsfolk and that made her one of them. She was falling for it,
this town with its historic row of storefronts along Main Street

and its brick sidewalks all encircled by mountain peaks. Some of the smaller mountains, to be sure, yet she could look past those towering peaks and feel like she could touch the clouds.

Abby felt good, a deep in the bone contentment, about her life in general. It could be the oodles of wine, but she knew in her gut that it had a lot to do with Nate. His friends were in the backseat—minus Miles, of course, who was staying at his mother's house and being her escort this evening. Abby liked Nate's friends. When had she ever liked a guy's friends before? This place fit her, and was something she knew she had to add into her *pro* column when she made her decision. But enough about what might or might not be, she wanted to live in the now, preferably with Nate.

Sam was semi passed out, and Jacob stared pensively out the side window at the passing darkness. The mood was lighthearted as Nate drove them home. He held her hand and drove one-handed with the confident ease of someone who'd driven these roads for years. She enjoyed that he always seemed to be touching her tonight. It was nice, comforting. Abby hadn't experienced warmth and affection growing up and oh, how she'd yearned for it. With Nate, it was a natural extension of him, and all Abby wanted to do was hold on and never let go.

The thought should terrify her, but it didn't. Normally she was so much more levelheaded than this, but for once in her life, she was choosing to enjoy rather than avoid. It was a whole new world opening up for Abby, one she wanted to explore in depth.

She didn't know whether Nate planned to stay at her place again, or if he was going to stay home with his friends. She chewed on her bottom lip. She hoped he'd stay with her but didn't want to ask in front of Sam and Jacob, especially if the answer was no. Did he want to be with her again? From the looks he'd given her tonight, she hoped he did. Her pulse thudded at the thought he might decide to turn away.

Abby wanted to hang her head in shame as he turned onto their street. She was being one of those girls who worried instead of taking what she wanted. If Nate said no, he said no. There would be other nights. His friends were leaving in another day or so. They weren't here forever.

Nate pulled his SUV into his driveway. The headlights illuminated the front window, where Rufus stood with his face pressed against the glass. The big black ball of fur danced around in excitement. The rascal—Abby adored him, and heard his woof of enthusiasm at the prospect of company and Nate arriving home.

Before she opened the car door, Nate leaned across the center console, cupped her chin and placed a gentle kiss on her lips, then said, "I will be over in a few minutes, after Jacob and I haul Sam into my house and get him squared away. Is that all right with you?"

Her breath strangled in her throat, and she nodded. "Yes."

"Good." He closed the distance again and locked lips with her. She sighed into it. The tiny niggles of doubt had been for naught. It wasn't a lengthy kiss, or necessarily a deep one, but the significance that he kissed her in front of his best friends wasn't lost on her. That had to mean something, like he was seeking more than just a simple fling.

It made butterflies erupt in a cacophony in her belly.

"Would you guys get a room?" Sam quipped drunkenly.

Nate reluctantly released her lips, then shot a look to the backseat and addressed Jacob. "Help me with the moron, would you?"

"Absolutely."

As if on cue, Nate and Jacob exited the vehicle and met around the left side, then opened Sam's door. In unison, they hauled Sam out. The drunken lout began singing a rendition of *Baby's Got Back*, and something about his anaconda. Abby shook her head at him; the guy had some issues, clearly.

She slid out of the SUV and walked around the front where they were half carrying, half dragging Sam. She asked, "Do you need some help? Is there anything I can do?"

"Actually," Nate replied, holding out his keys, "open the front door for us if you don't mind, and then I can just head over with you."

"Sure." She accepted the keys from him, enjoying the tiny jolt from his fingers touching hers. As the group neared the front door, Rufus was inside, losing his mind. She hurried her pace, which was not a cake walk in the slightest after having been in heels all night, and climbed the steps to Nate's front door. She realized this was the first time she was seeing inside his house. Born with enough curiosity to impress a cat, she admitted to herself that helping him with Sam was also an excuse to see the inside of his house. Just to make sure he wasn't hiding any dead bodies, or wasn't really the key master who would incite the doll army to rise. Things like that. Yes, she had likely seen far too many horror films for her own good.

Rufus woofed in an excited frenzy as she slid the key in the lock. Abby braced herself as she shoved open the door and all hundred and fifty pounds of black fur bounded out. Even though she braced for impact, Rufus jumped with the force of a small freight train and knocked her to the ground. She landed on Nate's porch with a *thunk*.

"Christ, Abby, are you all right?" Nate asked and started to release Sam, who began to fall without his support.

"I'm fine. I'm getting rather used to it by now. Take care of Sam." To prove it to Nate, she shifted her gaze to the mound of dog currently dancing around her in his joy at seeing her. "Hey, sweetheart. How are you?"

Rufus gave her sloppy kisses on her face, then darted out in the yard to do his business. Nate gave her a hand up. Dusting herself off, she held the door open as Jacob and Nate carried Sam inside. They lugged him straight past her, down a hallway, and out of sight. Then she heard a yelp and a holler as the sound of running water came on. They must be tossing him into a shower. Not a half bad idea. It would sober Sam up a bit at least. She waited near the front door for Rufus to finish his business.

When he started to wander off, she hollered, "Rufus, come on in, bud."

At her call, Rufus sprinted toward the door as if the hounds of hell were nipping at his paws. After he'd charged into the house, she shut the front door. Rufus followed her as she walked through Nate's living room and found his bed in the corner. This must be due to the remodeling he'd mentioned before. He definitely had ample space to live down here while he worked on the second floor. Not to mention, it now made perfect sense why they'd done the deed at her house and not his, because here they would have an audience.

Nate's home was Victorian in style but much more modernized. The floors were a glossy hardwood in a mild, medium cedar shade that leaned more toward nutmeg than mahogany. The walls were a dark taupe with ivory crown molding and baseboards, all of which had that freshly painted, new appearance.

But it was his kitchen that was the pièce de résistance. He had a professional grade gas stove a world-famous chef would lust over. The appliances were all stainless steel, new, and still had the sheen. Granite countertops and dark cherry wood cabinets complemented each other. But unlike the sedate taupe in the rest of what she'd seen, the walls were a cheerful yellow that made Abby think of school lunches and chocolate-chip cookies, lazy Saturday morning brunches and Thanksgiving.

"There you are." Nate's hands slid around her waist from behind, breaking her out of her reverie, which was a good thing. She shouldn't dream about little boys with cornflower blue eyes or little girls with the same smile as his.

She pressed back against him, enjoying the feel of his arms around her far too damn much. She murmured, "Sorry, didn't mean to be nosy. Is Sam okay?"

"Yeah, Jacob will make sure he's fine. Ready to go?" He placed a light kiss on the sensitive spot on her neck right beneath her ear. Oh, hell yeah, she was ready.

"Sure."

He released her enough so she could turn and accepted his outstretched hand. He threaded his fingers through hers. A banked fire blazed in his gaze and her knees wobbled a bit as he towed her out of the kitchen.

She had to admire the man's backside. She hadn't gotten a good look at it last night or this morning, having been more concerned with holding on to him. But crikey, did the man wear any type of pants well. As they walked back through the living room, she said, "I've got to ask. How bad does it look upstairs, since you're living down here? How much progress do you still have to make on the remodel?"

"Oh, that. Here, let me show you." He led her up the stairs into a full construction area. White tarps covered the floor. Walls were missing or had the skeletal structure of two-by-fours with no drywall enclosing them.

"See, this is where my bedroom will be eventually. There was a fifth bedroom that was the size of a walk-in closet and really nothing more than dead space. So I knocked down the wall here. And then I also wanted to create a master bathroom that was connected to the bedroom, so I'm pushing the walls out here."

"You did all this?" she asked.

"Yeah, before I became a cop, I worked construction, remodeling houses. And when I bought this place on the cheap, it was because of the shape it was in. It's taken me a while. I had to tackle the exterior, put on a new roof, fix the porch, and give it a new paint job. Then I worked on the first floor first. The kitchen was the worst and most time consuming. During those few weeks, I lived on more take out than I care to remember. Once it was done, though, it was worth every minute turning it into what it is today. After the first floor was completed, I started up here."

Abby saw Nate in a whole new light. He was layers deep. And knowing he had done the work on the beautiful kitchen downstairs made her realize he hadn't just bought a house, he was building his home, little by little, with steadfast progress. He didn't mind getting his hands dirty or side stepping the hard work, and that told her more about his character. If anything, he'd grown in her esteem, not diminished. She couldn't keep the wonder out of her voice as she said, "This is incredible, Nate, truly. I can't believe you've done all of this yourself. And what do you plan to do with the rest of the rooms up here?"

His gaze simmered and held hers for a long moment before he said quietly, "Here, I'll show you. Come with me, and watch your step."

Nate led her through the second story, explaining all the modifications he planned to make. It was a rather massive project, but as he described his plans, she could visualize everything and see his vision for how it would look. Nate wasn't just remodeling the place. He was building his future. And god help her, but she wanted to share in that future for however long he would have her—or until it was time for her to leave Echo Springs.

Nate was thoughtful, steady, and had a keen eye for beauty and aesthetics. But it was his dream of what this place could be that grabbed her by the heart. She yearned for it, wanted to be the one he would turn to at night during the cold winter months, wanted to be the one to share in the joys and laughter that were destined for the place he was building. He was fixing up a place where little boys with his eyes would run their grubby fingers along the balustrade, and little girls would splash their dad with bubbles during bath time. And then, at night, he would pull her close—to keep the bogeyman away, of course. One never knew when a mass murdering sociopath would strike. Abby wanted that family, wanted the love inherent there with an intensity that left her dazed.

Anxiety and dread suffused her at how swiftly he was coming to matter. She couldn't fall for Nate, but feared it was too late for that.

"What?" he asked, his dark brow scrunched with concern.

She felt vulnerable and terrified all in the same breath. Her fear was inexplicable and gripped her with enough force to bring her to her knees. As she stared at Nate, the realization sank in that she might finally have found everything she wanted, and everything she hadn't realized she needed. She didn't know how to process it all and it knocked her off her center of gravity. Doing her best to ignore her fear, she plastered a sexy smile on her face instead. There would be a time to confront those fears, but not tonight. "Nothing, I just was fantasizing about seeing you wear a tool belt."

"Is that right?" He tugged her close, stroking his knuckles gently down her cheek.

"Yeah. Want to go to my place and I can show you?"

"I thought you'd never ask." Nate escorted her back down the stairs. In the living room, Jacob was reclining in the brown leather La-Z-Boy, while Sam was passed out on the leather couch with a waste bucket next to his head.

"Everything cool here?" Nate asked Jacob and indicated Sam with a tilt of his head.

"Yeah, I think he's going to have one hell of a hangover, but I'll see that he doesn't hurt himself more," Jacob said with a small grin hovering over his lips.

Nate saluted him and said, "Good man, I'll see you in the morning."

"Yep, you kids have fun. Don't forget to wear protection," Jacob jibed.

"Thanks, Dad," Nate joked, sliding an arm around Abby's waist and shooting her a wicked grin as she giggled. Thank God he didn't say anything about her industrial sized box of condoms or she might just have to kill the man.

"Night, Jacob," Abby said.

"Abby. Rufus, what do you say, boy? Should we make something to eat?" Rufus, delighted at the prospect of food, raced back into the kitchen, with the hulk of a man following him.

And then Abby thought of them no more as Nate whisked her out the door and over to her house. Her stomach trembled in anticipation of the night to come.

Nate took her keys from her hands, unlocked the door for her, and then drew her inside. At the site of last night's epic scene, the flutters inside her core shifted into fiery embers. Taking his hand in hers, she led him up to her bedroom. They were barely inside her door when Nate spun her into his arms and his mouth claimed hers.

With a moan, she wrapped her arms around his neck. Nate walked her backward until her legs brushed against her mattress. This was what she'd been waiting for all night long. She returned his heated, open-mouthed kisses with her own. She couldn't seem to get enough of him. Deep down, she knew there would never be another man to kiss her like this, as if he were calibrated on an atomic level to mesh with her molecules.

She surrendered to the tempest as it built between them. As far as Abby was concerned, he could have been leading her into the fiery pits of hell, but as long as he kept kissing her, she didn't care. Bring on the army of undead. He seduced with his kiss. He teased and thrust his tongue inside, his hungry lips drinking her gasps and her fervent mewls as his tongue plunged inside to duel with hers. In this moment, she was happily drowning in him.

Nate's fingers were a whispered caress on the exposed skin of her back before he drew the zipper down, baring her back to his magic hands. Seducing her with his touch, he released her lips and slid the spaghetti straps off her shoulders, tugging the rose material so it slid into a heap at her feet.

"Christ, Abby! It's a good thing I had no clue what you were wearing underneath that dress because we never would have made it to the party," he growled, his fingers teasing the flesh of her abdomen as he stared at her like a starving man about to feast.

"I'm glad you like it."

"I more than like it, I plan to remove it," he hauled her close, "with my teeth."

She'd bought the lingerie to wear on a whim while out shopping with Tessa and Cybil. The coral bustier fit perfectly to her midriff, and it had matching coral lace panties. Her impulse buy had been a good bet if the lust darkening Nate's face was any indication. Tremors flared in her core. No man had ever looked at her the way Nate did.

In a flash, Nate hoisted her up—like she was his bride he was carrying across the threshold—and laid her tenderly on the bed. She protested, reaching for him when he pulled away, but then stared transfixed as he removed his clothing. She adored his firm chest, covered with dark hair that tapered into a narrow line over his abdomen and trailed beneath his trousers; the way his muscles bunched and flowed as he tossed the tie and shirt behind him, uncaring where they landed. And how his arms flexed as he stripped off his slacks and shoved his boxer briefs off and down his powerfully built legs until he stood naked, a veritable mountain of naked, lean, gorgeous man.

A guttural moan emitted from her very soul. Desire pulsed in frenetic waves as she reached for him, desperate to touch him, taste him. Her gaze dropped to the part of his anatomy that had brought her such joy and would do so again. His shaft jutted from the apex of his victory lines, hugely erect. But then he finally joined her in bed. Nate knelt and settled his weight between her thighs, and her breath caught at the back of her throat.

His blue eyes deepened, lust permeating his gaze.

And then her thoughts scattered to the breeze as he reclaimed her mouth in a torrid, potent duel of lips and teeth and tongue. He possessed her mouth, kissing her with such wicked desire she wondered if she would expire from the fire building inside her. Abby returned his kisses, her need boiling over and overriding any thoughts but him and his incredible mouth. He surrounded her, dominated the very air she breathed, and she reveled in the feel of his steely frame against hers, pressing her back against the mattress, the firm ridge of his shaft fitted intimately against her.

His hand caressed her sides, teasingly playing with the material of her bustier. His fingers were like hot brands against her flesh. Every place he touched, sparks of pleasure ignited. Then they traveled down to the little pink bow at her hip. His calloused fingertips caressed the exposed flesh at her midriff, toying with the delicate lace of her panties before they slipped beneath the gauzy fabric to her center. Trembling, she groaned into his mouth, her hips undulating against him.

Abby was slowly but surely going up in flames. Her hands slid over the contours of his muscular frame, enjoying the way they flexed and quivered beneath her hands. She continued south on her exploration while her eyes crossed at the exquisite sensations spiraling in her body because of Nate's magic hands.

He released her lips, his fingers stroking her intimately, and her mouth opened with a series of mewls. Her hands clasped his neck. When she whimpered, trying to draw his marvelous mouth back to hers, Nate murmured, his voice rumbling deep with his desire for her, "Just lie back and let me love you tonight."

"Nate," she sighed. He hovered, unmoving, until she nodded in agreement. The sensual smile he gave her, the lust darkening his features at her compliance, nearly sent her into the stratosphere. Biting her lip to try and contain her moans, Abby wondered if she would melt into a permanent puddle of need around him. Nate traced her collarbone with his teeth, placed nibbling bites on his way down her chest. He caressed her mounds of flesh above the bustier with his tongue and Abby thought she was going to come right out of her skin.

He upped the ante and did exactly as he'd promised, taking his time, unhooking the front buttons on her bustier one by one, revealing her body to his gaze and erotic touch at a languorous pace. It was as if last night had been a race to the finish line but tonight he tabled the faster pace as he savored her body like it was an incredibly rich, full-bodied, hundred-year-old Scotch.

When the bustier fell open and the expanse of her breasts lay bare before him, he treated the plump mounds like an all-you-can-eat buffet. His mouth closed around one taut nipple as his hand toyed with the other. His tongue tasted her, laving her skin until she burned, her mouth formed in a permanent O as she mewled in a constant stream of syllables. He nuzzled and nipped at the sensitive underside of her breast, kneading and suckling until she burned. And then he paid homage to its twin. Her fingers slid into his hair of their own accord and held him in place against her breast.

The fire built inside her with every flick of his tongue and graze of his teeth. All Abby could do was hold on for the ride. She whimpered when he traveled farther south. Her hands gripped the sheets as he caressed and tasted her belly, as if he was learning the flavor of each part of her body. She quivered beneath his touch.

Then he did as he'd promised; he nipped at her hips, and tugged and pulled her panties down over her thighs with his teeth. His tongue would flick over the little love bites, soothing her flesh, and turning her into a writhing mass of desire. Abby was certain she would expire from the sheer force of need battering her being. She yearned to feel him inside her. She whimpered and moaned, straining against his touch as he sat back on his haunches, proof of his desire for her bobbing under her gaze.

And then his broad shoulders were nudging her thighs wider as his head descended, hovering over her most intimate flesh while he held her gaze. The guttural moan she emitted when his mouth lowered and claimed her center sounded inhuman. Nate stroked her folds, lapping and teasing her until he plunged inside her quivering sheath. Her body rocketed to the brink of passion. Her hands dug into the sheets. She undulated her hips against his mouth until he held her steady, holding her prisoner as he ruthlessly decimated her control and she surrendered to his torrid onslaught. In the deep recesses of her soul, Abby knew she'd never been made love to so thoroughly.

With his gaze trained on her, Nate propelled her system to a bright shimmering cliff. Ecstasy cascaded through her, rending the very fabric of her being. Abby cried out, "Nate, oh god."

She shuddered, her limbs heavy at the molten mass flowing in her veins. But his exquisite, earth-shattering attention continued. His mouth plundered her depths as she came apart. He didn't allow her to come down from one peak before he swept her up another steep bluff. Again and again, he coerced her toward the glistening precipice, molding her body, reshaping it, vanquishing every man who'd come before him with his masterful skill.

When Nate finally slipped inside her, filling her to overflowing with his length, tears formed in the corners of her eyes. With his intense gaze—suffused with need—trained on hers, he caught her tears with his thumbs. She kissed him, tasting herself on his lips as he slid home. As Nate moved, Abby wrapped her legs around his waist, her hands digging into his back as she held him close. His breath became her breath and hers became his. Abby canted her hips, meeting him thrust for thrust in their erotic dance. The feel of his length pressed against hers, the way their bodies seemed to fit as if attuned and formed specifically for the other, added to her pleasure. Their twin moans filled the air as Nate lifted his face, releasing her lips.

"Look at me," he demanded.

Abby opened her eyes, staring into the vibrant blue orbs hovering above her as he propped himself up on his elbows. Her image was reflected in their depths. It sent her over the edge. Her system imploded. Fireworks erupted as her orgasm shattered whatever composure she had left, as well as her ability to remain indifferent. She moaned. She writhed. And pleasure more intense and more devastating barreled through her until she was trembling from the sheer volume of explosions as they ricocheted throughout her body.

"Abby," Nate groaned as he strained, his body stiffening as he thrust. She held him while his climax quaked through his body. He buried his face in her neck as tremors wracked him before he stilled. She cradled him against her. Her hands lightly traced the lines of his back, her eyes half-closed as their twin heartbeats slowed to normal.

He kissed her, and Abby knew in that moment that she had lost whatever semblance of distance or objectivity she'd had. Her heart trembled as it opened, and she poured her feelings into the kiss.

Then Nate shifted, withdrawing from her body, and she felt momentarily bereft at the loss of his weight on top of her. He rolled to his back, but took her with him, so that she lay nestled against his side. His arm was around her and his hand rested on her hip. Their legs were tangled together, her head pillowed on his chest, her eyes closed as Abby fell asleep. Just before she did so, she wondered how she was going to leave Echo Springs now that her heart was fully engaged.

Chapter Fifteen

From Old Man Turner's Journal:
A man without a plan isn't ready to date.

The next day, after she and Nate spent the morning tearing up her sheets, Abby sent him on his way to go play sheriff. That afternoon, she opened her front door to the sister duo who were fast becoming her best friends. Who would have thought for a second it would take moving two thousand miles away to find people who accepted her as she was with no thoughts for improvement?

Yeah, her heart not only existed but it was becoming her most used body part in the little mountain town.

Cybil and Tessa were always such contrasts in their styles. Cybil was looking classic, in jeans and an ivory peasant top, whereas Tessa's black, ripped jeans and tee-shirt with some superhero Abby didn't recognize splashed across it was a study in chic geek.

"Hey, come on in. I'm so glad you guys could make it," Abby said as they entered the foyer.

And was she ever. She'd given up the pretense of trying to concentrate on her dissertation today. After her amazing night with Nate, the memories had been on instant replay. All she seemed to do here lately was end up daydreaming about him. It was becoming a bad habit of hers that she didn't see any signs of stopping. It also didn't help that there were parts of her body chafed with whisker burn. Instead of progressing on her dissertation, she'd spent the last few hours in the kitchen, meal-prepping for the week and baking.

"It's so cool in here. Are these the original light fixtures?" Tessa asked, examining one of the brass wall sconces.

"It smells wonderful," Cybil said, sniffing the air in an imitation of a bloodhound.

"I believe so. Much of this place is the original. And I'm glad you think so because I've been baking today and will need your help to eat everything. Would you like a tour, or do you want to eat first?" Abby said.

"The tour," both sisters replied in unison.

"All right, the tour it is. Here on the left, as you can see, it was originally a living room and is now used as a repository for the undead doll army," Abby explained as they moved into the room. She lifted the first sheet from the couch. The beady stares from at least twenty or so dolls looked at them lifelessly and she shivered at their frozen porcelain expressions.

"Gah! You weren't kidding about the dolls." Cybil recoiled like Abby had exposed a nest of venomous snakes.

"Nope. Creepy little suckers, aren't they? A part of me wants to have a bonfire in the backyard with them. Except, I know Evie loved them, and I feel guilty for even thinking that way."

"I don't blame you. In fact, if you change your mind, I'll bring the matches to help," Cybil said, giving the dolls a wide berth as she walked through the room.

"I think they are wicked cool," Tessa countered. She leaned against the couch, examining them much more closely than Abby, who kept as much distance between her body and their limbs as she could while still holding the sheet up for the girls' inspection. Because Tessa was acting as if she were studying a gold mine deposit. Didn't she realize that's when those minions from hell would attack?

"You would." Cybil snorted.

Tessa shot Abby a quizzical glance and said, "Do you realize how much these things go for at auctions and such? You could make a pretty penny off these beauts."

Abby understood that but replied, "The money doesn't matter to me, not really. It's partly the sentimentality of them. Not to mention, my time has been thoroughly consumed by trying to finish my dissertation, in addition to teaching at ESCC, and it has left little time for doll sorting."

"And let's not forget all the hot monkey sex with Sheriff Stud Muffin. If I was getting nightly action with the sexy sheriff, I wouldn't be as concerned with the undead doll army either. It just means you have your priorities in order," Tessa joked with a gamine grin.

Heat infused Abby's cheeks as she blushed. It was really great sex. Spectacular, even. The best she'd ever had. Even thinking about it, about him, made tingles curl inside her belly. God, the way he kissed her. His mouth. The way those stellar lips moved against hers. How could she want him again so soon? Inhaling a breath and deflecting, Abby asked, "But didn't I see you dancing with Jacob, cozying up to him last night, Tessa? You seemed pretty into him, so I'm not the only one who could be doing it."

She left out the fact that it was far more than just raunchy bouts of hot sex with Nate. Much more. And those pesky feelings terrified her. Her time here was temporary, which meant any relationship with Nate was temporary. She couldn't have feelings for him.

Tessa snorted and shook her head. "You did see us dancing, but Jacob's not into me. I know he finds me attractive. I mean, hello, what guy wouldn't? But even with the skin I flashed his way last night, the man did nothing about it, despite ample urging on my part. He acted more like a monk than the hunk of burning love I thought he'd be."

"Well, you have to admit, Sam getting shit-faced didn't help," Abby tried to give Jacob the benefit of the doubt. She'd witnessed the way he had glanced at Tessa—with unrequited longing in his lonely gaze.

Cybil shrugged. "Totally my fault. How was I to know that he was already half drunk when I suggested we do shots? It's not like he confessed or said no thanks."

"You have a point there, Abby, I didn't consider. Way to cock-block me, Sis." Tessa shot Cybil a miffed glare that lasted all of two seconds as they toured the rest of the house. Abby took them through the second floor and then down the back set of stairs that exited into the kitchen.

They gathered around the kitchen table where she had set the spread. Looking at it, she realized she might have gone a teensy bit overboard. There was a cheese board with four different kinds of cheese, fruit, mini quiches, mini pizza muffins, cheese puff pastries, and cherry tarts. Tessa cracked open a bottle of chardonnay.

"It's like the promised land," Cybil said, filling a plate up.

"Baking, cooking in general, really, relaxes me."

Tessa took a bite of a cherry tart and moaned. "And it was so worth it. Can I just come for dinner every day? Man, these are so good."

"I will send some of this stuff home with you, how about that?" Because then it would keep Abby from eating it all herself. As it was, she'd have to get in a run tomorrow and she hated running. Typically, if anybody saw her running, they might want to consider running, too, because it meant something bad, or that someone was chasing her. And, in this instance, it would most likely be the possessed dolls.

Munching on a slice of cheese, Cybil exclaimed, "I can't believe you live in this big place all by yourself. Are you planning to sell it?"

That was the question of the hour, wasn't it? Abby replied with a sigh, "I don't know. I haven't decided if I'm even staying past the fall semester."

Tessa asked around a bite of pastry, "Does Nate know that you may not stick around?"

Abby glanced down at her wine glass, shame eating away at her. Why did her life have to be so complicated? All she wanted to do was enjoy her time here, this tiny reprieve that she had garnered from her real life. How sad was it that she needed the vacation from her real life? What did that say about her real life that she needed a vacation from it? Except, she was keeping the probability of her departure from Nate.

She was torn over the omission. On the one hand, she knew she was withholding rather crucial information. In the scheme of things, it was wrong, she understood that, but she feared if she did tell him the truth, he would walk away. In the event that Echo Springs was just a stopover, the relationship would end anyway. Long distance relationships rarely, if ever, worked. Then, on the other hand, the right thing to do, the honest thing, would be to tell him her stay in Echo Springs was most likely temporary —meaning any relationship between them was temporary as well —then allow Nate to decide the best course of action for himself. Deep down, she knew he would put a kibosh on the relationship. Which would mean no more knock her socks off kisses. She wasn't ready to give those up just yet.

"No. I hadn't planned on getting involved with him. Or anyone, for that matter. It just kind of happened. Please don't say anything to him, I'm begging you. I just need a little more time." Before the brakes were thrown on the toe-curling kisses.

Cybil refilled their wine glasses and asked, "When do you plan on telling him?"

Abby resisted the urge to squirm in her seat. She wanted to avoid this topic, preferring to play ostrich, then deal with the messy reality of her situation at a much later date. Which may be childish and rather chicken of her but, in her defense, she had never had such an intense connection with a man. With a sigh, she replied, "I don't know. Everything is still so new, and the sex…"

They leaned forward, eagerness dotting their faces, and Tessa urged, "Tell us more about you and Sheriff Hot Pants having all the sex."

"I think her term is Stud Muffin," Cybil countered with a wry grin.

"Other than that it's the best sex of my life and he makes me feel like the most beautiful woman on the planet? What would you guys do? Because I'm stumped. I don't want to lose this amazing guy, whom I might lose anyway if I don't stay. And every time I think I should say something, he kisses me and I forget everything else," Abby said, needing some guidance, because her heart was already in play. She worried about doing irreparable damage if she kept the possibility of her leaving Echo Springs from him. Because she knew how it must look to the casual observer: that she was building a life here, entrenching herself with the townspeople, and building a foundation for the future with the sexy sheriff. Even though they had not talked about the future, it felt like that was what they were doing.

Plus, most likely, Michael Myers was nearby sharpening his axe. That's what he did when unlikely couples finally got together and were having lots of hot monkey sex.

"In my opinion, and I know it doesn't mean much since I'm not currently dating anyone, you need to confess and come clean. Otherwise, your relationship is built around a lie, and I can tell you from experience, it won't end well," Cybil remarked, staring into her wine glass with a pensive expression clouding her face.

"For once, my sister's right. Confess like it's a drink-and-dial session, Ab, or it will bite you in the ass," Tessa agreed and popped one of the pastry tarts in her mouth.

"I'll think about it," Abby promised. And she would. Because she was always practical, she needed time, as this thinking with her heart thing was completely new territory for her. Instead of on bedrock, she suddenly found herself on unsolid ground and she was blindfolded, wandering in the dark, to boot. What better way for the undead army to strike? She sighed.

"Now, about the dolls. I think I can help you unload the undead army in there," Tessa said, jerking her thumb over her shoulder in their general direction.

"I'm listening," Abby said, willing to off-load those creepy little suckers the first chance she had. The sooner the better, before they rose up and destroyed the town. It was a kindness, truly, for her to get rid of them.

"Well, it's really more of a proposition," Tessa replied and gave her a calculating glance.

"Sweet Jesus, you're not bringing those suckers home," Cybil interjected with a warning.

Tessa crossed her arms and sat back in a chair with a caustic stare toward her sister. "No, I wasn't planning on it, but with that attitude, I just might. Our place is as much mine as it is yours."

"Great, you see what I have to put up with. I'll end up waking up one morning with one of those things sitting on the end of my bed." Cybil rolled her eyes and took a long drink of wine.

"It would serve you right. Anyhow, as I was saying, Abby, I know a legion of vendors in the comic book world. Who, as it so happens, also do vintage antique shows, and have contacts with owners of steampunk retail shops who would freak over the collection."

Abby studied her. She trusted Tessa, liked both her and her sister. And she knew that Nate thought highly of them, which was good enough in her book. "I'll make you a deal. If you help me catalog them and find buyers, I'll give you twenty percent of the profits."

"Fifty," Tessa responded.

"Twenty-five."

"Forty-five," Tessa countered.

"Thirty, take it or leave it," Abby commented with her counter-offer.

Just when Abby thought she might have miscalculated, Tessa grinned and said, "You drive a hard bargain, but you have yourself a deal. We can get started with the cataloging tonight."

"Don't you ever not hustle?" Cybil said, exasperated and glaring at her sister like she was Beelzebub rising from the fiery pits of hell.

Tessa shot her a modest smirk and exclaimed, rather dramatically, "Please, you know me better than that. This is about being efficient, as I have a looming deadline on the latest comic, plus classes this week."

Abby asked Tessa, realizing she had no clue what her stuff was about, "What's the name of your comic series?"

"The one I am currently on deadline for is *Tales of a Zombie Space Pilot.* I have another vampire series out as well," Tessa replied proudly.

"So, does your character eat the brains of all the passengers?" If so, Abby thought she might really be interested in reading it. She'd never given a thought to extending her love of horror films into comic books. But then again, perhaps her imagination was too wild and stuffed with horror references already. Couldn't hurt to try a new medium though, could it?

"Nope, she only zombies out if she doesn't get brains. And she delivers cargo between Earth and Zincain Planet Delta while evading space pirates and their sworn enemies, the Caden, who are these lizard type humanoids attempting to overthrow the Intergalactic Planetary Union," Tessa explained with a small shrug.

"Really?" Abby said, perplexed. She'd always thought the whole point of a zombie was that it was driven by the need to feed and consume human flesh. That they were no longer a sentient being. A zombie with deductive reasoning skills was outside her paradigm, which wasn't necessarily a bad thing, just different.

"It doesn't make sense to me either," Cybil muttered with a shake of her head.

"Hey," Tessa responded with a wounded expression.

"I'm proud as can be," Cybil answered. "I just don't get it."

Tessa shrugged and rolled her eyes. "Whatever. Let's take this party into the living room and start cataloging what you've got."

"Only the makings of Chucky's evil army. Nothing to be concerned about," Abby imparted with droll wit.

The three of them laughed as they headed into the living room, where they spent the remainder of the evening poring through her aunt's collection. Abby and Cybil viewed the pasty, beady-eyed objects from the sane perspective: that they were creepy demon spawn from hell that should be destroyed before they could kill everyone. Whereas Tessa acted like she'd discovered a gold mine and the keys to Disneyland.

All told, Abby enjoyed herself immensely.

ABBY NOTICED Nate's second floor lights were on when the girls left. As much as she yearned to see him again tonight, she held herself back; kept herself from crossing the divide between their houses and knocking on his door. There was a gorgeous macho man who wanted her, and she was avoiding him. How messed up was that? How many women would kill to be in her position? Both Cybil and Tessa had ribbed her over it.

Deep down in her heart, Abby knew Cybil was one hundred percent right. Nate deserved the truth: that there was a chance, a very likely one, that she wouldn't be in Echo Springs past the fall semester. How was she supposed to tell him that? Especially when he was someone she had feelings for and wasn't ready to let go of quite yet. It was selfish and self-serving, because she understood that, in all likelihood, the moment she did say something to the effect of, 'Hey, Nate, I realize we're kind of dating and all but we shouldn't get too serious because I'm likely leaving you and the town by Christmas,' it would all be over.

It sounded cold, callous, and was exceptionally bitchy. Abby understood the moment she did explain, the lovely, insulated bubble of world-altering sex and incredible kisses would end. He'd walk away from her. And she wouldn't blame him—she would do the same if their positions were reversed.

Her behavior was selfish and made her a hypocrite. But he mattered—much more than she wanted him to or had bargained for when they'd begun—and it petrified her into non-action. Abby would rather face a terrifying man in a hockey mask with a knife dripping blood than confess her sins to Nate.

So instead of heading next door wearing nothing but an overcoat and stockings, she occupied her time by working on lesson plans for the coming week and then went to bed alone. His light was still on when she switched hers off and snuggled under the covers. She smelled him on her sheets and sighed. If only he'd made the decision for her, crossed the expanse of lawn between them and invaded her space. She knew instinctively that if he had come, she wouldn't have turned him away.

The following week flew by for Abby. Between classes, final dissertation submission prep, and a faculty meeting with stale donut holes, she worked from sunup to sundown, collapsing into bed each night. And a little niggle of doubt had begun to take root. She was right next door to the man, and he'd never once crossed the divide. Had it just been a weekend fling? They'd never discussed any level of commitment, but it had been implied for sure. Perhaps, if that was the case, she should take it all for what it was, an incredible, life-affirming gift.

However, she lay awake at night, missing him. Reliving how every time she'd been in his arms, it had felt like coming home. All week she felt achy and needy, and wanted nothing more than to march across the expanse of yard between them. Except, if she wasn't staying in Echo Springs this solved the issue of her coming clean with him, didn't it?

She didn't go over, and neither did he; the thirty yards between their houses became an ocean.

On Friday, she stopped in at Papa Beau's Pizza for lunch. She was meeting Tessa, who had said in her message, 'Wait until you see what people will pay for those dolls.'

She spied Tessa in the small parking lot, with Cybil not far behind. Today Tessa had bright pink in her hair, and the funky streaks went well with her gray cargo pants and *Rainbow Brite* tee shirt. Cybil was dressed from top to bottom in yoga gear, from her gray pants to her powder blue top with *Namaste* scrawled over her chest and a cashmere cardigan in eggshell white.

"Hope you don't mind that I'm crashing lunch," Cybil said, twining her arm through Abby's.

"Not at all," Abby murmured. She would really miss these two if or when she left town.

Abby held the door for them into the pizza place that reminded her of a Western saloon—or what she imagined a Western saloon would have looked like back in the day. The heady scent of cooked dough, basil and garlic hung in the air. She followed them to an empty golden pinewood table booth, with faux leather chocolate seats, and was brought up short. She almost tripped over her own feet. The curse of tiny towns— besides them being a mass murderer with a chainsaw's favorite type of place, was how difficult it was to avoid other people. Namely, people you'd done the hanky-panky with all hot and heavy the prior weekend, and then didn't speak to all week long.

Nate. He was here.

She ran smack-dab into Sheriff Stud Muffin and two of his deputies eating lunch at a nearby table. Hot, shivering need battered her system. She still wanted him. Over the last week, he'd lost none of his potency. Abby's stomach churned. His blue gaze lasered in on her approach, and her knees trembled. It was going to suck monkey balls if she was this affected by him, and he didn't want anything more than that one weekend. If anything, he had grown more handsome over the last few days.

How was that even possible? He wore a black and ivory flannel shirt, the cuffs rolled up near his elbows, exposing his muscular forearms. He laid his half-eaten slice of pizza on his plate and wiped his hands on a paper napkin, and watching his forearms flex with the movement was enough to melt her from the inside out. She could recall with perfect clarity the way those long, sturdy fingers had caressed her skin.

"Sheriff, fancy running into you here," Tessa said, sliding into their booth. What a way to break the ice. Not that there was a shy bone in Tessa's body.

Nate's gaze never left Abby as he replied, "Good to see you, Tessa, Cybil. Abby, could I have a word?"

"Sure," Abby replied, wishing for a gateway to hell to open and swallow her whole. Was this the part where he explained it had been fun but that's all it had been? And why it even mattered, since she most likely wasn't staying in Echo Springs, was beyond her at the moment. This was just a temporary situation. She shouldn't get attached—couldn't allow herself to, because there was a part of her that was already in mourning over the coming separation.

"What do you want on your pie, Abby? I'm starved," Cybil asked, not even bothering with a menu as she slid into the booth. Abby's mind went blank with Nate standing nearby. She could smell him, his distinctly male scent, mixed in with pizza spices, and her system went berserk.

Hot and melty and tasting like sin.

She realized they meant the pizza and not Nate.

"Surprise me," Abby replied. Nate's patience obviously at an end, his hand closed around hers and he tugged her away from the table. He wove them through the crowded restaurant. Her feet followed of their own accord. She bit back a moan. Just his damn hand holding hers caused liquid heat to course through her veins and jangle all her ovaries into making kissy noises at him. Not to mention the view of his spectacular butt, lovingly cupped by his jeans. The two exited out the back door into the alleyway. Before she knew what hit her, Nate backed her up against the wall and was kissing her as if his life depended on it.

Her ovaries screamed in ecstasy and began swooning at his passionate embrace. Nate was kissing her again. He did want her. Oh god, his mouth. It was hot and needy, and just obliterated any misgivings.

She slid her hands up around his neck and into his hair, holding on to him, surrendering to the potent need she found in his embrace, giving as good as she received until Nate finally broke the kiss.

His gaze searched hers as he panted, "Sorry, didn't mean to accost you like that. I know you've been avoiding me…"

"Nate, it's not that," she denied. Oh, but it was exactly that and so much more than mere avoidance.

"Then what is it? Why did you shut me out this week?" he asked, rubbing her bottom lip with his thumb, his gaze intent, searching her face for answers.

And the truth—some of it, anyway, that were her deepest fears—spilled out. "I thought you didn't want me anymore. I figured, since you didn't come by, that you had gotten what you wanted."

His gaze noticeably softened and warmed. "Abby, I do want you. Much more than I'm comfortable with at times. I've missed you this week. Part of me, my ego really, figured if you wanted more you would come to me. But I see that I'm going to have to step up my game if you doubted I want more from you."

"What do you mean?" Her heart beat a staccato rhythm in her chest. She couldn't seem to stop touching him. Her hands caressed his back through his flannel shirt. She itched to slide her fingers beneath the material and feel his skin.

"Have dinner with me tonight," he insisted, then began nibbling on her jawline, placing tiny, feather-light kisses there that were doing melty things to her resolve.

"Um, you mean like a date?" she gasped as he sucked on her

earlobe, and her eyes closed at the pleasure streaking through her system.

"I mean that exactly." He spoke low, near her ear, and then his mouth moved to that one spot on her neck—the one that made her brain cells implode and tingles erupt along her spine. It made her ovaries whimper. And oh god, what was he asking? Couldn't he just kiss her now and stop talking? She did better when there was no talking, when their mouths were all but fused together and the world fell away, leaving no room for doubts.

Did she want to go on a date with him? He nibbled on her shoulder. As much as she knew she should walk away, make it a clean break, the undead doll army couldn't have dragged her away. She sighed. "Yeah, I'd like that."

He raised his face, lust darkening his cornflower blue gaze so that it was almost cobalt, and stroked a hand in a whispered caress down her cheek. "Good. I'll pick you up at six thirty. Oh, and Abby," he nipped her bottom lip, "if you have any more sexy underwear like the other night, take mercy on me and wear it."

"I'll see what I can do." She kissed him, needing his mouth on hers to assuage her until that evening. She loved his mouth, the way he slanted his lips over hers and assumed control.

Then he groaned, a deep, masculine rumble she could feel in his chest. He lifted his mouth, leaving her panting and achy as he pulled away. Regret swam in his eyes. "We need to get back inside, because it would be bad form for the sheriff to be discovered having sex in an alley, and if we continue like we are, I can't guarantee I won't ravish you where you stand."

Her breaths came in short, shallow pants. Desire and need clamored at her resolve and in her mind, she imagined doing just that. It didn't sound so bad—in fact, it sounded precisely like what she needed. She said, "When you put it that way…"

He yanked the door open and gave her one final, soul-stealing kiss. Then he ordered, "In, now. As tempting as that scenario and you are, waiting until tonight will build anticipation."

With her cheeks burning and her body in a fervent state of need, Abby gingerly walked back into the pizza parlor. Nate prowled behind her, setting her teeth on edge, because all she craved, all she wanted was to sink into his heat and the explosive passion that was always present between them. By the time she arrived back at their booth, there was a loaded extra-large pizza on the table, and Tessa and Cybil were already chowing down.

"We couldn't wait. Hope you don't mind," Tessa sheepishly commented around a bite of pepperoni as Abby joined them in the booth.

"No, not at all," she replied, slipping a slice onto a plate. Nate's presence made it hard to concentrate. Abby went to great pains to avoid looking at him. If she did, she couldn't be held responsible for her actions—like dragging him back out into the alley and making him finish what he'd so blithely started. All throughout lunch, as she and Tessa discussed her aunt's doll collection and the prospective buyers, she felt him.

Then the police force stood up en masse and exited Papa Beau's. Abby's gaze fixated on Nate's buns. They were so expertly formed in his jeans, she could bounce a nickel off them.

"So now that he's gone and not within earshot, what happened outside, hmmm? I've never seen someone blush precisely that shade of red before," Tessa teased Abby with a knowing smirk.

Abby winced. "Oh, brother. Was it that obvious? Do you think anyone else noticed?" She whipped her head around, glancing at the other patrons in Papa Beau's, feeling like she was wearing a scarlet letter. No one was staring at her or paying her any heed. That was good. Maybe they hadn't noticed.

Cybil snorted as she chuckled. "Sweetie, the whole pizza joint noticed. You two are like magnets around each other and don't even realize it."

"You haven't told him you're not staying, have you?" Tessa accused her.

Guilt assuaged Abby, turning the pizza into lead in her stomach. She wiped the grease off her hands onto a napkin. "No. Until today, we hadn't spoken to each other since last weekend. And besides, nothing has been decided on any front. I don't even know what he and I are yet. It's not like we're dating. I mean we've done the hanky-panky but surely Nate has a bevy of women in this town lusting after him to choose from." She was deflecting—or attempting to. Abby recognized there was an expiration date fast approaching when she would have to come clean. But it wasn't today.

"That's exactly what you are doing with him. As far as I've seen, you're the only woman Nate has shown any interest in over the last year or so. Beyond that, I can't remember. What did he ask you outside, or did you do it in the alley?" Cybil asked with a curious, yet sympathetic glance.

He wasn't a serial dater. She was the only one Nate wanted. Warmth speared her system. Couldn't the guy have a flaw? Any flaw? He was honorable and steady, good with his hands, and could kiss her brainless in ten seconds flat. "To go on a date with him tonight. And no, we did not have sex in the alley. Sex with Nate takes a whole lot longer than the short time we were in the alley."

She made the comment before her brain realized what had come flying out of her mouth. See? The man short-wired her brain, maybe because she had sex on her mind—sex with *him* on her mind—which tended to eclipse anything else in her system. Her statement got their attention, and both sisters leaned in with smirks on their faces.

"Really, do tell about your marathon sexcapades," Tessa said, wiggling her eyebrows.

"Why don't you two tell me about your relationships? Tessa? Cybil? There has to be someone each of you are seeing."

"My ass has been grabbed so many times over at Smitty's, the next guy to do it is going to get clocked. It tends to keep the guys away when you're smacking them all the time. And other than that, my sex life is non-existent, at least with something that isn't battery powered, so I have to live vicariously through my friends," Cybil stated with a huff, pointing at Abby.

"Besides, we are not talking about my failed dating record. The last guy I hit on ran for the hills faster than his feet could carry him, and don't even get me started with online dating. We are here and discussing yours, so stop changing the subject, missy," Tessa warned Abby, batting her lashes expectantly for her response.

As much as she was coming to count on these two, Abby didn't want to discuss her potentially leaving Echo Springs and that she had not told Nate yet of the possibility. The alarm on her phone chimed a warning that her next class was in fifteen minutes.

She took that as her cue to exit, literally saved by the bell, and with a saccharine sweet smile, said, "Gotta go. I have a class still to teach in fifteen."

"Abby, we're only trying to help," Tessa murmured with understanding written all over her face.

"I know that. I will figure out a way to tell him, I promise. I just need to do it in my own time. Thanks for having lunch with me. I've got this one." Abby tossed down enough cash to cover lunch, plus the waitress's tip, then left the pizza joint without a backward glance.

The reckoning with Nate regarding their potential future was coming, much sooner than she liked. But for today, she just didn't want to worry about it. She wanted to enjoy having an attractive, sexy man take her out. And if that meant she was acting like a selfish coward, so be it.

Chapter Sixteen

From Old Man Turner's Journal:
No sex on the first date.

Abby dressed with care for their first official date, unsure whether the form-fitting, deep cobalt blue cocktail dress that stopped right above her knees was the best option. As far as she was concerned, the retirement party for his friend's mom didn't count. Not really, no matter how wonderful an evening it had been or how incredible the night afterwards. The main concern she had with the dress was how skintight the material was—as in: it displayed every curve and line, which meant she couldn't wear any panties. Even a thong would show a panty line. She knew that because she had tried a few different pairs of panties. So, she opted to go commando. The top of the dress was a halter style that left her shoulders bare and came with a built-in bra that supported her boobs quite nicely. So at least she didn't have to worry about that portion, and only had to contend with the no panties issue.

She debated the pros and cons of such a move, imagining all

the horrible situations that could potentially occur. Abby practiced sitting in the dress from a few different angles and positions, just to make sure that her commando experience wouldn't end up in a disaster lane. While it wasn't ideal, it worked, and although the likelihood of some big bad monster interrupting their date since she was being so reckless was a distinct possibility, she chose to think positively. She wanted tonight, one perfect night with Nate, before she interrupted the dream with her potential future reality.

The pièce de résistance of her outfit were her shoes. They were silver, strappy stilettos that one could compare to ice picks but which made her calves and butt look awesome. As long as she didn't trip, fall, break her neck, and come back to life as a brain-eating zombie, they were perfect.

She fastened her hair into an artfully arranged topknot with a few strands framing her face that would be easy for Nate to undo later at their afterparty. Then she applied makeup, especially around her eyes, creating a smoky-eye look that made the green in her hazel eyes pop while giving them a sultry, sex kitten appeal. But now that she was ready and waiting for Nate, Abby had bullfrogs hopping around in her stomach.

Perhaps it was because, after this date, their relationship would be like a real entity. She'd no longer be able to hide behind the flimsy excuses she'd given Tessa and Cybil earlier today. It would transform their connection from two people merely enjoying a physical relationship, into a deeper and potentially long-lasting connection. Even though he had staked his claim on her in front of his friends, this was different. She felt it in her bones. And it unnerved her composure. Fear riddled her. Nate mattered to Abby, and that scared the hell out of her. It was quite the shock to learn that she was the commitment-phobic one.

At the sound of the doorbell chiming, she grabbed her clutch purse, sliding her phone inside it, and headed downstairs. She inhaled a deep breath as she closed the remaining distance to the door, praying she didn't stumble in her ice-picks, and pasted a smile on her face. Then she opened the door.

Holy guacamole! The man is a walking wet dream.

Nate didn't just knock her socks off—if she were wearing any —he blasted them out of the solar system. His deep mauve dress shirt draped and flowed over the contours of his torso, emphasizing his broad shoulders and muscled chest. The smoky gray slacks were perfectly tailored, hugging his lean hips and powerful thighs. Gone was her mountain man and in his place was a suave, debonair hunk who left her panting with need. He reminded her of the men who would board the train in New Jersey each day bound for Manhattan, where they went to work at the stock exchange or some other multibillion-dollar corporation. But it was his smoldering gaze that did her in—while externally, her mountain man was missing, the blaze and heat emanating from him said that he was just lying in wait for tonight.

His sensual stare traveled the length of her body, practically undressing her with his eyes as he entered her house. Nate didn't say a word as he withdrew a bouquet of roses from behind his back. Except, he didn't have to, his face said it all: that he not only approved of what she had on but couldn't wait to get her out of her dress.

"Hi," Abby said. "Don't you look handsome?"

"I'll talk in a minute, 'cause I just lost the ability to think with you in that dress. Christ, Abby, you look good enough to eat."

Pleasure speared her chest and spread, igniting a fire in her blood at his words. She'd known the dress was the perfect choice for tonight. She couldn't wait until he discovered the whole commando situation happening underneath the dress—he'd really blow a gasket then.

"Ah, these are for you. No daisies or anything that may cause an allergic reaction this time."

"Thank you. Just let me put these in water and we can leave.

What did you have in mind for this evening?" she asked over her shoulder as she headed down the hall to the kitchen.

"At the present time, I can only think about getting you out of that dress," he asserted, his baritone rough and sexy with uninhibited longing as he followed her into the kitchen. She could feel his eyes never leaving her body, and she hid her smile. Score one point for the book nerd. When she'd finished arranging the roses in a vase and filled it with water, Nate's solid arms slid around her from behind. An unbidden image of him bending her over the counter sprang to mind and she bit her tongue to contain her moan. He whispered huskily into her ear, "I'm tempted to just toss you over my shoulder, take you upstairs, and not let either of us come up for air until morning."

Intoxicating desire pumped in her veins and she leaned back against him, then replied, "And if I told you I'd be okay with that scenario?"

"Don't tempt me," he growled and nipped the exposed skin of her shoulder. She hissed at the pleasure his touch ignited. And then her stomach rumbled noisily in a *Feed me, Seymour* type of way that made her groan internally. It definitely painted the exact opposite of the portrait she wanted to display.

Nate chuckled, his mouth against her neck in that one spot that drove her mad. "All right, message received loud and clear. Feed you first, before I make love to you all night."

Her body trembled.

"That would be a good idea," she murmured, her voice rough from the carnal imagery his words presented. She fought the urge to turn in to him because she wanted a night out with him. One night out in public with him before it all came crashing down.

He placed one more kiss on her neck that seared itself all the way into her bones before he retreated, putting some distance between their bodies. Then he said, "Whenever you're ready, we can head off."

"I'm ready," she said. Abby turned and slid her hand into his, shivering at the intensity of his stare. Then she led him back to the front door whereupon he escorted her outside. She locked the door behind them. Nate ushered her over to his Explorer and assisted her up into his cab, since that step up was a bit of a doozy, especially when a girl had toothpicks that masqueraded as shoes on her feet.

"So where are you taking me?" Abby asked, once they'd buckled in and Nate was navigating the small winding mountain road into town. She still wasn't this confident on these roads yet, and would never be if her future reality came to fruition. She shoved the dark thought away. Tonight was just for them.

"To the only nice place in town, unless we want to go to the nearby ski resort. Porto's Steakhouse, off Main Street. They have the best steaks you'll find without having to head into Denver. Not that we couldn't do that one night. I hope that works for you."

"That sounds like an excellent choice. I don't remember the last time I had a decent steak. So how was your day? Did you catch any bad guys?" She peered at him in the low light of his dashboard, enjoying studying his handsome face.

He shot her a half smirk. "Sadly, no. Other than a few parking tickets and two speeding teens who thought drag racing would be cool, the day was fairly uneventful. Out here, there's typically more paperwork to my police work than danger. Although on the weekends, if there's a rowdy crowd at Smitty's, things can get a bit dicey. But otherwise it's fairly uneventful and boring. You?"

"Well, I did get my dissertation submitted today, so there's that." And why wasn't she happier that she'd finally finished the damn thing? It had taken her three incredibly long years, researching, and reading, then researching some more as she wrote it.

"And what happens after you submit a dissertation?" Nate asked as they parked near the steakhouse.

"Well, my doctoral advisory board will read through it. The

three of them will make any final notes on what I might need to change or add, if there is anything. Then, when those are fixed, it will be submitted to the doctoral committee for review. After they have read my dissertation, I will have to head back to Cornell and defend it before the committee, which is on a pass, fail basis. If I pass then I get my doctorate, if I don't, then I spend another year working on the bloody thing."

"That's quite a process," Nate responded as he helped her climb out of the Explorer.

"It really is and I'm so ready to be done with it," she murmured.

"Then you'll pass and we will celebrate. I believe in you. I've never seen anyone work so hard," he said as he guided her into the restaurant with his hand on her elbow.

"Spying on me again, are we?" she asked with a raised brow as happiness radiated through her. Even when she thought he wasn't paying attention or avoiding her, he was still looking out for her.

"Always," he murmured next to her ear.

"Ah, Sheriff Barnes, we have your table ready." The hostess, a woman in her fifties with salt-and-pepper hair and a sturdy frame, pulled two menus out as she turned to have them follow her in.

Porto's seemed to be the hot spot for dates in town. Unlike the other local restaurants, where you'd find families and teenagers hanging in groups, here Abby spied mainly couples on their walk to their table. Nate said hello to a few people they passed and so did she. Abby was surprised how many town residents knew her name.

Dark cherry wood dominated the interior décor, from the gleaming hardwood floors to the wooden paneling lining the lower three feet of the restaurant walls. Above the paneling was a satin burgundy wallpaper that glimmered with the light spilling from the golden wall sconces. The dining room made Abby think of a turn-of-the-century drawing room, complete with a massive marble stone fireplace.

The square tables were covered with burgundy linen table-cloths and in the center of each, adding to the romantic under-tones of the venue, was a small, clear glass candle holder with a burgundy tealight flickering away behind the glass. She adored the place. And the delicious smells emanating from the kitchen made her mouth water in expectation.

"Here you are," the matronly hostess said, putting the menus on a table near the back.

"Thank you, Clara," Nate said, then drew Abby's chair out for her and seated her before sliding into the chair on her right. There would be no across the table gazing with Nate. She had a feeling it would be more along the lines of whispering naughty things in each other's ear. She'd try to restrain herself, but really, she had only to come within ten feet of Nate and could hardly think about anything except wanting to get naked with him.

"So what's good here?" Abby asked, flipping open the black binder style menu and staring at the rather impressive selection. They had a really decent wine list for a town in the middle of Colorado.

"The New York strip sirloin. It's done really well here."

"I will take your word for it, then."

A waiter by the name of Casey, who looked like he was twelve, took their order. The sirloin for both of them, salads, and a bottle of cabernet. When Casey strode off with their order, promising to return with their wine and some pumpernickel bread, Nate shifted his attention back to her. Abby sighed inter-nally when he threaded his fingers through hers. "Just so you know, we may have to forgo the second part of the date I had planned for tonight."

"Why's that?" Her internal panic button blared but she tried to hide it, keeping her smile in place. Had she done something wrong? Had Tessa and Cybil ratted her out? If so, she'd make damn sure her undead doll army rose from the dead tonight and attacked the town, starting with their place first.

"Well, because I had originally planned on the two of us going bowling. But I think, given the circumstances, we may need to reserve that for another night."

"Bowling, really? Why not? It's been ages since I've done that. Or we could go to Smitty's and I could kick your ass at pool again." She grinned at his deep rumble of laughter.

"Touché. We could. Except I'm not sure how I feel about taking you to Smitty's, since I will have to fend off every red-blooded male in the joint. I'm sure the mayor would frown on the sheriff beating up every able-bodied man who came within walking distance of you in that dress." His gaze dropped down, caressing her form, and blasted her with his hunger—not for food, but for her.

She refrained from fanning herself, just barely, and replied, "Who knew Sheriff Stud Muffin was such a charmer?"

"Sheriff Stud Muffin?" Nate asked, his eyes widening at the name, his dark brows nearly disappearing into his hairline, and Abby wanted to slink under the floorboards. See? The man messed with her internal combustion. She couldn't think straight when he was nearby and looking at her like she was a fine delicacy.

And she was just as bad. She'd been staring at the way his mouth moved and not really paying attention to the words that she was saying. How could she have let that moniker slip? Maybe because every time she was around the man, her ovaries took her system hostage and her brain stopped functioning at higher levels.

"Yeah, sorry, it's what I called you in my mind the night we first met."

"Oh, you mean when you were bludgeoning me with a golf club?" he joked with a wide smile on his handsome face.

She winced at the memory of that night. "Yeah. Did I ever say how sorry I was about that?"

"Stud Muffin, huh?" he remarked, a sly, carnal smirk dotting his handsome visage.

"Yeah, can we switch topics please? Are there any sports teams you want to tell me about in some championship I really don't care about?"

That earned her a bark of laughter from him as she sipped her wine.

The smell hit her first, like charred flesh mixed with burning cedar. A cloud of gray smoke poured from the kitchen into the dining room just as smoke detectors blared. Before anyone could move or panic, the sprinkler system kicked on, raining buckets of water from the ceiling overhead and dousing every person in the restaurant.

And that's when all hell broke loose. Diners' panicked screams and cries competed against the shrill din from the fire alarms. The crowd scrambled en masse to the front door to escape the smoke and water.

"Shit, let's get you out of here." Nate stood, apparently unfazed by the commotion, and assumed command. "Folks…" His voice boomed above the panicky crowd. "If all of you could file out in an orderly fashion into the parking lot while we get this handled…"

At the controlled order and calm in his voice, people responded to him. It was amazing. They shifted from a panicked crowd where someone was bound to get hurt into a fast moving, but organized procession to the door.

He had his phone to his ear as he helped her out of her seat. "This is Sheriff Barnes, badge number two-nine-four-five. There is a possible fire at Porto's Steakhouse on Main Street. I need you to send fire and EMT services to this location on the double."

With his hand on her elbow, he escorted her from the restaurant as the rest of the inhabitants did as he had instructed. Abby saw him through new eyes. He wasn't just her sexy-as-sin neighbor who made her weak-kneed anytime he cast a glance in her direction, and could remodel an entire home into a show piece that rivaled *Better Homes and Gardens*. Nate the Sheriff was the calm buffer amidst the storm, able to take charge during a crisis, and was the man others looked to for guidance. Once at his vehicle, he wrapped her shivering form in a blanket he had stowed in the back of his Explorer, then deposited her in the front cab.

"Stay here. I'll be back as soon as I can." Then he returned to the heart of danger and chaos.

Watching Nate in his official capacity as fire trucks and ambulances blazed onto the scene was the sexiest damned thing Abby had ever witnessed. The firefighters and EMT personnel all deferred to him as he directed what amounted to a three-ring circus. She could tell a few patrons were being treated for smoke inhalation as they had oxygen masks over their faces. She watched the diners who weren't injured give their statements to Nate's deputies and then get waved off to head home. One of the cooks was bandaged and loaded into a waiting ambulance. The firefighters doused the flames the sprinkler system hadn't extinguished.

In the parking lot, amidst the flashing lights, an older gentleman she'd noticed at the grocery store the other day stood with a woman Abby assumed was his wife. It was the hostess who had seated them earlier that night. Gray blankets were around their shoulders. The woman leaned against the gentleman for support and their faces were awash with devastation at the water and fire damage. They must be the owners of Porto's. Abby didn't know what had caught fire in the kitchen and felt awful for them.

She shivered as night settled and the temperatures dipped. And through it all, her Sheriff Stud Muffin was the damn rock of Gibraltar, never faltering or fumbling in the midst of chaos. If she hadn't already fallen for him, she would have in this moment. He was epic and solid, and he made her want things she had no business yearning for with him.

Abby wasn't certain how much time had passed before he

finally climbed into the cab with her on the driver's side and shot her a glance.

"Sorry about our date," he said, and she noticed the first signs of weariness on his face.

Leaning across the center console, she laid her palm against his cheek. It was her turn to soothe and take care of him. Her turn to be his rock. She murmured, "It's not your fault in the slightest. And I've gotta say, Sheriff, I'm impressed."

"Yeah?" He gave her a half grin and kissed her palm.

"Uh huh."

"Well, I guess we could try Smitty's if you—"

She kissed him, just a gentle, *I'm here for you*, light brush of lips, and then said, "Why don't we pick up some burgers and a six-pack? There's a horror marathon playing on cable this weekend."

He leaned his forehead against hers and said, "That sounds like the best plan I've heard all week. Deal."

They stopped at The Emporium and grabbed some loaded burgers and fries to go, then picked up a cold six-pack at the Quick Stop Gas Mart before they headed home.

"I need to let Rufus out," Nate said apologetically when they finally pulled into his drive.

"Why don't we eat and finish our date at your place tonight? As long as you have cable, we should be good there," she offered. It wasn't like there was anyone waiting for her back at her house. Well, other than a possessed doll army, and of the two, she'd pick Rufus as her preferred third wheel companion for the night.

"Most women are not this easygoing," Nate commented as he helped her out of the Explorer while she held their dinner and drinks. But there was also deep in the bone appreciation in his gaze as he stared at her, like he had expected her to blast him over a disaster of an evening that wasn't his fault. Poor guy. Made her wonder about the women who had come before her.

She shrugged and gave him a saucy grin. "I'm not most

women. I'm a firm believer in shit happens, you just have to roll with it."

"No, you're definitely not," he murmured, studying her as he opened his front door.

Rufus rocketed out and pranced around, sniffing at them in greeting for all of two seconds before he darted into the yard to do his business.

"Why don't you head on in. I'll get him squared away," Nate said and brushed his lips against her forehead. Then his stare flicked to Rufus nosing about the bushes, mindful to keep the fur ball from running off into the woods, scanning the area to ensure there weren't any predators around. As big as Rufus was, against a black bear or mountain lion, he'd be mincemeat.

While Nate took care of Rufus, Abby headed inside and arranged their dinner on the wooden coffee table in the living room. It wasn't five-star dining, but it looked and smelled delicious. They were both starved at this point, anyhow. With a mild groan, she stepped out of her heels. Then Rufus bounded into the room to say hello and sniff at their dinners, Nate trailing in behind him.

"I hate to say I'm sad to see those go," Nate said, his eyes on her shoes as he approached.

Abby handed him a beer and replied, "Yeah, they look great, but after a few hours they're a killer. Not like *Freddy Krueger* killer, mind you, but more *Shaun of the Dead*."

He chuckled and shook his head. "I'll bet. Let me feed Rufus and I'll join you in a minute."

When he returned, they relaxed on his couch and ate in near silence. The burger tasted like sheer blissful heaven. Rufus finished his bowl of chow and trotted in to watch them. It was comical as he swiveled his head back and forth between them, drool leaking from the corners of his mouth. His expression clearly said: *Puh-lease, I know you are gonna give me some. You were gone all night and I was worried because you are my master and the lady I love to lick.* Abby obliged and tossed him a few French fries. By the time they finished dinner, she felt awesome, her belly finally satiated, and the beer created a warmth in her veins. Although it could be the man at her side too. She snuggled against Nate as he turned the television on, and one of her favorite slasher films, *Creeper*, was playing.

"I can't believe you like this stuff," Nate remarked. His arm around her felt wonderful. She wanted to sink into him but knew he needed some entertainment after tonight and she planned to give it to him. In more ways than one.

"Just wait, it gets so good," she promised.

"Abby?"

"Hmm?" She lifted her face toward his and held her breath at the tenderness in his gaze, mixed with another emotion she couldn't name. Yet it created a fluttering in her chest and drove the air from her lungs.

"Thanks for being you," he said, caressing her cheek with the backs of his knuckles. His simple touch scorched a path into her heart.

"That's the nicest thing anyone has ever said to me." She leaned her face into his caress. Considering her family's propensity to tell her precisely where they believed she was failing in life, and the direction she should recalibrate her life to head in, having someone who cared and liked her as she was, without attempting to change her or mold her into what they thought she should be, left her reeling and not a little awed.

"Really?"

She nodded her head and instead of explaining, she reached her hands up, sliding them around his neck, and tugged his mouth down to hers.

This time, Abby kissed him, pouring sentiments she couldn't voice, and didn't know if she ever could, into her kiss. Her favorite part of the film, where the murdering fiend chases the heroine, was playing, and she couldn't care less. This man had in record time become the sole focal point of her existence. And she emptied herself into her kiss.

The movie forgotten, she shifted on the couch until she was straddling his thighs. The action made her skirt ride high. Nate's hands skimmed her bare legs in a whispered caress. Shivers of pleasure whirled into her core like a funnel cloud forming. He murmured against her lips, "Did you wear one of those sexy thongs again?"

She nipped at his lips, pulled back a bit so she could watch his expression, and said, "Even better. I'm not wearing any at all."

His gaze shifted from turned-on to *holy hotness*, chock full of lust. "Christ, Abby."

His hands toyed with the hem of her dress for all of two seconds before sliding underneath to cup her naked butt. His mouth covered hers in a sweltering kiss that drugged her with his seductive lips. They brushed against her mouth, claiming her, possessing her, and her entire system became enveloped in flames. She craved him, and she was as terrified as the movie heroine screaming bloody murder in the background. There was no walking away from what she felt for him without bruises. If she had to leave Echo Springs, it was going to rip her burgeoning heart to smithereens. Then she shoved her fears away. They were for another day. Right now, the man, her man, was kissing her brainless. Her hands trailed to his shirt and Abby unbuttoned the silken material. She glided her hands underneath the fabric as she exposed his firm, ripped torso. She loved his chest, how the muscles rippled and quivered beneath her fingertips.

"Gah," she exclaimed when Nate stood with her in his arms. Her hands slid up to grip his neck.

"Hold on to me. I just want to move this to the bed. I want you in my bed," he growled.

Abby couldn't have agreed with him more. The movie was completely forgotten. And since his bed was in the corner of the living room, there was less travel time to get there. With her body plastered around his like a second skin, he carted her over to the king-sized bed, which was swathed in earth-toned blankets. As he walked, he unzipped the back of her dress. She loved how efficient he was when it came to divesting them of their clothes. When they reached his bed, he tugged the dress up over her head —with her help, of course.

"You should always be naked," he said like a benediction as he laid her back on his bed, his eyes caressing her form with hunger and need pulsing in their dark blue depths. Nate shoved his shirt off, then stripped away the rest of his clothes. Before he joined her in bed, he sheathed himself.

"I know it might be bad form, but tonight, I just need you," he explained as he knelt above her, searching her face.

She reared up and grabbed his neck, nipped his bottom lip, then said, "We can worry about finesse later."

"Thank God," he said, slipping between her legs.

One minute Abby was empty, and the next, she overflowed, filled to the brim and surrounded by Nate. She moved with him, rocking her hips. He claimed her mouth for a drugging, thorough kiss that left her breathless.

And then he stilled. She was about to speak up and lobby a protest when he roared, "Rufus! Get your nose out of there!"

Abby couldn't help it. She laughed. "Where was his nose?"

Nate shot her an exasperated glance with his brow raised as he withdrew from her body, then shoved the mammoth dog off the bed. The image of pissy man and recalcitrant beast staring each other down only made her laugh harder. Rufus had goosed him. Tears of mirth ran down her face.

"I'll deal with you in a minute," Nate declared with a heated glare her way as he vaulted off the bed. Then he hauled a whining Rufus into the nearby bathroom.

Abby had just about calmed herself when Nate strutted back in. The vexation he wore on his face was comical, and she erupted into further peals of laughter. Her sides ached. She couldn't stop laughing. Tears streamed down her cheeks. He climbed back into bed and said, "How would you like it if Rufus put his nose on your bare ass?"

"Not something I want to experience, thank you. You've gotten enough for the both of us. Or should I say a nose full?"

"I'm never going to live this down, am I?" he replied with consternation. Nate readjusted his big body, shifting until he was back between her thighs. Her hands glided up his chest and he slid inside her. She gasped as her body welcomed him back.

"Nope," she replied with a moan as her tears dried, trailing her fingers soothingly over his back, loving the shiver of his muscles until she gripped his butt. "But I promise, it will remain between you, me, and Rufus."

"Thanks for that." He gave her a lopsided grin.

And then he thrust deep, seating himself fully inside her. The laughter died in her throat. Her body responded with pulsating need, her hips canting and writhing beneath him as he drew her into the eye of the heated storm. There was no end and no beginning as they moved as one. Nate's fingers threaded through hers, fusing their connection as they raced toward the glistening peak of ecstasy.

When her climax finally hit, Nate was there to draw it out. He turned one into two as he played her body with all the finesse of a conductor, staying with her as he found his release, his body trembling and straining in her arms. He rocked within her until the final strains of their quaking tremors subsided. Cupping her face between his hands, Nate brushed a tender, soul-stirring kiss against her lips. The kiss was everything. It brought tears to her eyes. He moved her in ways she never thought possible. And the most terrifying prospect was that she never wanted it to end.

Abby was silent as he withdrew from her body. A wealth of emotions swelled inside her and she didn't know what to do with them because she had never felt their like before. She wanted to cling to him and never let him go. And she was more afraid than she had ever been in her life, terrified that he was the only one who would ever make her feel this way. With a last lingering, satisfied stare, Nate slipped from the bed and strode to the bathroom to dispose of the condom and allow Rufus out of confinement. She was quiet when he padded back into the living room and shut off the television that had moved on to the next horror film. Rufus settled himself with a *harrumph* on the floor by the bed. Nate shut off the lights and climbed back in beside her, where he gathered her into his arms. She went willingly, needing the connection as he tucked her against his side.

Abby drifted asleep, knowing the tethers she'd tried to place around her heart to keep herself from falling had snapped at some point tonight. Love for Nate overwhelmed her, silencing her voice with the sheer magnitude of her feelings.

Love wasn't part of her plan.

Chapter Seventeen

From Old Man Turner's Journal:
It's the little things, the small daily actions that matter most.

Abby cracked open her eyes. Early morning light peered in golden beams through the curtains. She was warm and completely cocooned in the king-sized bed as a chorus of snores from two different males played near her ears—two males she was sandwiched between. One male was big and naked, the length of his muscled form snug against her back, acting as her own personal space heater, and his hand lay against her abdomen as he spooned her. The other was nearly as large, covered in black fur, his head resting beside hers on the pillow, his back cuddled up against her so that she was inadvertently spooning him.

She couldn't help the smile as it formed.

Out of all the things she'd expected and hoped to find when she drove cross-country, this was not one of them. She loved them both. *We are talking big, crazy, stupidly in love with them.* It permeated every molecule of her being and expanded exponentially from her heart in all directions. And didn't it just bite the big one that she had no clue what to do about either of them?

Granted, Nate was a bit of a package deal with the big furball. Where Nate went, so too did Rufus. But the black one was easy and harmless to love, returned that love in spades and asked nothing in return but a few belly rubs and dog biscuits. Nate was the wild card in her deck, the unexpected prize for her leap of faith and she wanted to keep him. Build a bubble around this perfect time and keep the outside world from penetrating so that it was just the two of them—well, three. She'd always wanted a dog but in her parents' home, dogs were considered messy and required time they felt was better spent climbing the academic political ladder. So, getting to love Rufus and spend time with him was the scoop of ice cream on her slice of warm apple pie.

Unable to resist his soft, short fur, Abby scratched Rufus behind the ears, and he did a giant wriggle, pulling the covers with him until his chocolate eyes stared at her, his tongue hanging out, happily panting his doggy breath in her face. "Morning, sweetie. Could I tempt you into moving so I can get up?"

If Abby didn't know better, she'd have said he laughed at her and shook his head no. In his eyes, he said: *Nope, now that you are here and have spent the night, I'm not letting you leave, ever.* Rufus had decided he wanted to snuggle, her bladder be damned, and was now acting like a saner version of Kathy Bates in *Misery* in his adoration.

Then Nate's arm around Abby tightened, his hand slid up and cupped her left breast. She hissed at the delicious sensations his touch engendered against her sensitive flesh. He nuzzled her neck, his unshaven stubble rasping against her skin, and she broke out in goosebumps just as Rufus laid an *I love you so much* wet, sloppy tongue kiss against her cheek, inadvertently catching Nate across his jaw.

"Yuck, Rufus. What have I told you about sleeping in my

bed?" Nate grimaced.

Rufus rolled his eyes with a look that said: *Oh please, don't you know I'm always on the bed when you're not here? Besides, she's mine, I slept with her first.* The dog snuggled more tightly against Abby, almost like he was attempting to burrow against her. She didn't mind. There hadn't been a whole lot of hugs when she was growing up, or in her life in general, and it filled her with a warm, fuzzy contentment.

"Jesus, Rufus, get down," Nate commanded, tucking Abby more firmly against his body while he and Rufus played a sort of tug-of-war over her. She giggled and that made Rufus ecstatic. It inadvertently provided Nate the upper hand and he was able to maneuver Rufus onto the floor. With a loud *harrumph* and blast of doggy breath, Rufus slumped onto the floor by the bed with one of his squeaky toys. In all the commotion, Abby had been abandoned entirely and was about to crawl out when Nate lay back down beside her.

Cocking her head to one side, she asked with a tiny smirk, "So, should I leave the room for the two of you with your bromance?"

Nate tugged her back into his arms and she noticed how very up he was now.

"No, please don't," he murmured, nuzzling her collarbone, his lips grazing the sweet spot. Whenever he brushed his five o'clock shadow or lips against that one spot, she was willing to do whatever he wanted, even if it meant making a sacrifice to the devil and raising the undead doll army next door.

"I'm just saying, between last night and again this morning —" She gasped, her eyes crossing from the pleasure of his open-mouthed kisses over her neckline. *Sweet Jesus.*

"Haha, you're very funny." He ran his hand down her side, unerringly close to her apex, his fingers teasing along her hip bone, dipping down. Anticipation hummed deliciously in her bloodstream.

"I like to think so. Can I ask you a really important question?" She cast him a deadly serious look.

At her expression, his exploration of her body stalled. A wary look entered Nate's eyes and he nodded. "Sure."

"You do have coffee, right?"

Nate chuckled and resumed his seductive caresses over her abdomen. "As a matter of fact, I do."

Hallelujah! No sacrifices would have to be made. She quipped, "And what does a girl have to do to get a cup around here?"

His eyes heated to thermonuclear levels and he said huskily, "I'll show you."

"Can you show me after I use your bathroom?" As much as she didn't want to interrupt their morning in bed, she couldn't help it.

He sighed, gave her a swift kiss—just a simple brush of his lips over hers—and said, "I'll join you in there, after I let Rufus out."

"What? Why?"

"We may as well put the shower to good use." He wiggled his eyebrows, his eyes blazing innuendo, and gave her what could be called the king of sensual smiles.

Her belly fluttered. The man made her weak-kneed, and her breath clogged in her throat as he winked at her and slid from the bed. Nate stood, comfortable and confident in his naked glory, his powerful and sleek, muscled sinew on display. Her gaze lowered to the part of him that brought her so much pleasure. His shaft bobbed, fiercely erect as he strutted the short distance from the living room to the front door to let Rufus outside. Hunger and need stirred within Abby. She licked her lips and inhaled a deep steadying breath until she was certain her knees wouldn't buckle from the force of her desire.

And that was all tangled up with her new-found feelings for him. Biting her lower lip, she steeled herself as she climbed out of bed, then padded into the bathroom to relieve herself. Nate's promise to join her swimming in her mind, when she'd finished taking care of bodily functions, she switched the shower on.

The bath was a stand-up stall enclosed on three sides, the walls tiled in a cobalt and gray pattern. She closed the glass door, sighing as she stood underneath the hot spray.

She felt good—physically, at least, she was satisfied and content. Nate made her burn and touched her heart as no one had done before. The love she held for him left her dazed and unsure of the path forward. She'd lived her life by following her intellect—at least she had until she'd rebelled against her parents' life plan for her and left the world of science. So, she had been attempting to live a more fulfilling life with passion and zeal, when in reality, she'd discovered a lot more of the same humdrum existence. That didn't mean she didn't love literature, she did, but it had taken on a dull, repetitive sheen, where all she could do was ponder whether this was it for her: a stale, uneventful, boring yet safe life.

Inheriting Evie's home had been a godsend. It had broken her out of her insular shell and provided her with a place in which to decide her path forward. And then Nate had invaded her aunt's home on that very first night and upended the entire paradigm of her life. He'd taken up residence in her heart, her mind, and altered the fabric of her being. Could she really give that up and return to the existence she'd had before she arrived? Spend the rest of her days at an institution that would demand excellence from her and end up leeching her passion for life?

Nate entered the bathroom and shut the door behind him, ensuring that Rufus, who was whining on the other side at being excluded, wouldn't follow him in. Her body attuned to Nate's as he stepped inside the glass enclosure, and Abby bit her lip to contain her moan. The man was perfect and gorgeous, and she couldn't seem to get enough of him.

He crowded her back against the tile and she shivered. All thoughts of getting clean evaporated. Nate lowered his head until his mouth hovered over hers and his hungry, dark gaze bored into her.

Her hands splayed over his chest, slid around to his back, and she sighed as she felt his muscles flex and bulge. "Nate, I—"

Her words were cut short as his mouth covered hers and she simply turned into putty in his hands. It was a while before Abby had another thought enter her mind that wasn't consumed by and with Nate.

When they exited the bathroom, limp and sated, Nate let her borrow a pair of his boxers and a Henley tee that dwarfed her but also protected her skin while they made breakfast together at the stove. The scent of bacon and French toast filled his kitchen. Nate, being such an alpha, deemed the bacon his territory, which was fine by her. Abby's French toast was near legendary in her family and she couldn't wait to see Nate's expression at first bite. He'd be her slave after that, which wouldn't be a hardship to handle at all. Plus, making it put her closer to the coffeemaker.

Ah. She sniffed the dark brew and then all but inhaled that first glorious cup of steaming goodness.

"You really do love coffee," Nate murmured, studying her as she helped herself to a second cup.

"Coffee equals life, my good man. Without it, I don't do the walking, the talking, or functioning of any kind, really." Abby was pretty certain if the world ran out of coffee, she'd have no problem starting the nuclear apocalypse, because truly, life wasn't worth living without it.

"I'll make sure to keep my supply stocked." He shot her a smile while he removed crispy strips of bacon onto a plate.

"I'd appreciate that. But what do you do when you run out?" The mere thought of not having coffee readily available was an unfathomable idea. She'd already been making plans to head back to Gundry's Bulk Superstore and stock up on more of that staple for winter. She figured she could stockpile a whole shelf in her basement hoard with nothing but extra coffee. The world would keep spinning if she had a fully stocked supply of her favorite coffee bean because if she didn't, and happened to run out, she would consider summoning a demon to destroy the planet. Coffee equaled life.

He shrugged his massive, sexy, bare shoulders, then replied rather nonchalantly, "I usually just wait until I reach the station."

She gasped and remarked, "People would die if I had to wait that long."

"You do realize you are telling an officer your plans to commit murder should you not have coffee when you wake up."

"No jury would convict me," she assured him, withdrawing the pan with their French toast from the oven.

Nate raised a cocky brow and said, the hint of a smile hovering on his face, "I'll keep that in mind. What are your plans today?"

"Well, if you aren't doing anything, I was hoping I could help you upstairs," she said. This was the first free day she had where she didn't have her dissertation to work on, and while there were papers to grade, along with other tasks to complete for her classes at Echo Springs Community College, she wasn't going to worry about those today.

"You want to help me with the remodeling upstairs?" he asked, his voice full of skepticism.

"Sure, why not? I may not be able to put up drywall, but I can take instructions, and I have painted a room before." Once, a long time ago, and not well, but he didn't need to know that. It gave her an excuse to watch him in action.

"Well, if that's what you want, who am I to stop you?" he said, his bemused gaze studying her like she was playing a prank on him.

"You couldn't," she murmured, carrying their plates over to the table. Nate joined her and said, "I could try to distract you with other activities."

A slow burn engaged in her lower extremities. She sighed at the mix of sugary carbs and crispy bacon. "Perhaps, but I'd still like to help out."

After breakfast, Abby ran home next door for a change of

clothes and then headed back to Nate's. They worked together for the better part of the day, until Abby just couldn't lift her arms anymore. She'd held drywall up while he positioned it in the future master bathroom, using a nail gun to attach it to the studs and wooden frame he'd built. She helped him carry two-by-fours into the smaller bedrooms that were nothing but open frames at this point.

Later, when they took a break, they sat near Rufus on the floor in the master bedroom, and Nate handed her a bottle of water. Abby spied the journal sitting on top of his radio.

"What's that?" She gestured in the general direction with her water bottle.

"Old Man Turner's journal. He's the former owner of this house."

"And he left it here?" Why would someone leave a part of themselves behind like that?

"Oh, I think it was done on purpose. It was left on an inlaid bookshelf between the bathroom and bedroom that had been drywalled over. I found it when I was demolishing the wall."

"So if you hadn't been remodeling, you never would have found it." Weird. Why would someone leave a journal behind for others to find one day?

"Pretty much," Nate said, taking a long draught of water. She watched the way his throat muscles worked and had to divert her lustful thoughts. As much as she wanted to do nothing but make love with the man, all day and all night—not that he would be opposed to that suggestion, of course—Abby knew if they had any chance of being something, they couldn't be in the bedroom all the time. This was her way of determining if there was substance and depth to their relationship outside the bedroom. They were already so compatible in that arena that they could give lessons.

"Well, what does he say in it?" she asked, curious about the contents.

"He talks about his love affair with your aunt, among other

things."

What? "No, get out. Aunt Evie? As my dad described her, the crazy spinster who never married, Evie?"

"Yeah, it was pretty serious too. He asked her to marry him and everything."

"Really? Well, what happened?" Evie had never married. What had happened? Why had she chosen to live her life alone? And why, if they loved one another, had they lived next door to each other?

"I was getting to that, but life, mainly, intervened and ended up separating them." Nate glanced at her with a wealth of meaning. His gaze was hot and suffused with emotion. If she had been standing, her knees would have given out.

"Read it to me." She was dying to know what had happened to her aunt's relationship. Her dad had never said boo about it, which meant he probably hadn't known. Then again, Dr. Phillip Callier the Fourth didn't consider much worth his time outside his physics seminars and lab work, including his daughter. She grimaced. She wasn't like them; her life was filled with passion and an exuberance for life he'd never displayed.

"You sure?" Nate asked, picking up the mahogany leather journal.

"Yep." She snuggled against his side, staring at the worn leather as he opened it. The book smelled old and a bit musty, a scent she had adored since she was a child. Abby listened as Nate's deep baritone filled the room.

"I was barely into my first campaign in Europe when I received a letter from Evelyn. There are times in life where a tragedy will define your life, alter it into something else. This was mine. Evie, my beautiful fiancée whom I loved more than life itself, had miscarried our child. Half a world away, and all I wanted to do was hold my precious Evie. It is said that men don't cry. Well, I'm here to tell you that we do. The promise of that child, with all the ugliness happening in the world, had kept me sane.

"I lost something that day, more than just the babe. Maybe it was an innocence that had yet to die off in war. Perhaps it was the belief that good

always triumphed over evil for decent people. Although, looking back now, I think in some respects, it was a part of myself and hope for the future that died that day, along with our unborn child. Knowing that our child, the proof of the love Evie and I had shared, would never take its first breath, crushed a part of my soul that I still have never regained.

"And it wasn't just the promise of that child I lost that day, but my precious Evie too. For, you see, in order to save Evie's life as she miscarried, the doctors had to remove parts of her uterus. After that, she would never be able to bear a child. Her letter that day was a double whammy of grief as eviscerating as the bombs that fell around us. She called off our engagement, told me to move on and find another woman more suitable, one who could bear my children with ease. She had been discharged from her service and was moving away from Echo Springs. She asked me to let her go and not try to find her.

"There were days after I received that letter when I wanted to die. A part of me did die. It was as if, upon opening that fateful letter, all the vitality and perseverance for living had been sucked from my body. I moved through the next few months of my life like the walking wounded, not really existing, just putting one foot in front of the other. Men died all around me, and none of it fazed me.

"While I served in Europe with the United States Seventh Division Army as we landed in Sicily in 1943, I felt like my life had ended already, and I was rather reckless. I considered it divine providence that I was destined to die on the battlefield and if I could take out a couple Nazis in the process, then that's what I would do. When I think back about that time, and remember just how hollow I was, I am actually thankful for it. It removed my fear of death, and instead of getting me killed, it did the exact opposite. It saved me.

"During our campaign in Italy, I was wounded by enemy fire. Three bullets in my left leg—one of which, had it have been two inches farther over, would have hit an artery, and my story would have ended then and there.

"But it didn't. I survived, cursing my rotten luck when I wanted to die. But something was keeping me tethered here. It was while I was cussing my very existence, doing my damnedest to join the rest of my brethren who fell that day and whose bodies were being shipped home in pine boxes, that I met

Lila. She was a nurse from San Diego, and she brought me back to life. She, more than anything, helped heal both my body and my heart.

"That didn't mean I forgot about Evie. She was always in the back of my mind and in my heart. But Lila resurrected me from the depression that had taken hold the day Evie left my life.

"I need to say now that I did, in my way, love Lila. Was she the great love of my life? No. That distinction had already occurred, and it was Evie. Even when I fell for Lila, I knew in my soul that there was a part of me that would forever belong to Evie. That doesn't mean I loved Lila less, just differently. But Lila helped me recover, and we both stayed in Europe through the end of the war. I didn't see any fighting after that, and helped serve in the medical unit.

"When the war ended in 1945, Lila and I were married. I knew the moment our vows were said that I had made a mistake. But I was a man of honor and I held my vow sacred. We settled in Lila's hometown of San Diego. It's where our son, Charles, was born in 1946. That was one of the most precious days of my life. It's a humbling and, I'll admit, rather terrifying experience to hold your child in your arms that first time. There's no love greater, or anything else quite like it.

"Over the next decade, we gave Charles two sisters, Rebecca and Marjorie, who gave their big brother a run for his money. Lila and I, while we didn't have the flash-burn, all-consuming love that Evie and I had shared, shared something that was steadfast and true. In the end, we loved one another but were more each other's companions than lovers.

"In early September of 1965, a storm, Hurricane Emily, moved in up the coast from Baja California, dumping torrents of rain on our city. Charles was driving his mother and sisters home from school that day when a truck lost control and hydroplaned into their vehicle. My dear sweet Lila was killed on impact. Charles sustained a concussion, a broken shoulder, and severe internal bleeding.

"It's one kind of pain to lose a spouse and partner, quite another when it's your child. I was there when Charles emitted his first squalling cry, and I was there to hold his hand when he took his last breath. Both of my girls, thankfully, only sustained minor cuts and bruises, but after we buried Charles and Lila, I moved us back to my old hometown of Echo Springs. I thought it

would be good for the girls to have the change of scenery, and as my mother was still alive, I knew that, as a single parent, I could use the help with two teenage girls.

"It was back in Echo Springs—now middle-aged, with more years behind me than before me—that I had my world turned upside down yet again. We had survived the rather brutal winter in our new home in town, and temperatures had finally crossed into spring-like territory, so I took the girls for a drive to one of my favorite spots. It was where Evie and I had spent so much time together in years past. It was on our way up to the lake that I spied the land where the old shack had been, where Evie and I had stowed away in that ramshackle wooden place during a freak snowstorm. The hunter's shack was gone. Now, there was a row of Victorian two-story homes. And in front of one house, where I knew the shack had stood, was a lone woman, her golden head cocked at an angle as she sat at her easel with her paints, contemplating the skyline beyond.

"It was my Evie."

Nate closed the journal. "I think that's enough for now, don't you?" He wiped the tears from Abby's cheeks that she hadn't even realized were there.

"It's just so sad. I never knew that Evie couldn't have children. I just always thought what my dad had told me; that she was a spinster who never married and was crazy. Instead, she had loved and lost in ways I know my father would never understand." Once again, Abby felt her buttons burn over her father's narrow-minded, unemotional viewpoint.

"It is tragic, but they did see each other again. Old Man Turner lived here, right next to your aunt, for forty years." Nate ran his hand comfortingly over her arm.

"Yeah, but what happened? We should read some more." Evie had chosen to walk away from the man she loved, and Abby had to know if things worked out for them in the end. Especially when she was still trying to determine the right direction for herself. Her head wanted one direction and her heart, well, she knew it existed because it was clamoring to be heard and to stay here.

224

"Not tonight." He kissed her temple as he bookmarked the page and set the journal back on top of the radio.

"But why not?" she commented, reaching for the book, but Nate caught her hand and lifted it to his mouth, where he placed a light kiss on her knuckles.

"Because what I'm gleaning from Turner's story is that you have to grab joy and life by the throat. Not to waste time over trivialities and things that don't matter. And because I'm hungry, and not just for food." He kissed her, and the passion was like a pressure cooker exploding and walloping her. Desire, unbidden and uncontrolled, raged hotter than any forest fire and she tangled her tongue with his as he covered her mouth. His kiss reverberated clear to her soul and she prayed that he was as moved by the combustible passion between them as she.

Nate was right. The journal wasn't going anywhere tonight. And Abby craved the affirmation, that her feelings might be returned and reflected in his gaze, sealing her choice once and for all. He nipped her bottom lip, and her stomach rumbled, causing a smile to spread across his lips. She lifted her head and said, "Okay, feed me and then take me to bed."

"As you wish." His eyes simmered with longing as he gave her another kiss, just a brief brush of his lips against hers that made her shiver. Nate released her and stood, then held his hand out to her. She took it without question. Together, they headed downstairs for the evening, bantering back and forth while they made tacos for dinner.

They were at the table, enjoying soft tacos and beer when Nate asked, "What does your family think about your horror film obsession?"

"It tends to put me in the category of one of their science experiments. Then again, it's kind of the way they view my entire existence." She took a swig of her beer.

"And why is that?" He cocked a dark brow as he studied her.

"Because I'm the proverbial black sheep that has never really fit in," she said, looking down at her plate with her half-eaten meal.

"Abby, I'm sure they love you," he scoffed.

"They do, in their way, but they don't approve of me and my life choices. They aren't the warmest people in the world. For the longest time, I thought the lack of emotion was in me, that it was something about me that made them so cold and distant. It wasn't until I was in undergraduate that I realized it was them. And if it wasn't for Evie encouraging me, I never would have broken free of the mold they wanted to place me in."

"I don't know. I think you would have, eventually. You're too strong to have allowed it to continue forever. I'm proud of you. Not everyone has the gumption to go after what they want, especially with parents pressuring you to do otherwise."

"Is that how you became a cop?" she asked, desperately needing to change the subject from her family. It only depressed her, and that was the last thing she wanted to be tonight.

Nate shook his head. "Quite the opposite. My dad lit out on us when I was seven. I don't remember him much, and haven't had any contact with him since. My mom was dealt a crappy hand, and through those circumstances she became an alcoholic. She drank through any extra money that came into the house, and was constantly getting into trouble with the police here, but the old sheriff took pity on her. He let things slide, more than he should have, because he knew my sister and I would have been tossed into the system if he put my mom away. And he had plenty of opportunities."

She laid her hand over his. "I'm so sorry, Nate. That couldn't have been easy."

"It wasn't, and I was a bit of a shit-stirrer myself as a teen. It was the old sheriff who sat me down in my senior year of high school and told me that I had two options. Either I cleaned up my act and went on to become someone, or I could continue down the path I was on and end up doing hard time when the law finally caught up with me."

"I can't see you on the other side of the law." She looked him over, trying to imagine him as a teenager, capable of pulling juvenile stunts that would land him in jail.

"Believe it. I arrived home after that to find my mom in a pool of her own vomit, passed out drunk, and had to call nine-one-one. I knew then I didn't want to end up like my mother, and that the sheriff was right. He'd done more for me than my own father had ever done. So I went to college, because I wanted the four year degree in criminal justice before I went and applied at the police academy," he said, picking up their empty plates and taking them over to the kitchen sink.

Abby followed him over to the sink with the empty beer bottles. Just when she thought she couldn't be more impressed by him, he proved her wrong. And here she'd thought her own stuffy, emotionless upbringing had been hard. At least her parents had been there. She might not agree with their methods, but she'd never wanted for a thing, had grown up with a comfortable wealth, and never once had to worry about their wellbeing.

She cupped his face in his hands and turned his gaze toward her. "You're pretty amazing, you know that?"

Warmth filled his gaze. "You think?"

She nodded. "Yeah, I do. Why don't you leave those until morning and come into the living room with me?"

"I did promise to ravish you, didn't I?" he said as a wicked grin spread over his face.

She slid her arms around his neck. "That you did. Have I ever told you about my handcuff fantasy?"

His eyes darkened. "No, you haven't. But that can be arranged."

With that, he scooped her up in his arms, the dishes forgotten in the sink, and carried her into the living room. Nate did as he had promised—he kept doing that—and made love with her until the wee hours of the night, when they fell asleep entwined with each other.

Chapter Eighteen

From Old Man Turner's Journal:
Enjoy your time together, for every breath is a precious gift.

The next two weeks for Abby were as close to idyllic as she'd ever experienced. During the day, she and Nate went their separate ways, he off to play a big bad sexy sheriff while she taught freshman co-eds about the literary works of Emily, Edgar, and Walt. In the evenings, they met for dinner either at her house or his—mainly his—where, after they'd eaten, they worked side-by-side on remodeling his second floor until one of them could no longer stand it and dragged the other into bed, or the shower, or really any other semi-stationary surface in the house. Who knew kitchen tables and the laundry room could be so multi-functional? Abby helped Nate choose the different shades of paint for the bedrooms, tiles for the bathrooms, and the lighting fixtures.

Then there was the night in which they had gotten carried away with paint brushes. It had taken Abby days to remove all the mint green color from her hair. But holy smokes, it had been one hot night.

And then each night, after they read another entry in Bill Turner's journal and they discovered more about the love he had for Abby's aunt, Nate took her to bed and made love with her into the wee hours of the night. Sometimes they would talk, like last night.

She had lain, limp and sated, curled up against Nate, with her head resting on his strong shoulder. Her hands grazed the tiny whorls of dark hair covering his chest.

"I have a question for you. Why were you unattached when we met? I mean, you're easygoing, honorable, can hold your own in a battle of wits," she said, propping her chin up on his chest so that she could look at him.

"Don't forget, a stud muffin to boot." He gave her a lopsided grin.

"That too," she admitted, the corners of her mouth twitching.

He sighed, his fingers lightly stroking over her back. "I wasn't a monk before you barreled into my life and clobbered me with that nine-iron, but I also haven't been serious about anyone in quite a while. During college, and the first few years afterward, I was with Stacy. We met freshman year at the University of Boulder at a frat party and were inseparable after that. After college, we both tried to make our relationship work, even though it hadn't for quite some time. However, when it came down to living in the real world, she decided she didn't want to be a cop's wife. She hated the hours I had to put in and the fear of something happening to me. It's not an unusual response in my profession."

"And there's been no one else?" Abby found it so hard to believe because to her, he was incredible. Did he have flaws? Sure. He was rather stubborn and could be domineering, but he was also kind, caring, always willing to lend a hand. And he looked like a god naked.

He shook his head. "Not that I've been serious about. My job comes with risks, Abby. That scar on my left shoulder is from a knife a suspect had with him on a traffic stop in Denver that he used on me to try and escape. All because he had a warrant out for possession. A few inches further south and better aim, and I wouldn't be here."

"That's awful." It was something she had to digest. She knew his job came with risks, but staring at the scar, at the tangible proof that he could lose his life on the job, was jarring.

He shrugged slightly. "It comes with the territory. And it's one of the reasons I moved back to Echo Springs after our relationship imploded. As much as I am doing what I'm meant to be doing, in a city like Denver, I'm more likely to die on the job than to make a real impact in the community. For me it's part of the oath I took, to be of service to my community and make life better for those in it."

"I think you have made an impact here. Just because she couldn't see that and live with it, doesn't mean it wasn't right for you." How could he be this deep in the gut good? Wasn't there some law that men like him didn't exist—couldn't—because it would rip apart the space time continuum or something?

"I don't regret that my relationship with Stacy ended or that I came back here. If I hadn't, I never would have bought the place next to your aunt and learned all about your rebellion."

"She told you?" Abby gasped. She hadn't got around to telling him yet and wanted to thunk her head against the wall.

"About you bucking your parents and going after what was right for you? Yep. Whenever I checked on her, she would tell me all about you and the letters you sent her."

Abby could feel the blush heating her cheeks. "Those were private. I can't believe she shared them with you."

"Maybe it's why I've felt like I've known you forever. Because in a way, I did. And the reality of you has far surpassed the image I had created in my mind from her stories."

Abby's heart trembled at the fierce, solid emotions in his gaze.

He was… everything. Still not ready to voice what was in her heart, she leaned forward and claimed his lips, silencing any declarations.

But most often, during the course of those two weeks, they were in too great of a hurry to squeeze as much passion into their nights together as humanly possible, until their bodies were worn out. And every day, Abby fell deeper in love with Nate, more so than she ever thought herself capable of loving someone. But she never told him that she loved him; it was on the tip of her tongue so many nights and it would stall on her lips. It was fear, mainly. Fear that he wouldn't love her back. Fear because she didn't know if Echo Springs was more than just a stopping point for her.

Abby had tried to say something about her potential departure from the town every day over the last two weeks. But every time she worked up the nerve, Nate distracted her with mind-melting kisses or she chickened out, too afraid of losing his hungry glances and nights spent in his arms. Or there was that night when Rufus had bolted after a squirrel into the forest and they'd had to chase after him. Abby knew it was the two-ton elephant in the room. Perhaps Nate sensed her disquiet, too, because he'd not divulged his feelings for her.

Now, Abby sat in her minute office at the Echo Springs Community College, her lectures done for the day, holding a letter from the University of California at Berkeley. One of the advisors on her dissertation had been so impressed with her work that he had forwarded it to their head of the literature department, who wanted to offer Abby a grant research position with a fast track to tenure.

Abby should be thrilled, ecstatic by the offer. This was the dream job she'd been working steadily toward her whole life, it seemed. But the stately, expensive letterhead with the UC Berkeley Crest on it didn't engender feelings of joy or excitement —rather, confusion and sorrow. After everything she'd experienced, receiving the confirmation that she knew would make her parents proud and look at her not like she was one of their science experiments gone wrong, but worthy of their love, was anti-climactic. The chair of the literary department wanted her to come visit the campus and meet the team she'd be working with if she chose to accept the position.

Two months ago, she would have jumped without looking, and taken the opportunity with a snap of her fingers, but now, she didn't know. Was it the right choice? Because Echo Springs had begun to feel like home. And while she knew that had a lot to do with a certain sexy sheriff, she'd started to enjoy life here in a way she'd not experienced before. She looked forward to meeting Tessa and Cybil for lunch at Papa Beau's or drinks at Smitty's. Did she want to throw all of it away for a job she didn't know if she would like? Abby sat, staring, flummoxed that, in the short months since she had arrived, she'd entrenched herself into the rhythm of small town living and insinuated herself into Echo Springs, building a pretty spectacular life here.

At the knock on her door, she folded the letter, slipping it back into the outer pocket of her purse. "Come in."

Barry Stein entered, appearing as frazzled as ever. He wasn't a typical administrator but she enjoyed his company. He looked more at home in a lab coat away from people than he did managing the academic political landscape that was always present at a college, no matter the size, and seemed to do the job grudgingly, since no one else wanted the headache.

"Barry, what can I do for you?" Abby asked, pasting a congenial smile on her face and ignoring the melancholy suffusing her being.

He took a seat in the chair on the other side of her desk, looking rather serious. "I'm so glad I caught you before you left for the weekend. I realize we still have some way to go this term, but I wanted you to know that I've been extremely impressed with your lectures and performance. I realize you will probably have a million offers from universities across the country once you receive your doctorate in the spring, but I wanted to toss

Echo Springs Community College into the ring for your consideration. I understand that we are a small school, but I do believe what we do here makes a difference, and we have more of a one-on-one interaction with our students. In fact, if you would agree to stay on, Professor Lawrence is retiring at the end of the year, and I wanted to offer you the position as Head and Chair of the English Department. It's more responsibility, and we have wiggle room in our budget to make you a nice offer."

"Um, wow, thank you," Abby replied, a bit stunned. Her own department to run? Most professors worked years on the off-chance that they might reach that distinction. She was flattered that Barry thought so highly of her skills. Meanwhile, the damn letter from UC Berkeley burned away in her purse.

"You don't have to give me an answer right away if you need some time to think it over," Barry commented, his gaze studying her, and she wondered if he saw her fear, the indecision plaguing her, or the uncertainty she felt every time she tried to imagine her future.

She sighed almost inaudibly. "I do need some time to consider the position. It's a very generous offer, but…"

"But you have some bigwig universities courting you. I completely understand. And no hard feelings if you should choose to accept another offer." Barry gave her a small smile, like he knew she'd choose another institution over this one, but he was offering on the off-chance that she might accept.

"Thanks, Barry. I mean it. I will give it some serious thought and let you know in a week or so, if that's okay with you." She prayed that in that time, lightning would strike her with an ah-ha image and she'd have a clear vision for the direction she should go in. That feeling she'd had when she'd first arrived, of wanting to pull the covers over her head and ignore everything? Yeah, that was there again. Only this time, she wanted Nate under those covers with her so she didn't have to think about anything but her next orgasm.

"Absolutely. Have a nice weekend, and I will see you on

Monday." He stood from the chair and left her office, giving her a quick nod filled with compassion and warmth.

"Yeah, you do the same."

Abby sat there, stunned, after he left her office. She could stay in Echo Springs if she wanted to, continue seeing Nate and give herself the chance to dream more about little boys with his eyes and her nose, baking cookies and Thanksgiving dinner in his kitchen together, building a life that she'd never dreamed she could one day have. And there was a part of her that wanted it so fiercely, her heart squeezed and ached to even hope that was a possibility.

Well, didn't that little kernel just thicken the muck around her decision.

Abby left work, not really paying attention to where she was driving. In fact, instead of stopping at her house—when did it become hers and not Aunt Evie's?—she followed the winding road past the stately Victorian, up the mountainside until she arrived at a crystal-blue lake with a small pavilion containing some picnic tables, and bathrooms off to the side.

She parked her car, spying a set of diverging trails from the pavilion out into the mountain terrain with some stone benches set along them. Abby left her car, absorbed the chilly air at the higher elevation, and sat on one of the benches. She let nature seep into her pores as she stared at the forest of evergreens reflecting in the lake and the craggy gray mountaintop beyond covered in glaciers. Crows cawed and soared overhead while she contemplated what she wanted for her life. Dream job or dream man? Play it safe and be logical, or risk it all and potentially suffer heartbreak. Either way, wasn't she short-changing herself? It was like asking her whether she wanted to cut off her right or left arm.

Abby tried imagining herself at UC Berkeley, the sun, the warmth, the smog even. She'd be surrounded by like-minded individuals all pursuing knowledge and truth. She'd live in a much more liberal state, maybe learn to love kale, and take up surfing. Who was she kidding? She'd always hate kale, and would like nothing more than to send her undead doll army after whoever had created that idiotic fad. But she could see it all: teaching a classroom full of students, all of whom were some of the best and brightest young minds around. Abby could imagine studying her dissertation in even more depth, publishing papers, and doing all manner of academic climbing whereupon she'd have a book published one day.

And two months ago, she would have said that life was exactly what she wanted above all else. That it was her most cherished and eagerly anticipated dream. But was it? Or was a life like that just an extension of her parents' dream for her, with the hope that they would finally love her?

She wasn't sure. And that was the crux of the matter.

She stared at the lake, attempting to divine some wisdom from it. And hell, if a mythic being appeared out of the water to offer her advice about the right path to choose, she'd take it.

Because Abby could also see herself staying in Echo Springs. The little strip of a town felt like home, like she could build a life here. That's what she felt she and Nate were doing. They weren't two people just having fun, they were creating something together. What, she wasn't certain, because neither of them had discussed their feelings.

They'd talked about everything else as they worked on his house, from the probability of extraterrestrial life to the proper way to cook a steak, and everything in between. Abby had told him about her upbringing, and her rebellion that had led her to her current path. Nate had told her about his time in Denver with his ex-girlfriend, and stories about college with Miles, Jacob, and Sam. He'd talked about his mom, and his scarred upbringing. And how the former sheriff had treated him like the son he never had up until he passed two years ago.

They knew each other's strengths and weaknesses and neither of them had run. Quite the opposite, in fact—with the exception of this secret, one she'd tried so many times to bring up but in the end had let fear be her ruler and chickened out. It wasn't fair of her, not telling Nate, she knew that. But now she worried what it would do to their relationship when he learned she'd withheld information.

No matter what, she felt like either way she chose, she'd lose something important to her.

Abby fell deeper in love with Nate every night. The feeling was so potent and tangible, she could almost hold it. The thought of leaving him stole the breath from her body.

She was no closer to an answer when Nate's SUV pulled up alongside hers. He exited his vehicle, garbed in his sheriff gear. She wished he'd wear the hat that came with the position, but he had nixed it. Although, when she'd told him it was because she thought he'd look sexy in it, he'd given her a private show. Totally worth the rug burn too.

"Abby, something wrong?"

She gave him a smile, attempting to hide the turmoil swimming in her heart. "No, I just wanted some fresh air. And I hadn't been up this far."

He sat on the bench beside her. "It's beautiful, isn't it?"

"Yeah, it is. Want to neck like a couple of teenagers?"

Nate laughed and slid his arm around her. "If I wasn't here in my official capacity, I would in a heartbeat."

She leaned her head against his shoulder. "I'll take a rain check on that."

"You got it." He kissed her brow, and the letter in her purse burned that much hotter. What should she tell Nate? How could she tell him?

"What are you doing up here?" she asked.

"I'm closing the trails off. There's a storm coming in this weekend, and forecasters are saying the higher elevations will get some accumulations."

"Accumulations of what?" she asked, confused.

He looked at her with a raised brow and an *it's a good thing you're cute* expression. "Snow."

236

This early? "But it's the end of September," she exclaimed and looked skyward for impending frozen white flakes.

"Welcome to Colorado. Not to worry, I'll make sure you stay warm and toasty when it blows in tomorrow night."

"Thanks, I appreciate it. That's crazy, to think of snow in September." And then she thought about cuddling with Nate inside, soup bubbling in the crockpot while the white stuff kept them homebound. Not a bad image.

Nate murmured against her brow, "I have to go close them up. If you wait, I will follow you down to your house and will be off duty the rest of the night. Maybe we can go take in a show or something."

"That'd be nice. Why don't I go get dinner started for us at my place while you finish up here? I'm starving anyhow, and you can meet me at my place." Where she could ply him with food and sex before confessing the choices before her. She had to do it tonight, tell him. No matter the outcome.

With a smile that made her heart melt into a gooey pool, he brushed a light kiss upon her lips that left her breathless with anticipation and then said, "Sounds good. See you soon."

"Watch out for bears," she warned as she climbed in her Rover. On the way back down the mountain, her heart fluttered in her chest over the conversation to come tonight. She went over in her head how to tell Nate about both of her offers. Perhaps if she told him about both, his response would give her some direction and an idea of which route to select. If he said it didn't matter, then perhaps he wasn't as enamored of her as she was of him.

She pulled into her driveway, went next door and let Rufus out first, as had become her habit here lately. Rufus blasted out of the house and into her arms with glee.

"Hey sweetheart. Go potty real quick and then you can come to my house."

He swiped a wet kiss across her hand then, with a sharp woof, trotted to the nearest bush. He followed her the short distance to her house. As she climbed up the stairs, her feet crunched over broken glass and she saw the nearby window had been smashed.

What in the world? At her side, Rufus growled, a deep, menacing rumble in his chest. When she discovered her front door open a crack, she pushed inside and spied destruction beyond. Her heart thumped madly in her chest. She gulped air into her lungs, trying not to scream. What if whoever had done this was still in there? She stumbled back unsteadily, backpedaling away from the door with Rufus guarding her, tense at her side. As she put distance between herself and her house, she groped inside her purse for her phone and called Nate.

Nate answered on the first ring, thank god. "Hey, Abby, I was just thinking about tonight, maybe we could—"

"Nate, my aunt's house, it's… I need you to come." Her voice sounded hollow, even to her ears.

"Go to my house and lock the door behind you. I will be there soon. Promise."

"Okay," she said and hurried to his front door. Thank goodness he'd given her a key. Rufus didn't leave her side for a minute. Sensing the danger, he became her stalwart protector. She locked the front door once they were inside, just as Nate asked. Then she walked over to the window and stared out at her house.

Nate did as he'd promised, appearing in front of her aunt's house with lights blazing barely a minute later. She didn't know how he'd made it so fast and didn't care. Her knees wobbled in relief at spying him. But he didn't come to check on her first. She watched, Rufus standing beside her, through his front window as he entered her house with his gun drawn.

❧

NATE PUSHED his vehicle as fast as he could down the winding mountain road. He forced his fear for Abby back, compartmentalizing it as he pulled up in front of her house. He'd already called O'Leary and instructed him to bring backup.

Nate exited his Explorer and drew his gun from its holster. He noted the broken glass on the porch and avoided it. He had no idea if the perp was still here or if he had already been there and left.

He entered through the front door hanging slightly ajar, pushed it the rest of the way open and stepped inside warily, searching for any signs or sounds of the intruder. He cleared the living room with the dolls shrouded in sheets before heading down the hallway toward the kitchen in the back. He inched down the hall, his footsteps silent as he moved. Halfway between the front and back of the house, he heard it, coming from the second floor above: the distinct sound of heavy footsteps. *Gotcha!*

Nate crept back toward the stairwell and got into a crouched position so he remained unseen until the perp was in position as those same footsteps pounded down the stairs. His adrenaline hummed. Time slowed down to a crawl. His body tensed and coiled, ready to spring into action as the footsteps neared.

When the intruder reached the main floor, Nate rose from where he'd been crouched and pointed his firearm at the man's back. "Put your hands where I can see them, asshole!"

Even though the guy had a noticeable paunch, he sprang forward, heading toward the open front door. Shit! Why did they always try to run? But Nate was faster. Nate rushed him, leapt and tackled him to the ground. The black bag the perp was holding fell and slid along the hardwood, out of reach.

"You have the right to remain silent," Nate snarled as the guy tried to buck him off.

The man turned his body, just enough for Nate to see his profile. Shock riddled Nate—otherwise, the asshole never would have gotten the upper hand. He bucked Nate off and came after him. They wrestled around on the floor, with Deputy Filbert reaching for his gun that Nate held above his head with one hand while he tried to subdue him with the other. Filbert punched him in the gut, taking the wind out of him with his ham-like hands. It gave the bastard the edge he needed, and he tried to take the gun from Nate's hand stretched over his head.

Filbert squeezed. It caused Nate's finger to press on the trigger and a shot erupted from the chamber. Porcelain and plaster exploded where the bullet hit one of the dolls on a bench against the far wall. Nate pushed his free hand against Filbert's windpipe and squeezed, cutting off the man's air just enough so that Filbert removed his hands from trying to take his firearm and fought against Nate's hold as his face turned beet red. Nate released his gun onto the floor and used that brief leverage to flip Filbert onto his fat belly, yank his hands behind his back, and slap his cuffs around his wrists.

Deputies O'Leary and Young entered through the front door with their guns drawn.

"Glad you finally made it. Give me a hand with this son of a bitch," Nate ordered his deputies. "Touch nothing until we can get the state boys here to help dust for prints."

"Filbert? You're the asshole behind these break ins?" O'Leary said with a scowl.

Nate nodded. "This one hurts. Help me get him the fuck out of here."

He grabbed his gun from where he had dropped it on the floor while O'Leary and Young hauled the man to his feet. Then Nate grabbed Filbert by the cuffs, one hand clutching his shoulder and led him out to the waiting police cruiser.

"You have the right to remain silent, Filbert. Anything you say or do can be used against you in a court of law."

"Piss off," Filbert snarled, red-faced and huffing labored breaths in and out.

"You best get used to it, asshole. Judges and prosecuting attorneys don't like it when it's one of us breaking the law." Nate shoved him into the back of O'Leary's car and slammed the door shut.

Then he called it in to the state boys and asked for their

assistance with this case. He had to, since it was one of their own, to make sure everything was done by the book. Betrayal and disgust fueled his anger.

And he couldn't help but think it was his fault that they had missed the signs.

~

FOR THE MOST PART, Abby never thought about Nate's job being dangerous. He'd explained the dangers, shown her the scar on his shoulder. But that hadn't prepared her for the deep in the gut worry. The other night, at the steakhouse fire, she had witnessed the good side of his job. And now she was experiencing the terror of it. If she wanted a relationship with him, a long lasting one, this was a fear she would have to confront time and time again, even in a town as small as Echo Springs.

He was good at his job. She had witnessed that first-hand. And he was an integral part of the community, making a difference in the lives of those in his small town every time he strapped on his gun belt and badge. He was a man of honor and compassion, and deep down yummy goodness.

But standing there at his window, wondering what danger he would find inside her house, she'd never been so afraid for another person in her life. She wrung her hands, and swore, and even said a few prayers to whomever would listen. With her luck, it would be Beelzebub, who would respond so he could take control of his undead doll army, but if they got Nate out alive and in one piece, she'd deal with the fallout. The minutes seemed to stretch out, and time slowed.

Deputies Greg O'Leary and Kate Young arrived on the scene and were about to enter Abby's house when there was a pop of gunfire from inside. The two deputies entered with their guns drawn, and Abby's heart felt permanently lodged in her throat. A lifetime seemed to pass as she waited. Her stalwart companion, Rufus, quivered at her side.

"I know, sweetheart, he'll be okay," she reassured Rufus, her throat raw with unshed tears at the intermittent terror building.

Then Nate exited her house and towed out a man in hand-cuffs. Deputies Young and O'Leary were on his heels.

The breath she'd been holding expelled in a rush and she sagged against Rufus. Deputy Young held the back door of O'Leary's police cruiser open as Nate shoved Deputy Denny Filbert into the backseat and slammed the door shut. Deputy Filbert had broken into her home? How? Why? Holy shit!

Nate trudged across the lawn. Abby flew to his door, opening it and raced outside, meeting him on the porch.

"Are you all right?" she said, examining every inch of his body, running her hands over him and not finding any bullet holes.

He cupped her face, his eyes searching hers and said, "I could ask the same about you. You okay?"

"I heard gunfire and I thought you'd been shot." She couldn't keep the fear contained any longer now that he was safe. Some tears seeped from her eyes and she sniffled.

Nate gave her a warm smile, his eyes tender as he wiped away her tears and said, "Yeah, Denny got off a shot. Unfortunately, one of the dolls didn't make it."

"I don't give a shit about the dolls. I'm just glad you are all right. That you weren't hurt or worse." She leaned into him and pressed her lips against his, needing the solid reassurance of his presence. He returned her kiss gently.

Then he lifted his face and said, "Abby, will you be okay here at my place for a bit? I just called in the state boys, since it was one of my deputies behind the break-ins. I need their assistance on the case from here on out. Will you be all right on your own? I could call Tessa or Cybil to come sit with you while I'm occupied."

"Cybil's working tonight, and Tessa has a date. I don't want to worry them. I've got Rufus with me for company. We will stay inside, make coffee and some food for anyone who needs it."

He kissed her forehead. "I'm not sure how long I'll be, and unfortunately, we can't take anything from your house until after we get through logging evidence. Should take twenty-four hours or so, give or take a bit."

"That's okay. I already have a few things here I can use. Besides, I can always sleep naked," she said, attempting to lighten the mood, and was rewarded with a flash of white teeth.

"I like the sound of that. Stay inside, please. I'll be back as soon as I can," he said, ushering her back inside.

"Absolutely." She gave him a last look and shut the door behind him. "What do you say, Rufus, want to help me make some dinner?" she asked as she trod toward the kitchen. An enthusiastic *woof* was his response.

Chapter Nineteen

From Old Man Turner's Journal:
Mistakes happen, always forgive, and trust that your heart knows best.

A bby loitered around Nate's house. She made sandwiches and had soup simmering over the stove. She brewed a full pot of coffee for what was certain to be the lengthy night ahead. She fed Rufus and then took a blisteringly hot shower to try and eradicate the cold that had settled into her bones as she anxiously waited for Nate. Police vehicles swarmed the street and were lined up outside. Instead of watching television and being distracted by flashing lights, she retrieved Bill Turner's journal from upstairs. She and Rufus curled up together on the couch in the living room, and she read.

Evie was back in my life after almost twenty-five years apart. I'll admit, I was more nervous than you can imagine as I parked the car and told my girls to stretch their feet. There had been a tiny stream back beyond the hunter's cabin I told them to go find as we disembarked. My stomach tied in knots, I cautiously walked up the gravel path.

Evie was still the most beautiful creature I had ever seen. She spied me halfway up the drive, set her paints down, and turned my way. I was so nervous, my palms were sweating.

"Well, hell, aren't you a sight for sore eyes? What brings you back here, Bill?"

"Evie, it's wonderful to see you again. My girls and I moved to Echo Springs this past fall. I had not realized there were houses up this way."

"They're new. So, do you want to come up and have a visit or are you just going to stand there like a fish with its mouth open?"

"You haven't changed a bit," I said with my heart beating a loud drumbeat in my chest.

"Oh, you'd be surprised."

I took her up on the visit, climbed her porch and sat. I can still remember the hummingbirds buzzing by us as we talked. It was about nothing important, nothing deep, as I kept an ear out for Rebecca and Marjorie's return. But by the time our visit was finished, I knew I would do anything to win her back. My girls met Evie, and I could see the ghost of a shadow in her eyes that were as beautiful as ever. I left that afternoon, dropped my girls off at the little house we were renting, and made an offer on the house next to Evie's.

At first, Evie was a bit put out with me for purchasing the house next to hers, but fate had sought to put us back in each other's path, and I was not going to let her get away from me a second time. Our first time in love, I was an unschooled boy playing at being a man. This time, I set out on a campaign to woo her back.

It took time. It took the patience of a saint, because for Evie, after all this time, life had been harder on her in some ways than it had been on me. Evie never married and, instead, followed her passion for art. She attended art school and found success in work, before deciding to move back to Echo Springs so that she could paint in solitude. She bought the land where the hunter's cabin still stood, and after painting it, she had it torn down and had her home built on the site. She told me it was a way for her to be close to what we once shared and that it no longer caused her the heartache it once had, but filled her with a bittersweet remembrance.

Since we were both seasoned this time around, Evie was a tougher nut to crack, but the things I have listed are what I did to win the love of my life *back. We never did marry. But I think, after everything we went through to find our way back to one another, we didn't need to.*

Evie said it wouldn't be fair to my girls, although I think both Rebecca and Marjorie would have been just fine with it. Especially as both of them grew up and went to college. Rebecca went back to San Diego State, and Marjorie attended Notre Dame.

Most nights, we would meet on Evie's front porch, when it was warm enough, and just talk about our lives. She held my hand and shed tears over Charles and Lila.

In the end, we lived our lives side by side and loved each other unconditionally for the past forty years, and as the cancer is eating away at my liver, I felt the need to put it all down. For the bulk of my life, I have loved one woman with all my heart and soul. I hate that I have to leave her once more, and this time for good. I like to think that if there's life after death, or if the soul does continue on, that my soul will find hers, always.

And so my final words to you are this: Love is always the answer. It is always worth fighting for, no matter how short a time you might have it. Loving Evie was the greatest gift of my life.

Abby closed the journal. Tears streamed down her face at the bittersweet beauty of Bill's love for her Aunt Evie. How she wished she'd known about it. Even in her communication with Evie, her aunt had not mentioned him once, and Abby had not seen the painting of the hunter's lodge. There were others that were Evie's decorating the house. Abby had always imagined Evie as this force to be reckoned with, who'd lived her life alone to the tune of her own band. But she'd been wrong, and her entire paradigm shifted and wobbled with this newfound knowledge. She didn't know what to do with this new information. Outside, the lights and sounds had diminished, and then the front door opened. Abby swiped at her tears.

Nate's face was composed in an unreadable mask as he entered the living room. Abby was about to ask him what was wrong when she spied a folded letter in his hand. Her heart stuttered to a shuddering halt in her chest. Fear licked its way into her breast.

"Can I ask, were you even going to tell me, or were you just going to pack up and move without saying a word to me?" Nate said, his eyes hot with accusation.

"Nate, I can explain—"

He cut her off, and muttered, "Was this just a fun fling with the guy next door while you searched for greener fucking pastures?"

Abby stood and approached him, but he retreated, keeping the wall he'd erected between them in place. Her heart ached and she defensively crossed her arms in front of her chest. "Nate, the offer just came in, and I was mulling it over. I was going to talk to you about it tonight."

"So you were going to tell me? You sure about that?"

Guilt swam in her chest and shame heated her cheeks as she said, her voice small, "I was going to, Nate. I just needed time to think. Don't you understand that this is what I've been working toward practically my whole life?"

"Abby, that's what I'm here for, to bounce your ideas off of—or at least, I thought it was. That's what you do in a relationship. We help each other become the best versions of ourselves. If this is what you want, I won't stand in the way. But dammit, Abby, the fact that you think so little of me... to keep something this huge a secret from me, just belittles everything I thought we were and were heading toward."

His words were like a sucker punch to her midsection. Her vision swam and she trembled at the sheer agony of pain that lacerated her heart into bite size pieces.

"Are you breaking up with me?" Abby's breath clogged in her chest.

"What would you have me do? Wait around for you to make a decision to leave at the drop of a hat? I've done that before. I have the scars to prove it, and I'm not looking for a repeat. So, I guess, yeah, I am." He ran a frustrated hand through his hair.

She reared back, shaking, and realized the heart she'd wondered whether she had was there for certain because it was breaking into a million pieces. "I can't believe you would compare me to your ex."

He gave her a dark look and snorted. "Shoe fits, don't you think? Look, why don't you stay here tonight? I have to head into the station anyhow, with this case, and will just sleep there. Then you can find lodgings in the morning if we aren't finished with your aunt's house."

It was no longer her house to him, but Evie's. Her pain transmuted into anger and she remarked as calmly as possible, "You know what? I will be fine on my own. Like hell I'm staying here."

"Dammit, Abby." He started to approach.

She backed away from him, shaking her head. "No, if you are calling it quits on this relationship without even hearing my side, you're a stubborn, mule-headed idiot and a fool. I hadn't decided what I was going to do. I was planning to talk to you about it, because I received an offer from Echo Springs Community College too."

"Like you would choose our little school over a prominent school like Berkeley. Do you think I'm just some dumb hick cop? I know the way the world works, and that a school like that can offer you opportunities this place never could."

"You don't get to make the choice for me, and you didn't think to ask me what I wanted. You just accused. I'll see you around, Sheriff." She grabbed her purse, snatched the letter from his hands, and headed toward his front door.

"Where will you go?" he asked quietly, and she glanced at him then. His expression was bleak. She committed his image to memory, the way his dark hair was mussed, and his broad shoulders were taut with tension. She dug her fingers in her palm to waylay the tears that were threatening to fall.

"I guess that's really none of your concern now, is it?" Abby replied, and stormed out of his house, feeling like she'd been hit by a truck. She drove blindly through tears and ended up on Tessa and Cybil's doorstep, realizing that it was nearly midnight.

"Abby? What's wrong?" Cybil asked, pushing open the screen

door, wearing a pair of Victoria's Secret pajamas with the words, *I'm an Angel* scrawled in glittery pink across the bust.

The tears Abby thought she had gotten under control spilled down her cheeks and she asked, "Could I stay here tonight? I hate to put you out, but I can't stay at my aunt's place because of the break-in and Nate and I—"

"Oh, honey, of course." Cybil slid a comforting arm around her and pulled her inside. "Tessa, break out the wine and chocolate. I think we have a long night ahead of us."

Chapter Twenty

From Old Man Turner's Journal:
Listen to what your heart tells you. It's the only way to be true to yourself.

"You were right." Abby sniffled and wiped at an errant tear before it splashed off her cheek onto her shirt. Tessa had lent her a pair of pajama bottoms so she wouldn't have to sleep in her jeans. Abby was a teensy bit wider in the hip area and the cotton leggings with the superhero logo on them stretched, distorting the image a bit.

Cybil grimaced, swirling the chardonnay in her wine glass. "But we didn't want to be."

"We were both hoping for the best. Well, and that you would confess a whole lot sooner. So why didn't you?" Tessa asked, refilling her wine glass. They were on their second bottle of wine already. And Abby's friends had brought out the big guns: one of those extra-large chocolate bars and broken it up into bite size pieces for them to nibble on.

"It just got so complicated so fast. I wanted to tell him. I knew I needed to tell him. But then… I didn't think I was going

250

to fall for him. And yet I did. I've never felt this way about a guy before and I let fear control me."

But Abby had known her chances for staying in Echo Spring were slim. She was curled up on their comfortable, deep-seated brown plaid couch. She liked their home. It was a two-story duplex. Basically, it was a two-story house that had a dividing wall clear down the middle. Cybil sat on the couch beside her, while Tessa reclined on the love seat.

"That serious, huh? We all tend to do stupid things in the name of love. It tends to happen when you're dating. So what happened tonight exactly? Beyond your house getting broken into, and I can't believe Denny Filbert was the perp." Tessa popped a piece of chocolate in her mouth.

"The break-in was pretty frightening. I won't lie, I nearly peed in my pants when I found the door open." And then she'd called Nate. He had been steadfast and calm, helping her push past her fear.

"I can only imagine," Cybil said, grabbing a piece of chocolate. "But how did it progress from Nate riding in to save the day to the two of you calling it quits?"

Because the entire day, from the moment I received the offer, had gone into the toilet. "I received an offer from the University of California at Berkeley for a research grant position with a fast track to tenure."

Tessa's dark brows rose up, nearly disappearing beneath her hairline. "Wow. That's quite the offer. You could do worse."

"And you're going to take it?" Cybil asked, studying Abby over the rim of her wineglass.

Wasn't that the million-dollar question? Abby peered into her own glass, hoping that some inspiration would strike. "I don't know. I used to believe that was what I wanted: to work at a prestigious university, garnering accolades and being at the forefront of the academic world. But truthfully, I've been burned out and a little apathetic toward my research. And yeah, it could just be that I've worked insane hours for years and years so it could just mean I need a break from it all. That was what my coming here was supposed to be, me shaking up my life a bit, making sure that my career path was still the one I wanted. And I'm not so certain it is anymore. I like it here in Echo Springs and I could stay here. Barry offered me the English Department Chair position for next fall. And I was going to tell Nate—about both of the offers and how I am struggling to make my decision. But then I got home and found my house broken into. My offer from Berkeley fell out of my purse and Nate found it after he came and arrested the bad guy."

"So he rode in and saved you, only to find out you were leaving him? This was after he discovered it was an officer who worked for him behind all the break-ins in the area?" Tessa asked.

"Pretty much. He was so angry. And did I forget to mention he's stubborn to boot? I tried to explain but he wouldn't listen to a thing I had to say by that point."

"He's a card-carrying member of the penis brigade. Stubborn kind of comes with the territory. But think about it, if positions were reversed, and you found out he was withholding some rather critical information from you, you can't tell me you wouldn't feel betrayed and hurt. If it was just a fling for Nate and he didn't care, he wouldn't have put up such a big stink about it. The real question is, do you love him?" Cybil asked, picking up another piece of chocolate and giving Abby a knowing look.

Feeling rather defeated, because Cybil was right, Abby sighed. "And if I do? What does it matter? He didn't even give me a chance to explain. It doesn't leave me much room to make amends."

"I think it matters a great deal if you love him. Sometimes love doesn't fix everything, and sometimes you can't make it work no matter how much you want it to. But I think you will regret it if you don't at least tell him how you feel," Cybil replied, her gaze rather pensive.

"I think you should check out Berkeley. I think you owe it to yourself to call them and go visit," Tessa added, finishing off the last sip of wine in her glass.

"Why? What purpose would that serve?" Wouldn't it just convolute the sad state of her life further?

Tessa cocked her head a bit and said, "Look. You won't know until you give yourself a chance to see the place for yourself, get a feel for the campus and where you would be working. Having an offer like that is a big deal. Before you say yes or no, you need to know exactly what it is you would be saying yes or no to. It will give you a better idea so you can make a pros and cons list if you need to, and I think it will help you decide what's right for you."

"And what if Berkeley is right for me?" Which would mean uprooting her life again, when she was finally feeling settled, and most likely saying goodbye to Nate, forever. He was too much a part of this town to leave it.

Cybil shrugged. "Then it's what is right for you. We'll miss you. But it wouldn't even start until next fall so you could spend the next six months here before heading further west."

"And who knows, it might give you enough time to fall out of love with Nate," Tessa added.

Abby yawned. She didn't think that was going to happen. Her feelings were not fickle. Once they existed, they tended to stick like white on rice.

"Why don't you get some sleep and we can figure it out in the morning." Cybil stood and grabbed the blankets and pillows she had brought down earlier and set on the nearby recliner.

Cybil was right. It had been an inordinately long day. "Yeah, maybe sleep will do me a world of good. Thank you, guys, for letting me crash here with you."

Tessa gave her a hug. "We're always here if you need us."

Cybil set the bedding on the couch and then gave her a hug too. "Things will look better in the morning. Yell if you need anything."

A sob lodged itself in Abby's throat and she nodded, blinking back tears. Cybil helped her make up the couch and they all cleaned up the wine glasses, bottles, and remaining chocolate spread on the coffee table, carrying it all over to the eat-in kitchen that looked like it was still the original nineteen eighties style cabinetry.

But then Tessa and Cybil headed upstairs, leaving her alone with her thoughts. Abby was tired, but the moment she lay down, her brain replayed her fight with Nate, over and over again. Maybe she did need to head out to Berkeley, check it out for herself, and see if it felt right. When Abby finally slept, she dreamed of little boys with grubby hands and cornflower blue eyes.

～

IN THE MORNING, sitting at Tessa and Cybil's dinette table, Abby contacted Dr. Ruth Greenberg. She'd given Abby a cell phone number to use in case she couldn't reach her at the UC Berkeley office number.

"Abigail, thank you so much for calling me. I just want to say, I loved your dissertation and really hope you will consider coming to work with us after graduation." Her voice was chipper and polite, with the cultured air one expected in the world of academia.

Even though her heart wasn't fully invested in it, Abby reckoned she owed herself the chance and said, "Thank you, Dr. Greenberg. I would like to visit your campus and see where I'd be working if I accepted your offer."

"Fantastic news. When would you like to come out?"

"I have a break in my schedule this next week. Is that feasible for you?" She chewed on her thumb, worrying over taking this leap.

"Lovely. I will make all the arrangements for you. Why don't we have you fly out here tomorrow so you can sightsee a bit? We have such a pretty campus. What airport are you flying out of?"

"Denver International," Abby said, her heartrate accelerating. It was happening so fast, but that was what she needed to soothe her battered heart, right? A change of pace and chance to get away from it all. That's what they had concluded late last night.

"Perfect. I will have my assistant get everything set up and will see you tomorrow evening for dinner. How does that sound?" Dr. Greenberg asked.

"It sounds wonderful," Abby replied, trying to sound happy, but her voice was brittle and sharp. Deep down in her heart, the only thing she wanted was for Nate to no longer be mad at her. And the heart she had worried she didn't have was definitely there, because she could feel the broken pieces throb in agony. She'd never felt so adrift. She gulped in air as a wave of anguish gripped her. But she would fake being all right until it no longer hurt to breathe.

Both Tessa and Cybil were right, she had to at least visit Berkeley and see what they were offering before she made a decision. It was the only way she could make a fully informed choice. When she had measured, organized steps to follow, she could ignore the pain for periods of time. So, she made plans, and contacted Barry Stein to let him know that she would be absent from this week's lessons but would send him her lesson plans.

Tessa graciously offered to fill in for her since Abby's classes worked with her schedule. Even though, as she explained, she didn't like those stuffy books. But Abby's classes would be covered for the next week while she figured her life out. With her eye on the clock and the approaching snow, she left their house and headed to the police station to meet with the state troopers on the investigation into Deputy Denny Filbert's moonlighting activities breaking into people's homes and stealing their belongings.

Abby entered the brick station, and gave the front desk clerk her name. She recognized the deputy from yesterday evening. The woman was roughly her age, with her blonde hair pulled back in a braid.

When she spied Abby, she said, "I'll let the officers know you're here. Just have a seat."

"Thank you," Abby replied, twisting her hands, wondering if Nate was here—and if he was, what he would do when he saw her.

She wasn't forced to wait long.

"Miss Callier?"

She looked up, a tight smile on her face. It wasn't Nate, but some officer she had never seen before. He was in full uniform, and quite the hottie with his short buzz cut and a body with the bearing of a soldier.

"Yes," she said, standing.

"I'm Captain Matt Clark. If you'd follow me, we can get through these questions fairly quickly."

"I'd appreciate that."

The captain escorted her back through the station to a small conference room. Abby glanced around for Nate as she followed the officer, but didn't see him. The man was probably avoiding her.

The captain took her through the events the day before—all very standard questions, he assured her with a congenial smile. But he also filled her in a bit more on the case. Apparently, Denny was a bit of a gambler and liked to head to the casinos. Only, he wasn't a good gambler, and owed a loan shark quite a bit of money. Instead of the loan shark taking it out of Denny's hide, Denny figured out a way to pay back his gambling debts. That a cop was the culprit in the crime was one of the reasons Nate's police force had had a difficult time cracking the case.

"The number you provided, is that the best one to reach you at? In case we need more information," the captain asked, looking up from his notes.

She nodded. "Yes. I am heading out of town for a few days, but that is my cell phone if you need to contact me. Would I be able to go home and get my things?" She was thinking about her clothes, suitcase, and anything else she might need for her trip.

"Yes. You can return home. We've already collected all the evidence we should need. And we will let you know if there is anything else."

"Great. Is that it?" she asked, checking the time.

"Let me walk you out," he said, giving her a kind smile, and he ushered her out to the front doors.

She left, breathing a deep sigh. She had not run into Nate. And for that she was supremely grateful. Abby couldn't face him yet. Her heart was too tender and bruised. She feared the tight rein she had on her emotions would snap and she'd crumble. And then there was the tiny little detail that the pigheaded man hadn't paused to let her explain or even discuss her side. All he'd done was jump to conclusions and toss her aside like their time together had meant nothing.

Except he was justified in his anger. This was a mess of her own making. Keeping the possibility of her leaving Echo Springs from him had been the wrong choice, the selfish choice. So on top of feeling like her heart was bleeding out in despair, she had boatloads of guilt over the way she had bungled things from the start. At this point, Abby was just trying to pick up the pieces without further implosions or disasters.

Instead of dealing with Nate and her broken heart head on, she packed a suitcase with what she would need for a week away, made a reservation at an airport hotel, and drove to Denver. With snow forecast for the mountains tonight, she left early so she wouldn't miss her flight tomorrow. Ruth's assistant had booked the flight for her as promised, and emailed Abby the ticket. It was easier this way. She hadn't wanted to stay in her house, not with Nate so close. The memories would suffocate her. And while she was certain Tessa and Cybil would have had no problem hosting her another night, she needed time away to think things through and couldn't do that with them hovering nearby. They'd been wonderful last night and if she did leave Echo Springs, she was going to miss them terribly.

Tessa and Cybil had her information for emergencies, and

knew what she was doing, and for now that was enough. Abby couldn't make an informed decision on whether she was going to stay in Echo Springs or leave until she'd seen for herself whether that greener pasture actually was greener.

Abby ordered room service that evening because she knew she wasn't fit for company at the moment. She needed the night to sulk and mourn and cry her eyes out to her heart's content. It was the only way she'd make it through her trip this week without breaking down at the most inopportune time.

It was one of the longest, bleakest nights of her life. She tossed and turned in the unfamiliar bed. Throughout the night, as she dozed, she found herself reaching for a warm body that wasn't there and then the tears would start all over again.

By the time her flight lifted off the following morning, Abby was hollowed out and knew deep in her soul the choice best suited for her. But she worried, because she didn't know if she was brave enough to take what she wanted.

ABBY SPENT the week getting to know the faculty in the literature department and walking around the stunning Berkeley campus under a blue, cloudless sky. Ruth Greenberg made sure she was shown all the sights and took her to dinner at nearby restaurants each night. She showed Abby where they had housing for incoming professors if they wanted to live on campus. Basically, she was trying to woo Abby to come work there after graduation.

The place was amazing. They were at the cutting edge on so many academic fronts. And each day, Abby grew more resolved in what she wanted.

The old Abby would have jumped at the chance to work here. This was where she could write and have the university recommend her for the Nobel in literature. Prestige oozed from the hallowed halls of every stone building on campus. The campus itself was enormous, stretching for what seemed like miles on end, with each building more grandiose than the last one she passed.

The problem was, Abby was no longer that woman. Her time in Echo Springs had proved that she was more like her great aunt than her parents. And she had remembered something Evie had said to her in a letter when she'd switched majors all those years ago: that she had to grab her happiness wherever she found it.

That was exactly what Abby intended to do.

Chapter Twenty-One

From Old Man Turner's Journal:
Give her your time, your effort, your loyalty, your smile and make her a
priority.

N ate could hardly live in his own house. Everywhere he
went, it reminded him of Abby and his heart squeezed.
The bulk of the investigation had concluded, with Denny—the
sycophantic bastard—babbling for immunity while he gave the
state boys much bigger fish to fry, with enough information for
the prosecuting attorney to take before the judge Monday
morning to issue an indictment. The promised snow had roared
into town last night and dumped half a foot of white powder.
Which meant Nate had spent all day today out on patrol, helping
with the snaggled traffic and idiots who thought they didn't need
to slow down because they had a four-wheel drive.

When he'd pulled into his driveway, he had noticed Abby's
house was dark and her Rover wasn't there. Nate sat on his
couch feeling sorry for himself, Rufus at his feet, and proceeded

to get rip-roaring drunk so he couldn't feel the giant hole gaping in his chest.

It was better than feeling like he'd ripped his heart out and thrown it away. He was a blathering idiot. He understood that now, in hindsight. He loved Abby. She drove him crazy and made him burn. She was much more intelligent than he was—by far. He loved her mind and her soft, generous heart. The way she would sneak Rufus treats when she thought he wasn't looking. Her fearlessness in tackling new things, the way she made him laugh, and her obsession with horror films. Shit. Nate didn't know if he could breathe without her, much less do anything else.

From the moment she'd beaned him with the nine-iron, he'd been a goner. He just hadn't realized it then.

Nate ended up passed out on his couch, Rufus snoring soundly beside him on the floor.

When he woke up Monday morning with the mother of all hangovers, he knew what he had to do. If he had to eat crow for the rest of his life, that was fine, all that mattered was that he was with Abby. To set his plan in motion, he made a brief trip into Denver and back.

Then he stopped at Tessa and Cybil's house, certain that was where Abby had decided to hole up for the time being, even though he didn't see her Rover parked nearby. The first tremors of unease rippled through him when he knocked on the door. Tessa answered a few heartbeats later. The woman was a trip. Today, her hair had bright pink stripes running through the ebony, and she wore a tee shirt that said *Bite Me* across the chest.

Nate shook his head.

"What can I do for you, Sheriff?" Tessa asked, leaning against the wooden door frame with her arms crossed. She was acting like a guard dog for Abby, which, while he appreciated her willingness to protect her friend, she didn't need to anymore. He'd come to apologize—among other things.

"I need to speak with Abby. Is she here?" Nate asked. His

heart pounded in his chest and he tried to see around Tessa into the duplex.

"Nope, she left a while ago."

His heart stalled. He asked, "When? Where did she go?"

"You're about a day late, Sheriff. She left for Berkeley yesterday morning."

"She what?" Nate's head spun. She'd left him, without a word. Then again, he was the moron. Perhaps if he hadn't been so furious about discovering that Filbert was behind all the break-ins, he wouldn't have lost his mind when he'd discovered the letter from Berkeley. But he'd blown it.

There was sympathy in Tessa's eyes as she said, "Look, Nate, I know it's none of my business—"

"It's really not." The last thing he wanted to do was have a heart to heart with Tessa.

"But, dude, come on. She was the best thing to ever happen to you, and like a typical dumb man, you went ballistic before she could explain," Tessa said, exasperation coloring her voice.

Her diatribe hit far too close to home. But Nate had thought he would at least have a chance to talk her out of going, that she'd wait for things to cool off after their fight before she made up her mind. Slipping his hands in his front pockets, he hung his head and said, "I realize that, and came here to apologize."

"Oh, Nate, really? I'm sorry that you missed her then. I was pulling for you guys. Truly. We all were. You know she's crazy about you."

He'd thought so, too, but she'd left him. He cleared his throat and asked, "Is she coming back?"

"Yes, I believe so, but whether she is coming back to stay or to pack up to move to Cali, I can't tell you. Hate to tell you this, dude, but you might need to man up and decide what it is you do want with Abby. If you don't want to be with her then you need to let her go so she can be happy elsewhere."

"Got it. Thanks, Tessa." Like hell he was letting her go.

"Anytime, Sheriff Stud Muffin," Tessa replied as she shut the door.

The name was a complete kick in the gut. But it also gave him hope. He headed home and looked around the place. As much expectation as he'd had for this house, it was just four walls. He and Abby had begun to build something, something solid and long lasting. If he had to follow her to California, well then, that was what he would have to do. And what he had to say to her couldn't be done over the phone.

Nate spent the next few days working like a dervish between his duties as sheriff and completing the upstairs remodel. If he had to move, he'd rather have the house finished so he could get top dollar for it. The entire time he worked on the house, he thought about Abby, replaying every moment, from the time she'd beaned him with the golf club to their last disastrous conversation.

Nate was a bloody fool, and he knew it.

He remembered that horrible night vividly. He'd already been in a foul mood after discovering their B&E culprit was one of his deputies, a man he had trusted. That still smarted. It had put him on edge as he'd begun cataloging evidence at Abby's house. He'd discovered the letter in the snake plant next to the front door and figured it had fallen out of her purse in her fright to get to safety earlier. Not thinking, he had opened it.

And had lost his ever-loving mind.

Fear had swamped him at the thought that she was going to leave him. In his rather feeble defense, when he'd found the letter, he'd just begun to sort out his feelings for Abby, realizing how deep they went and that he wanted a more permanent relationship with her. The discovery had thrown his world into a tumult and he'd spoken out of anger and fear that night.

He remembered the look on her face. It was one he would never forget, like he'd kicked a puppy. And then she'd left his house. His pride and his ego had let her walk out his door. He'd regretted it ever since.

That was why he was taking the steps he was taking now, to prove to Abby that she was it for him. After she'd left that night, he'd read the rest of the journal and couldn't stop thinking about it. The last part of Old Man Turner's final entry had hit home for Nate:

Love is always the answer. It is always worth fighting for, no matter how short a time you might have it. Loving Evie was the greatest gift of my life.

Nate knew Abby was the woman for him. That, if he had to, he would follow her to the ends of the earth so that she could pursue the career she wanted. Whatever she needed, he would do. He might even have a buyer for his house. His sister, Beth, was moving back to town and had just messaged him to let him know that she would be in town in two days' time to look at places.

He might have just the one for her.

For Nate, loving Abby was what he wanted for his life. The rest was just window dressing, as far as he was concerned. He just had to convince her to forgive him, and that they were better together than apart.

Chapter Twenty-Two

From Old Man Turner's Journal:
Stand up for what you believe in.

A bby returned to Echo Springs on Friday after a whirlwind couple of days. The University of California at Berkeley was amazing, but in the end, she knew it wasn't the right fit for her. A part of her, the last vestiges of her parents' influence, hated the fact that she'd turned down the job offer. It still tripped her out a bit. In fact, she'd hyperventilated on her cab ride to the San Francisco airport for her flight home, and then again on the drive from Denver International to Echo Springs because, truth be told, she had just made a life-altering, *there's no going back on it now* decision based on the mere hope that Nate would talk to her.

Abby wasn't so certain he would, not after what he had said the last time.

But she wanted to fight for him, for them. She loved him. And as much as she wanted to lay all the blame for their fight at his feet, much of it could be placed on her shoulders. She should have been upfront about her uncertainty about sticking around

Echo Springs beyond the fall semester. Then the letter from Berkeley wouldn't have caused such a rift between them. Abby could see her mistakes with complete and utter clarity. In the future, if he gave her another chance, he would be her sounding board.

But first she had to apologize for her omission, and even planned to grovel if necessary.

Before Abby had left California, she'd called Barry and accepted the offer to be the department head. While the position wasn't as glamorous and certainly not as lucrative as the one at Berkeley, Echo Springs was home for Abby. It was the right decision for her. Before her rebellion her sophomore year, her parents had controlled every aspect of her life, and she'd been afraid of handing the reins over to someone else—completely missing the point that in a true relationship, it wasn't about handing over control but presenting a united front against the world. And there was no one else she would rather have in her corner than Nate. That also meant she still had to deal with her aunt's pesky little undead doll army too.

When she turned onto her street, she spied a sedan in Nate's driveway that she didn't recognize and slowed her vehicle—and was treated to a bird's-eye view of Nate embracing a willowy blonde on his doorstep.

Her heart, the hope she'd carried since making her choice, exploded into flames faster than the Hindenburg. It felt like her heart had been ripped from her chest while it was still beating. Nate had moved on already. Abby didn't want to know the hows or whys of it. In a pained daze, she parked outside her house and carted her suitcase up the driveway, fighting back the sobs that threatened to escape. The last thing she wanted to be seen as was pathetic, especially when it was clear that he'd never cared for her. She escaped into her house, hoping to avoid any confrontation.

Okay, so that had not gone as planned. She glanced about Evie's home, at the undead doll army still shrouded in the living room. Maybe she could sell the place, or rent it out. Part of her decision to stay in Echo Springs had been due to the fact that she had a home fully paid for and would not have to worry about rent. She loved this house and didn't want to lose it. But the last thing she wanted to do was live next door and watch Nate date other women. The ache in her chest expanded and she fought to breathe. If he wasn't going to be with her and was going to move on just like that, she would survive. Not well, but she would, and she'd live on her own terms, like her great-aunt had.

Anger roiled and bubbled in her chest. Was she that easy to get over? She paced in her foyer, glancing at the amassed army of dolls, ready to take them on. *Bring on the possessed doll apocalypse.* Anything was better than this weight that bore down on her chest. It hurt to breathe. How could he treat her like she was disposable? Like what they had had meant nothing to him? With her heart in her throat, Abby headed upstairs to her bedroom. She couldn't stay here. There was a motel in town she could stay in for the time being until she found a place to rent. She began packing, feeling like her heart had shattered into a million pieces all over again.

~

NATE KNOCKED on Abby's door. It had been a week since he had seen her. A long damn week that felt like a lifetime. He didn't plan on being without her that long ever again if he could help it.

Abby opened the door, her eyes flat as she peered up at him. Gone was the light and warmth he'd begun to expect in their hazel depths. She was so beautiful, he ached, and promised himself he would put the spark back in her gaze. Beyond her in the hall, there were boxes stacked. He had his answer. She was packing up and leaving Echo Springs. He had to convince her that he was going with her.

"You're leaving. You made your decision?" Nate asked, his heart lodged in his throat.

"Yes," Abby replied, averting her eyes and avoiding looking at him. Like she couldn't stand to.

"It's just that easy for you? So I was just an itch that you needed to scratch and it's done, is that it?" he snapped furiously. His rehearsed speech flew right out the window when she wouldn't even look at him and caused his insecurities to rise. It was like she'd punched a hole clean through his chest, leaving a gaping hole where his heart once resided.

Abby snorted. "You're one to talk and cast accusations at me. I was gone for a week. One week. But you already moved on to a blonde bimbo. And I know I messed up by not telling you about the possibility of my leaving Echo Springs."

"What blonde bimbo?" Nate asked, taken aback by her accusation. There was no one but Abby in his life. He did not want another woman. It was then that he spied the moisture lining her inky lashes, tears she valiantly attempted to hide. His anger melted away. Nate was being a bloody fool—again—and almost laughed at himself.

"The one I saw leaving your house tonight after you were all cozy and hugging each other," she said through gritted teeth. "Besides, I have no reason to stay. Why does it matter so much to you anyway?"

He closed his eyes as hope speared through his chest. Abby was jealous. Her emotions were as raw and bruised as his. He gazed at her with everything that was in his heart and said, "Because I am utterly and completely in love with you, Abby. I'm not really sure when it happened. It was your eyes, at first. Every time you looked at me, I felt like I was on fire. They drew me in time and time again, until I didn't want to sleep unless you were by my side. I'm not easy, I'm stubborn, and can be rather thick-headed at times. But I do know that you're it for me. I'm sorry that I jumped to conclusions the other night without hearing your side of things. In the future, I swear to be a better listener. If your decision really is to move to California, I'll put the house on the market in the morning and follow you once it sells. Oh, and that bimbo you saw was my baby sister. She will think it's a hoot that you thought that. She likes to rib me over everything, so this one will make her howl with laughter for years to come."

"You love me?" Abby searched his face, studying him with that intense direct hazel gaze of hers. Her emotions made the green magnify. Yet, she must have seen the truth of his words. Her face softened, tears spilled down her cheeks, and his breath stuttered at what he found in her eyes. His future, with her. There was nowhere she would go that he would not follow.

"Yes, more than anything," he murmured, closing the distance. He cupped her face in his hands and caught her tears with his thumbs.

She sniffled, placed her hands over his and said, "I love you too. But why didn't you say that before I left?"

"Pride, mostly. I had just figured out my feelings for you but was blindsided by the possibility of you leaving. Remember my bit about being stubborn?" He grinned tenderly, knowing that his decision was right. How could he not want to follow this woman to the ends of the earth if necessary?

"Why would you give up your career and your life for me? You've put so much into that house." She searched his face for an answer.

"How's this for a reason?" He withdrew the ring he'd picked up last week. The half carat diamond sparkled in its white gold setting, and he heard her sharp intake of breath as he knelt down on her front porch on one knee. Gazing up at her, he gripped her left hand and said, "Marry me, Abby? Because I know there is no one for me but you. I want to build a life with you. Make a family with you. We can build our own house together. What do you say? Think you could love me forever?"

Abby blubbered, "Yes."

Nate's heart expanded in his chest. Then he slid the ring on her finger. It was like a key fitting into a lock, the rightness of it.

Rising, he drew Abby close. Joy mixed with peace, and certainty suffused him at having her back in his arms. It was where she belonged for the rest of their lives. Her hands slid up behind his neck and she pressed her body against him so that their torsos were lined up. She rose up, meeting him halfway as he lowered his mouth and claimed hers for a kiss that held all the promise of all their tomorrows. It was bittersweet and infused with love so powerful it nearly brought him back down to his knees. Nate lifted his head and smiled down at her.

"I'll put the house on the market in the morning and start making arrangements for California," he murmured, his heart nearly bursting with love for Abby. Rufus would get a kick out of the beach.

"But I'm not moving to California."

Not moving? "Wait, you're not? Then why were you packing?"

"I turned down the offer from Berkeley and accepted the position at ESCC. I made my decision before I even arrived in California. But I went to view the campus anyway, to see what my life would be like if I accepted the offer. The campus is spectacular, the faculty members I met were great and enthusiastic about me joining them in the fall. Except, the hours I'd be working would be killer, and wouldn't leave me with much of a life. The thing is, you brought me to life, Nate. I had been so enmeshed in my own little world of academia that I barely noticed the world around me and found myself questioning whether I had a heart at all. It was why I came here in the first place, to see if there was something else for me. And I decided I would rather live here with you and have a life than any pretense of a dream job that would keep me from living that life. And I was packing because, if you had moved on to someone else, I couldn't live in this house and see you all the time but never be able to touch you."

"So it's my body you're after?" he teased, his heart putty in her capable hands. He stroked her arms.

She shrugged with a cock-eyed grin. "Of course. And your house too."

"Is that right?"

"Uh huh, mister, be sure, because you won't ever be rid of me now, or my undead doll minions," she teased with her love shining in her gaze.

"That's something I can live with. Come home with me, Abby, to *our* home."

She slid her hand into his and nodded toward the house. "You mean that fixer upper over there? I thought you'd never ask."

Hand in hand, they walked toward the home they'd made together. It was a place they would continue to build on in the days, weeks, and years to come.

Loving Abby was the only thing in Nate's life that mattered. And he planned to show her every day of their life together just how much she meant. With a bit of fanfare and her surprised laughter, he scooped her up into his arms and carried her across the threshold as a symbol of his promise. They entered the house with Rufus maniacally jumping for joy around them. Then Nate kissed her, feeling all the promise of their sweet tomorrows, and reveling in the bliss of having her here with him today. Because Old Man Turner was right.

In the end, loving Abby would be the greatest gift of his life.

~The End~

Acknowledgments

This has been a project of my heart, and there are many people who have helped turn this dream of a book into reality whom I need to acknowledge. Joyce Lamb, for helping me piece this story together. My publisher, Blushing Books, for taking a chance on this book and series. My entire team at Blushing Books: my editor, Tahlia Blythe; cover artist, Patty Devlin; formatter, Courage Knight, and Allison Tee, you have my heartfelt thanks for all that you do.

And last, to Heather Graham for your generosity and fierce friendship. I am humbled and honored by them.

Maggie Mae Gallagher

Born in St. Louis, Missouri, Maggie grew up listening to Cardinals baseball and reading anything she could get her hands on. She remembers her mother saying if only she would read the right type of books instead of binging her way through the romance aisles at the bookstore, she'd have been a doctor. While Maggie never did get that doctorate, she graduated cum laude from the University of Missouri-St. Louis with an M.A. in History.

Maggie is a bestselling and award-winning author published in multiple fiction genres. She also writes erotic romance under the name Anya Summers. A total geek at her core, when she is not writing, she adores attending the latest comic con or spending time with her family. She currently lives in the Midwest with her two furry felines.

Visit her website here:
www.maggiemaegallagher.com

Visit her on social media here:
Facebook: FB.me/MagMaeGallagher
https://www.facebook.com/MagMaeGallagher/
https://www.instagram.com/magmaegallagher/
https://www.goodreads.com/author/show/
7846308.Maggie_Mae_Gallagher
https://twitter.com/magmaegallagher?lang=en
https://www.amazon.com/author/maggiegallagher
https://www.bookbub.com/authors/maggie-mae-gallagher

Don't miss these exciting titles by Maggie Mae Gallagher!

Echo Springs
THE FIXER UPPER

The Mystic Series
REMEMBER ME
CASKET GIRL

The Cantati Chronicles
RUPTURED
ANOINTED
ASCENDED

And if you like your romance with a bit of spice and kink, be sure to check out Maggie Mae Gallagher writing as Anya Summers!

CPSIA information can be obtained
at www.ICGtesting.com
Printed in the USA
LVHW111612070620
657606LV00005B/1349

9 781947 132665